W9-CKI-802

You'll Think of Me

This Large Print Book carries the Seal of Approval of N.A.V.H.

YOU'LL THINK OF ME

ROBIN LEE HATCHER

THORNDIKE PRESS
A part of Gale, Cengage Learning

GALE
CENGAGE Learning®

Farmington Hills, Mich • San Francisco • New York • Waterville, Maine
Meriden, Conn • Mason, Ohio • Chicago

GALE
CENGAGE Learning·

Copyright © 2017 by Robin Lee Hatcher.
Unless otherwise noted, Scripture quotations are taken from New American Standard Bible®, Copyright © 1960, 1962, 1963, 1968, 1971, 1972, 1973, 1975, 1977, 1995 by The Lockman Foundation. Used by permission. (www.Lockman.org)
Thorndike Press, a part of Gale, Cengage Learning.

Thorndike Press® Large Print Christian Fiction.
The text of this Large Print edition is unabridged.
Other aspects of the book may vary from the original edition.
Set in 16 pt. Plantin.

LIBRARY OF CONGRESS CATALOGING-IN-PUBLICATION DATA

Names: Hatcher, Robin Lee, author.
Title: You'll think of me / by Robin Lee Hatcher.
Other titles: You will think of me
Description: Large print edition. | Waterville, Maine : Thorndike Press, a part of Gale, Cengage Learning, 2017. | Series: Thorndike Press large print Christian fiction
Identifiers: LCCN 2017008965 | ISBN 9781410499745 (hardcover) | ISBN 141049974X (hardcover)
Subjects: LCSH: Single mothers—Fiction. | Widows—Fiction. | Large type books. | GSAFD: Christian fiction. | Love stories.
Classification: LCC PS3558.A73574 Y68 2017b | DDC 813/.54—dc23
LC record available at https://lccn.loc.gov/2017008965

Published in 2017 by arrangement with Thomas Nelson, Inc., a division of HarperCollins Christian Publishers

Printed in Mexico
1 2 3 4 5 6 7 21 20 19 18 17

To my Abba-Father, who holds me in His arms, even when I am unaware.

Two are better than one because they have a good return for their labor. For if either of them falls, the one will lift up his companion. But woe to the one who falls when there is not another to lift him up. Furthermore, if two lie down together they keep warm, but how can one be warm alone? And if one can overpower him who is alone, two can resist him. A cord of three strands is not quickly torn apart.

Ecclesiastes 4:9–12

CHAPTER 1

April
Reno, Nevada

Brooklyn Myers sat on the narrow stretch of lawn beside the brick apartment building, watching her ten-year-old daughter. On this balmy Saturday afternoon, Alycia lay on her stomach in the grass while reading a book they'd checked out at the library that morning. Reading, thanks to the public library, was one habit that Brooklyn not only approved of but could afford to encourage. When a mother and child survived on a waitress's salary, toys and other gadgets were a luxury. As was most everything else.

A headache threatened, and Brooklyn closed her eyes, rubbing her temples with her fingertips. Thank goodness she didn't have to work today. She'd put in a lot of overtime in recent weeks and was in need of rest. Rest that always seemed just out of reach.

9

"Brooklyn?" Esther Peterman called from the second-story landing. "May I join you?"

Brooklyn looked toward the stairwell. "Of course."

The rail-thin woman flashed one of her brave smiles before slowly heading down the final flight of stairs, a folded lawn chair clasped in one hand. She was only in her late forties, but she moved as if she were eighty.

Brooklyn's heart clenched at the sight. As far as she was concerned, Esther was — and had always been — a godsend. She couldn't begin to imagine how she and Alycia would have managed over the past decade without this kindly neighbor. Or how they were going to manage without her in the future.

Her temples throbbed, the headache full blown now.

Esther arrived at her side and unfolded the lawn chair. "What a beautiful day."

"I couldn't agree more." Brooklyn tilted her face toward the sun, hoping its warmth would ease the pain in her head — and in her heart.

When Esther spoke again, she sounded wistful. "I suppose San Diego will be just as lovely."

"I'm sure it will be. And you'll be with your family."

10

"Yes." Her friend drew a long breath and let it out on a sigh. "But they might as well be strangers. I haven't seen my cousins in years."

Brooklyn reached over and took hold of Esther's hand, gently squeezing it with her own. "I wish . . . ," she began, then let the rest go unsaid.

"I know, Brooklyn. I know."

Esther Peterman was the first person Brooklyn had met when she moved into this low-income apartment building over ten years ago. She'd been eighteen, pregnant, and all alone in a strange city. Chad Hallston, her husband of only a few months, had left Brooklyn soon after learning they were to have a baby. Esther and her husband, Joshua, had become the closest thing to family Brooklyn had ever known. But prostate cancer had taken Joshua, age sixty, three years earlier, and now bone cancer was taking Esther.

It seemed so unfair.

"God has this," Esther said softly. "I'll be all right, and so will the two of you."

Brooklyn swallowed the lump in her throat.

"Have you found someone to watch Alycia when you're at work?"

She shrugged, unwilling for Esther to take

11

on that worry. But honesty wouldn't allow her to leave it alone, and finally she shook her head.

"I'll keep praying." Esther spoke with confidence, although her voice was weak. "God knows what you need. He will provide."

Real faith was another blessing from Esther. Before meeting her, all Brooklyn had known were rules, restrictions, and God's wrath. She'd lived in expectation of the Almighty slapping her down whenever she displeased Him — which she had been guaranteed to do on a daily basis. That was the God Brooklyn had learned from her father. But Esther had introduced her to a God who loved her, to a Savior who had willingly died for her, to a Spirit who renewed her mind and gave her strength.

"It's going to be all right." Now it was Esther's turn to squeeze Brooklyn's hand. "You'll see."

From behind them came a male voice. "Hey. Are one of you ladies named Myers?"

Brooklyn twisted in her lawn chair. "I am."

"Got a delivery for you." He held up a legal-sized overnight envelope. "Need you to sign for it."

Brooklyn frowned, unable to imagine any reason for express mail. She wasn't behind

12

on her rent or her cell phone bill. Her few friends lived right here in Reno, and she never shopped online.

"Are you sure it's for me?" she asked as she stood.

The young man, dressed in a cotton shirt and shorts, looked at the large envelope again. "Brooklyn Myers. M-y-e-r-s. Apartment 12B."

Alycia appeared at her side. "What've you got, Mom?"

"I don't know," she answered her daughter. Then to the deliveryman she said, "That's me." She walked toward the breezeway where he stood, Alycia following along.

He handed her the stylus, then held the device toward her. She scribbled her name on the small screen, hoping it wasn't required that it actually look like her signature.

"Here you go." He took back the stylus and replaced it with the envelope.

"Thank you." She watched him stride toward the parking lot.

"What is it, Mom?" Alycia asked again.

"I'm not sure. Just a lot of papers, it feels like."

"Oh." Disappointment laced the word before her daughter returned to the grass and her book.

13

Brooklyn's gaze lowered to the sender's address on the thick envelope. *Hodges, Thurber, and Williams, Attorneys-at-Law, Miami, Florida.* Why would some lawyer in Florida send her overnight mail? Her stomach clenched with sudden nervousness as she flipped the envelope over.

Thunder Creek, Idaho

Derek Johnson stopped at the northeast corner of his three-acre farm. Since buying the property six years earlier, he'd slowly cultivated more and more of it, changing the land from pasture to neat rows of vegetables. In addition, a small apple orchard — six trees planted by a previous owner — sat in the northwest corner of the property. Eventually, he planned to expand the orchard, adding more apple trees and other kinds of fruit as well. Maybe next year.

In the beginning he'd sold his produce on weekends from booths at farmers' markets or from the back of his pickup at popular spots along the highway. But for the last two growing seasons, after receiving his organic certification, he'd been able to sell direct to a couple of small-town grocery stores. It had definitely made his life easier and his income slightly more certain.

One of his favorite books on the subject

of organic gardening for profit said it was possible, if done properly, to make a living of sixty thousand dollars or more per year on one and a half acres. Perhaps that was true, but as of yet he wasn't finding it that profitable. Besides, he wanted more than simply to make a living. He wanted to expand, to experiment, to offer the best produce available in this county and the ones surrounding it.

His gaze shifted to the neighboring land. All ten acres of the Hallston property lay in a tangle of weeds and bare ground. There was so much he'd be able to do with those additional acres once they were his. Another six months and he should have the down payment required by the bank.

"Lord willin' and the creek don't rise," he muttered to himself.

Impatience welled up inside him. What he wouldn't give to be able to buy that land now, to be able to expand his operation this growing season rather than next. He longed for the day he could quit working as a part-time sheriff's deputy and call himself a full-time farmer. But both of those dreams were on hold for now.

He sighed, consciously letting go of his frustration. At least Chad Hallston wasn't in a hurry to sell. His best friend from child-

15

hood had promised to wait until Derek had the down payment. True, it was taking longer for that to happen than either of them had expected. But the last time they'd spoken — more than nine months ago — Chad had assured Derek he would continue to wait. "Take as long as you need. The house has sat empty all these years. Another one or two won't matter."

Derek avoided looking at the two-story Hallston house with its boarded-up windows and faded yellow paint. He didn't understand why Chad had stayed away all of these years, letting the house go to ruin after his parents' tragic deaths. But then there were a lot of things about Chad that Derek didn't understand. His old friend had become almost a stranger to him over the years — a change that had started when Chad became involved with Brooklyn Myers.

With a shake of his head, he turned away from the neighboring property and headed toward the pasture where his two horses and the calf he raised for beef grazed on shoots of spring grass. In his head he heard his dad's voice: "Why on earth do you want to give up being a deputy for farming? What did you go to college for if all you're going to do is dig in the dirt? You could be elected

16

sheriff, given a few more years' experience. You would be a shoo-in."

He stopped, leaned down, and scooped freshly turned soil into one hand, bringing it to his nose and breathing in. He loved the smell of it. Healthy. Rich. Life giving. The way dirt was supposed to smell. It indicated the kind of earth that could produce foods rich in nutrients and flavor. Flavor that had been stripped from most of the produce available in grocery stores today. That was just one reason he'd decided to become an organic farmer.

As for leaving the sheriff's department? His dad was right. There were plenty of reasons to stay. He liked helping people. He liked the men and women he worked with. He didn't mind the danger that could come with the job — although real danger was rare in these parts.

But there were a number of good reasons to leave, a number of things he disliked about police work. What he hated most were the domestic dispute calls. Even in a county full of farmers, vineyards, and churchgoing folks, the deputies had to answer too many of those calls to suit Derek. Seeing the underbelly of the place he loved wasn't how he wanted to spend his life. He'd rather work the land.

17

The sound of car wheels crunching on gravel drifted toward him, and he turned away from the pasture. Beyond one of the sheds, he glimpsed his grandmother's car rolling to a stop. With a grin, he waved. "Hey, Gran," he called as he walked over.

His grandmother, Ruth Johnson, was a slender, spry woman in her seventies. Somewhat of an institution in Thunder Creek after more than fifty years as the wife of the town's physician, Ruth had come to the small town in western Idaho as a new bride. She and Derek's grandfather, Walter Johnson, had raised two sons and one daughter in a rambling Victorian house one block north of Main Street. Pappy had delivered most everyone Derek knew who was under the age of fifty and had set more bones and cured more fevers than anybody could count. Widowed for several years, Gran still lived in the same big house but had turned the attached doctor's offices into a tea and gift shop — a popular gathering place for the entire community.

His grandmother was out of the car by the time he drew close, and she greeted him with a kiss on one cheek, followed by a pat of her hand on the other. "How are you, dear?"

"I'm great."

"Not working today?"

He shook his head, still smiling. "I'm always working, Gran. You know that."

"Yes, I do know that. I meant the job that pays."

"My little farm pays. Not much yet, but it pays. I didn't do too bad last year, remember? And now that I've got my organic certification, I expect to do even better." He glanced toward his fields. "I was just walking around, making some mental notes of things to do differently this season." He took hold of his grandmother's arm and steered her toward the back door of his house. "So, tell me what brought you out this way."

"Do I have to have a reason to visit my grandson?"

"Of course not," he answered — although he knew good and well she had one. He could see it in her eyes.

Inside, Gran settled onto the padded rocking chair beside the large living-room window.

"You want something cold to drink?" Derek offered.

"Oh, no need. I have a bottled water I've been sipping on." She patted her purse.

"Fair enough." He sat on the sofa and allowed her to guide their conversation wher-

19

ever she wanted.

First they talked about his parents. His dad's job had transferred him from Nampa, Idaho, to Southern California over eight years before. Both his dad and mom loved living near the ocean, and ever since then they'd been after Derek to relocate too. He wasn't inclined to do so, no matter how much they raved about the great weather and ocean breezes. His roots went down too deep into the Idaho soil.

"I notice they haven't convinced you to move either," he said to Gran.

Her airy laughter filled the room "Your dad knows better than to try that with me. This is my home, and it's where I intend to stay until they bury me next to your grandfather."

"Which will be a long, long, long time from now."

"God willing." Her smile faded and she cleared her throat, clueing him in that they were finally getting around to the reason for her visit. "Have you talked to Hank McLean today?"

Derek cocked an eyebrow. "No. Why?" Hank was one of the full-time deputies with the sheriff's department and a close friend and mentor of Derek's.

"I saw Fran Tompkins at the market this

20

morning."

Before Gran said another word, he knew what was coming next.

"She was sporting a black eye."

His gut tightened. "Sorry to hear that."

"I just wondered if Hank knew about . . . about this latest event."

"Gran, there isn't anything he can do — that any of us can do — as long as Fran continues to lie about what her husband's doing. She always protects Mac. She always denies he's done anything to her."

"I know. But Hank's her cousin and a deputy. I thought maybe he —"

"Gran."

"I know." She sighed. "I know. If only she would confide in someone."

Derek wished the same, but before he could think of anything comforting or encouraging to say, the doorbell rang. He rose to answer it.

A FedEx driver stood on the front stoop, an envelope in hand. "You Mr. Johnson? Derek Johnson?"

"That's me."

"Here." He held out a small electronic device. "Need you to sign for it."

CHAPTER 2

Chad was dead.

Brooklyn stared at the three-page letter from the attorney in Miami and tried to make sense of what it said in the first paragraph. The rest was still unread because the first sentences contained a revelation she could hardly wrap her head around. Chad was dead. At the age of thirty-two, Chad was dead. Something about his heart.

The sorrow that welled up inside surprised her. She'd stopped loving her husband long ago. For a while she'd even hated him. But by the time ten years of silence had rolled by, he'd become nothing to her but distant memories. And yet she ached at the news of his death. In her mind he remained the boy who'd made her feel noticed and valued and, for a while, loved. Yes, he'd broken her heart in the end. But she'd never wished him dead.

And now he was.

She didn't know how or when or why Chad had ended up in Florida. She didn't know what he'd done for a living or if he'd thought of divorcing the girl he'd eloped with, married, and then abandoned in Reno. Had he regretted never knowing his own daughter? Had he even known if the baby she'd carried was a boy or a girl? Had it mattered to him how Brooklyn had struggled to survive, first on her own, then with an infant? Had he given them any thought at all until now?

Seated nearby in Brooklyn's small apartment, Esther let out a long breath and looked up from the thick packet of papers that had accompanied the letter. Her eyes were wide. "Brooklyn, he left you a house. For Alycia."

"A house?" Confusion filled her head, like a jar filled with cotton. She stared at Esther, the letter in her hand momentarily forgotten in lieu of this new puzzle. "What do you mean, a house?"

"A house. In Idaho." Esther reviewed some wording, then held the papers toward Brooklyn. "It looks like it was his . . . parents' house?"

"His parents' house." Even to herself, her voice sounded wooden, inflectionless. Unbidden, her thoughts flew across the miles.

23

Idaho . . . Thunder Creek . . . A chill shivered up her spine.

Esther noted the reaction and frowned. "Do you know the house?"

Large. Beautiful. Sunny. Warm. How could she forget it?

"I know it."

"And?"

Her friend and her surroundings momentarily forgotten, Brooklyn pictured Mrs. Hallston in the bright, airy kitchen, frilly curtains framing the window over the sink. She heard the woman's laughter, so full of joy. She remembered the way Mr. Hallston had taken his wife in his arms one Sunday afternoon and danced her around the kitchen as if it were a ballroom. She remembered the tenderness in his eyes.

Once upon a time, Brooklyn had expected Chad to cherish her in the same way. It hadn't happened. Why had she been surprised? Her own mother hadn't cared enough about Brooklyn to stay. Her father had thought Brooklyn worthless. What had made her think Chad would love her? Really love her.

"Brooklyn?"

She shook off the memories, both the bitter and the sweet. "It's a beautiful home, Esther. I've never been in one that I liked

24

more. And . . . you say Chad left it to Alycia?" She shook her head, bewildered. "But he never knew her. He didn't care about her enough to even meet her, let alone be a father to her."

She remembered the day he'd walked out on her. *"I can't do this!"* he'd shouted, duffel bag in hand. *"I thought we were going to have fun."* Then had come the slamming door. She winced.

Looking at her friend again, she began, "And what about Mr. and Mrs. —" She broke off just as suddenly, unwilling to hear the answer. Because there was only one reason that made sense. If Chad owned the house, if it was his right to leave it to Alycia, then his parents must be dead.

"You need to finish reading that letter." Esther pointed at the papers in Brooklyn's hands.

Her heart hammered in her chest. "I can't. I . . . I'm not ready." She held the sheets of textured paper toward her friend. "Please. You do it."

Esther gave her a patient smile, then took the letter and began to silently read. Brooklyn found it hard to breathe as she waited.

In her memories, Chad smiled at her. So handsome. So full of charm. Always in pursuit of a good time. "Oh, Chad," she

25

whispered. "You were so young. I'm sorry you died. I wish . . . I wish it all could have been different."

She pictured the Hallston house a second time. Had Chad really left it to her, to their daughter? Hadn't he known Brooklyn would have no desire to return to her hometown? When she'd run away from Thunder Creek — and from her father — as a seventeen-year-old, she'd run away for good. She'd never wanted to go back. Not ever. Not even when things were at their worst. Not even when she'd been hungry and homeless and scared to death. Because home to her had been every bit as dark, scary, and loveless as the streets of Reno.

Esther laid the letter atop the other papers on her lap. "Well."

"Well, what?"

"You really should read it yourself."

"No." She shook her head. "Just summarize it for me. Please."

There was a lengthy silence before Esther said, "Very well. Your husband died of a rare heart disease. Apparently he learned he was dying about six months ago. He hired an investigator to find you and your daughter. He also hired an attorney — this Mr. Thurber — to get his things in order." She glanced down at the letter again. "It says his parents died around nine years ago and left him their house, but he never lived in it. Like you, he never went back to Idaho. Now he wants his daughter to have the home. So he left it to you as her mother."

Once again, Brooklyn shook her head. "Why would he do it? He didn't care. All of those years, he didn't care . . ." Her voice trailed off as she stared at memories. Good ones. Bad ones. All mixed together. Memories long forgotten. Or so she'd thought.

"Brooklyn?"

"Hmm?"

"Has it occurred to you that this might be God's answer to your prayers? That this is how He has provided for your needs?"

Brooklyn stared at her friend. Her pulse thrummed at the suggestion. No, it hadn't occurred to her. Not at all.

Because why would God send her back to Thunder Creek, a place of so much unhappiness, after all these years?

The image of the Hallston home flashed a third time in her mind. It had two stories and five bedrooms plus an inviting porch that wrapped around the house. Tall trees shaded it on all sides, and Mrs. Hallston's beautiful flower beds, ablaze with color, lined the sidewalk — so glorious throughout the summer. In front of it all lay a

27

horseshoe-shaped driveway and an emerald-green lawn. She recalled the rope-and-board swing in the backyard and the day when she'd sat on it and Chad had pushed her over and over, making her go higher and higher. She remembered how happy she'd felt and the sound of their laughter mingling together. And when she'd stopped the swing, he'd kissed her for the first time. She remembered that too.

Unexpected tears blinded her. She turned away so that Esther wouldn't see before she blinked them away.

"Brooklyn, think about it. A home of your own instead of this cramped apartment with a kitchen you can hardly turn around in. No more city traffic to avoid and bus fumes to inhale. An actual lawn for Alycia to play on. And surely there are people you knew who would welcome you home again."

Brooklyn released a humorless laugh. How little her friend understood about Thunder Creek.

"You were only seventeen when you left," Esther added. "Perhaps you are being unfair to at least some of those people you remember."

"Perhaps," she admitted reluctantly, facing her friend again. "But my dad won't be one of them. Besides, what would I do there

28

if I did go back? It's a big house. Much bigger than Alycia and I need. We would rattle around in it. And there would be utilities and taxes to pay. I'd have to get a job, and there never were a lot of those to go around."

"Don't borrow trouble, Brooklyn Myers." Esther gave her a determined look. "Consider the possibilities first. Then look for solutions. If God can give you a house, He can surely take care of all the other details."

Brooklyn sank onto the chair. Once more she pictured the big yellow house — only this time she imagined it with Alycia on that rope swing going higher and higher. She imagined her daughter's laughter instead of her own. A house. A home.

"Esther." Disbelief mingling with wonder filled her chest. "Do you really think this could be God's answer to my prayers?"

After reading the attorney's brief cover letter, Derek wordlessly handed it to his grandmother. Then he opened the business envelope with his name written on the outside in uncertain cursive.

Derek, this probably sounds like a bad movie line, but if you're reading this, I'm dead. Sorry for the way you're hearing from my attorney about my decision regarding the property. Sorry I didn't have the guts to call you and tell you myself once I made the decision. I know we never had any formal agreement, nothing in writing, but I also know you were counting on the sale. I'm sorry for disappointing you. But you're a stand-up guy, so I know you'll get it. It's what you would do, too, if you had a wife and daughter.

Alycia's my kid, and leaving the house I grew up in to her and her mom is what's right, even if it means breaking a promise to the best friend I ever had. Maybe the only friend I still have.

But that's not the real reason for this personal note. I need to ask you something more important. I've never been around Alycia. I left before she was born and never went back. God knows what she thinks of me. Don't know what Brooklyn's told her about why I've never been around. Don't want to know, to tell you the truth. Because no matter how bad it is, no matter what her mom's said to her, I deserve it and more. Can't be bad enough, I guess. I don't know what you think of me now either.

But here's what I'm asking anyway.

30

When Alycia and her mom come back to Thunder Creek to live, like I'm counting on, I'm asking you to be the father to my kid that I never was. The kind of dad like I had and like you had. The decent kind. Not a lousy one like Brooklyn's or an absent one like me.

Do it for an old friend, buddy. It's the best thing I can leave Alycia now. I know having a home and property will help them, but not as much as Alycia having some kind of a dad in her life. Somebody she can trust and look up to. Now that it's too late, I wish it could be me.

Although Brooklyn's getting a surprise packet from my lawyer, I don't plan to tell her what I'm asking you to do. I don't have the courage to write what I should. You can tell her yourself, if you ever think the time is right.

Chad

His gut churned as he read Chad's note a second time and then a third. Finally, he passed it to Gran, as he had the more formal letter from the attorney. Then, without a word, he went outside, his gaze turning automatically toward the neighboring house with its faded yellow paint. Blow-

31

ing out a breath, he clasped the back of his neck.

Twenty or thirty minutes ago, his dream for expansion had been within reach. Twenty or thirty minutes ago, the possibilities had seemed endless. And twenty or thirty minutes ago, he'd believed his best friend from childhood was alive and well in Miami.

It was difficult to make sense of the reality, to grasp the fact he'd been monumentally wrong about all of it.

"What am I going to do now?" he asked himself and the sky.

"Derek," Gran said from behind him, "I'm sorry."

"Chad was only thirty-two." He shook his head. "How can he be dead?"

"Death is always a surprise to us, no matter when it comes."

And that was the moment the guilt swept over him. Because it wasn't just Chad he'd thought of. He'd thought of himself — of his farm and the lost possibilities — and the disappointment had tasted bitter on his tongue.

"It's all right, Derek," his grandmother said softly. "I understand. 'Hope deferred makes the heart sick.' "

He turned toward her. "The thing is, Gran, Chad was right to do what he did with his property. I know that in my head. I really do. The place *should* go to his daughter and Brooklyn. But it sure feels like it's ruined everything for me. I don't know what I'm going to do now."

What would he do? Decide to be satisfied with his three acres and what he could do with it? Give up on the idea of expanding and experimenting, of farming full time?

"You'll wait to see what the Lord wants of you," Gran said.

Derek barely heard her as disappointment washed over him again. Buying the Hallston property had felt like a done deal. He'd had the word of a friend. But that hadn't been enough. He should have gotten it in writing. Or he should have borrowed the down payment from a family member. Maybe his dad would have given it to him, but Derek had been too proud to ask. He'd wanted to do this himself. Look where that got him.

Resentment followed hard on the heels of disappointment. Brooklyn Myers had always been trouble. At least that's what Derek had thought from the moment Chad first took notice of her. After that, Derek had become the proverbial third wheel. He blamed Brooklyn for the change in his relationship with his best friend, and he blamed her for

33

making Chad take her away from Thunder Creek.

"And now she's coming between me and the prime ten acres of Hallston land I was counting on," he muttered.

There it was again. That twinge of guilt.

"Derek, what about Chad's other request?"

He met Gran's gaze.

"About Alycia needing a father figure in her life."

"I don't know." He shrugged. "What can I do about it? She's not here." He frowned. "The letter didn't say where they're living now, but I remember that Brooklyn couldn't wait to get away from Thunder Creek."

He couldn't help it. No matter how much he knew he should focus on more important things — the death of his friend, the idea of becoming a surrogate father figure — his thoughts turned like a beacon toward the land sitting in front of him. And despite his guilt, hope flickered in his chest.

"Maybe she won't even come back. Maybe she'll just sell the place."

And therein lay the million-dollar question. Was it possible this situation could be salvaged? Was there a chance he could buy the Hallston property from Chad's widow

34

instead of from Chad himself?

He supposed time would tell.

CHAPTER 3

June

With every passing mile, Brooklyn felt the knots in her stomach twist and tighten. Even Alycia's bright chatter couldn't erase the growing anxiety inside her. More than once during the six-hour drive, she'd been tempted to stop, turn the old car around, and return to Reno.

But she couldn't do it. For Alycia's sake, if not her own, she couldn't do it. Besides, there was nothing to go back to. She'd let her apartment go. She'd quit her job. She'd made her decision already. She and Alycia were headed to Idaho to make new lives for themselves. As Esther said, God had answered her prayers by opening an unexpected door . . . and by giving her a new dream for the future.

Literally a new dream. She'd awakened one night, about two weeks after receiving that overnight envelope from Mr. Thurber, with the dream so clear in her mind it had felt as if she could reach out and touch it. That big old house of the Hallstons would make an ideal bed-and-breakfast. Brooklyn had spent the next several weeks making plans, researching at the library, estimating costs. It would take time and money and plenty of labor, but it could be done. Perhaps not this year. Maybe not even the next. But it could be done.

"How much longer, Mom?"

Pulled from her thoughts, Brooklyn glanced into the rearview mirror at Alycia, who sat in the backseat surrounded by the remaining trappings of their lives, all boxed and bagged up. "Not long. Less than an hour, I think. We're in Idaho now."

"We are?" Excited, Alycia set down the Kindle Fire — a going-away present from Esther — and peered out the nearby window. After a short while, she sat back with a huff. "It doesn't look any different than it did before."

Her daughter was right. There had been little to see except sagebrush and desert for much of the drive. "As soon as we reach the river," she answered, "you'll begin to see farms and orchards. It's pretty." At least she remembered it as being pretty. But she supposed a lot could change in eleven years.

37

Brooklyn had been seventeen when she and Chad eloped, and she hadn't been back since. When she'd called her dad to tell him she was married, he'd made it clear she wouldn't be welcome in Thunder Creek ever again. She knew him well, knew he'd meant it. But when she'd found herself alone and pregnant not many months later, she'd called a second time, hoping for a change of heart. There hadn't been one. He'd told her she was as worthless as her mother and to never come back.

Too bad that's how he feels, because here we come.

The words in her head sounded brave. But other words tried to follow them. Other thoughts tried to remind her that she'd always been unwanted. By her mom. By her dad. Even by Chad in the end. More words told her she was a failure. She'd failed in the past. She would fail again in the future.

"But I'm not that girl anymore," she whispered. "I'm not that girl."

Brooklyn's anxiety eased a little. She would not let uncertainty change her course. She would not let fear rule her heart. She wouldn't be ruled by her past.

"Remember, you are a new creation in Christ." Esther's voice in her head was so clear — and with the memory came a sharp

38

longing for her dear friend. *"God has brought you this far. He will take you on from here. Never doubt it. Not even for an instant."*

The remainder of her apprehension drained away. She drew in a deep breath, along with renewed resolve.

She glanced again into the rearview mirror. "How about some music, honey? If we sing along, maybe the trip will go faster."

"Okay." Alycia closed the cover on the tablet a second time. "Sure."

Brooklyn turned on the car's stereo, adjusted the dial to a station with music she and Alycia would both recognize, and let the miles slip away.

Forty minutes later, she began to recognize farmhouses and fruit orchards. She turned down the volume on the radio. "Alycia, see that house?" She pointed to it. "My fifth-grade teacher, Mrs. Edwards, lived there. She was one of my favorite teachers."

"I'm gonna be in fifth grade when school starts. Maybe she'll be my teacher too."

"Maybe." Of course, Mrs. Edwards might not live in Thunder Creek any longer, for all Brooklyn knew.

"Mom, look over there! Horses! There's so many of them."

A quick glance in the mirror told her the direction to look. And her daughter was

39

right. There were quite a few of them. Twenty or so, grazing in a fenced pasture, the grass a deep green thanks to irrigation waters from the Snake River.

She recalled driving this same section of road on a spring night, stars twinkling in a moonless sky. Chad's arm had been around her shoulders as he steered the pickup with his left hand. "Let's get out of here, Brook," he'd said. "You and me. There's nothing to keep us here. I'm tired of living in this hick town. Let's have an adventure, you and me."

How surprisingly easy it had been for her to agree to go with him. It hadn't mattered where. Not as long as he loved her.

Only he hadn't loved her. Not really. And if she was honest with herself, maybe she hadn't truly loved him. Maybe she'd been in love with the idea of being in love. Maybe she'd wanted desperately for someone — anyone — to love her in return and she'd made herself believe that someone was Chad Hallston.

"Mom, do you think I can get a horse?"

Brooklyn shook off thoughts of Chad. The memories only made her sad, especially now that he was dead. Glancing again at the mirror, she answered, "I don't know, Alycia. It costs a lot of money to keep a horse."

"But if —"

40

"Honey, you'll have to wait. Maybe someday when you're older, but not yet. We just don't have the money for now."

The car crested a rise in the highway, and Thunder Creek came into view. Picturesque from this viewpoint, the town was home to about three thousand people, most of them lifelong residents. Victorian-style houses as well as 1950s bungalows lined a perfect grid of streets shaded by tall trees.

It looked exactly the way she remembered it.

She swallowed. "There it is, honey. There's Thunder Creek."

"Where? I can't see." Alycia leaned forward, trying to peer between the two front seats.

"Wait a second. You'll be able to see it out your side window when the road curves."

No more had the words left her lips than the engine made a strange sound — something like a cough, followed by a gasp — and then died.

"No. No-no-no-no-no-no."

Amidst the litany of her denial, she steered the old car to the side of the road. It coasted to the bottom of the hill and came to a stop. For a moment, she just sat there.

"Mom? What happened? Why'd you stop?"

Rather than answer, Brooklyn tried turning the key.

Nothing.

She tried again. Still nothing. Dead. Dead. Dead.

With a sigh, she sat back and assessed the situation. It could have been worse, she told herself. This could have happened back in Nevada. It could have happened in the middle of nowhere instead of within walking distance of Thunder Creek.

"What's wrong, Mom?"

"I don't know, sweetheart. The engine isn't working. We're going to have to walk the rest of the way." Better walking than calling for a tow truck she couldn't afford.

"Walk?" Thankfully, Alycia sounded pleased with the prospect. Anything to get out of the car after all these hours.

Brooklyn opened the driver-side door. "Stay put until I come around." She checked behind her for traffic, although this stretch of highway wasn't exactly busy at any time of day. Or it hadn't used to be, anyway. Seeing nothing, she got out and hurried around to the passenger side of the car.

"We'll leave our things here and come back for it all as soon as we can. It'll be all right until then."

Alycia slid out of the backseat, bringing

42

the Fire with her.

Out of habit, Brooklyn locked the car doors before taking her daughter by the hand. They began walking, but before they'd gone more than a few yards, she heard the crunch of tires on gravel and looked behind her. A black SUV — a sheriff's vehicle — rolled to a stop behind her disabled automobile. Relief rushed through her.

Moments later, a sheriff's deputy unfolded himself from behind the wheel. As he straightened, he tugged at the brim of his black baseball cap. He was tall, over six feet, and broad shouldered. He looked like a man who could solve problems.

But as the deputy took his first couple of strides toward her, Brooklyn felt her nerves erupt in tension. Of all people . . .

"Derek Johnson."

Recognition crossed his face an instant later, and he hesitated. Then, his jaw hardening a little, he continued toward her. "Brooklyn Myers," he said when he stopped again. "I hadn't heard you were coming." His gaze flicked to her daughter. "You must be Alycia."

Brooklyn's eyes widened. How did he know her daughter's name?

Alycia nodded. "Yes, sir," she said softly.

43

"I'm Deputy Johnson." He paused before adding, "A friend of your mom's."

A friend? Not the way she remembered it. He'd been Chad's friend but had never seemed to care much for Brooklyn. *Tolerated* was a more accurate term.

"Trouble with your car?" he asked, looking at her again. There seemed to be an accusation in that single word. As if he'd added, *"You're always in some kind of trouble, Brooklyn."*

"The engine died." She tilted her chin. "It wouldn't restart."

"Out of gas?"

Insulted by the question, she had to work to keep the irritation out of her voice. "No. There's still plenty of fuel in the tank."

"Well, let me have a look. See if I can find what's wrong."

With more than a little reluctance, she removed the car key from the ring and handed it to him.

After he'd walked away, Alycia tugged on Brooklyn's hand. "How did he know my name?"

"I suppose your dad told him." She frowned, wondering if she'd guessed right. But how else could he have known? Still, it was strange to think Chad had talked about the daughter he'd never met, never seen,

44

never supported until his dying act.

"Is he gonna fix the car?"

"I don't know, honey. Maybe." She glanced over her shoulder, her gaze finding a large rock. "Let's sit over there while we wait."

Half an hour later, when it was obvious nothing Derek had tried would make Brooklyn's old clunker of a car start again, he put her and her daughter, along with some of their belongings, into the department's black SUV and drove them the rest of the way into Thunder Creek.

But when he turned onto Sharp Street, toward her girlhood home, Brooklyn protested. "Not to my dad's house, Derek. Take us to the Hallston place instead."

"What about —"

"We need to go to our home."

Their home. The words made him want to grind his teeth. Nonetheless, he turned the vehicle at the next street, then again at the next, and headed west, toward the edge of town. Houses soon thinned out. The road began to wind and curve, in opposition to the straight streets in town. Regular lots became acreages, which then became small farms. And at last, the Hallston house came into view. With its faded paint and its

45

windows boarded over, it was far from the warm and welcoming home it had been when Chad's parents were alive, back when Derek and his best friend had run in and out of that front door countless times a day.

"Oh," Brooklyn whispered. "It looks so sad."

He glanced over at her. "Nobody's been inside of it since right after the funeral. The day after his parents were buried, Chad had the windows boarded over, the power turned off, and the pipes drained. Then he left town again." Fair or not, Derek had blamed Brooklyn for Chad's second departure, as he'd blamed her for most things involving his friend. "Although he was thinking about selling the place, last time we talked."

Selling it to me.

"You were in touch with him?"

"Rarely. But yes. Every now and then."

She was silent a few moments. "I'm glad."

He wasn't sure what she meant, and he didn't know how to respond. So he said nothing as he pulled the SUV into the horseshoe-shaped driveway, stopping near the sidewalk that led to the wraparound front porch. "Not sure what you're going to find inside."

"It doesn't matter. We'll manage. Won't we, Alycia?"

46

"Sure, Mom."

Softly, Brooklyn added, "I've stayed in worse places."

Derek looked at her again, his mind suddenly full of questions, but he found no answers in her closed expression.

He was tempted to drive away the instant she and her daughter got out of the SUV with their few belongings. Only he couldn't do that. He couldn't leave her there with boarded-over windows and who knew what on the inside. So he opened the driver door and got out too.

Brooklyn and Alycia stood on the sidewalk, holding hands. He saw Brooklyn square her narrow shoulders and stiffen her spine. Then mother and daughter moved toward the porch, like soldiers marching into battle. An unwelcome feeling — sympathy, perhaps? — tugged at his chest, but he shoved it away and followed after the pair. He caught up with them in time to hear Alycia ask her mom, "How do we get in?"

"I have the key, honey. It's our home now. Your father left it to us. Remember?" She opened the small purse hanging from her shoulder. "Let's see what it's like inside. It's been a long time since I was here."

She stuck the key in the lock. When she pushed the door open a moment later, cool

47

air flowed out of the dim interior.

More boyhood memories flooded Derek's mind. Happy memories. And they made him wonder again what had gone so wrong for Chad.

"I never imagined it had come to this," Brooklyn said, drawing his attention to her again.

Derek watched as she stepped through the open doorway.

"It was such a beautiful home." She moved deeper into the house, becoming a shadow within shadows. "Mrs. Hallston would be heartbroken to see it so uncared for." Another pause, then, "It makes me want to cry."

Strange, the way her words affected him. They made him feel as if he were at fault in some way. Guilty because he hadn't cared about the house. If he'd been able to buy the property, he would have torn it down, making room for more crops. He hadn't given any thought to Marie Hallston and the home she'd made for her husband and son.

But Brooklyn was right. Chad's mother would be heartbroken if she knew the home she'd cared for had come to this.

"It's kinda spooky in here, Mom," Alycia said in a near whisper.

48

Brooklyn laughed softly. "We'll take care of that." She moved to a wall switch and flipped it upward. Nothing happened. No lights illuminated the room. "Oh no. I arranged for the power to be turned on today. I guess it hasn't happened yet."

Derek heard the slight frustration in her voice. He moved into the doorway. "You can't stay here without power. Without electricity there's no pump to run the well. You can't get by without water. And you won't have lights or the use of the stove. Besides that, you don't have any food here and no way to get it until you've got a car. Let me take you to the motel."

She turned toward him, but she was too far inside the house for him to make out her expression. "I can't afford for us to stay in a motel. Especially now that my car needs some kind of repair. Alycia and I will have to get by for a while. I'm sure the power will be turned on before dark. We'll manage until then."

There was no way to escape it. He knew what had to be done. He was going to have to help Brooklyn. She was the last person on earth he felt like helping just now, but he would have to do it anyway.

Ruth Johnson stood on the porch of her

49

home, shading her eyes against the afternoon sun with the flat of one hand. Her grandson hadn't expected Brooklyn and Alycia to return to Thunder Creek. At least not without advance notice. But like it or not, they were here, and Derek had turned to Ruth when he hadn't known what else to do. He hadn't given her many details when he called, but details hadn't been required. She had long ago learned not to refuse when God brought a need to her attention.

The sheriff's SUV turned the corner onto Maple, the sight causing a flutter of anticipation in Ruth's chest. She was curious for that first glimpse of Brooklyn Myers after all these years. She had been such a pretty girl, but an unhappy one — with good reason, given her home situation.

Ruth wondered if Brooklyn had let her father know she was returning to Thunder Creek after all these years. "Surely he wouldn't turn them away if he knew," she said aloud.

But that wasn't true. Reggie Myers was a hard, unforgiving man, and his bitterness had made him more brittle, unbending, and unkind with every passing year. He could — and probably would — turn away anybody who displeased him in the slightest. Even his only daughter and grandchild.

50

Derek parked the vehicle in the private driveway on the opposite side of the house from the entrance to Ruth's tea and gift shop, Sips and Scentimentals. As he got out, he gave her a brief wave, then rounded the SUV to open both front and back doors at the same time. Moments later, Brooklyn slipped to the ground, joined soon after by her daughter. The two quickly clasped hands.

Brooklyn looked smaller than Ruth remembered. Maybe that was because Derek, who stood right behind her, was taller and broader than he'd been in high school. As for the child, Alycia had her mother's coloring — dark-brown hair and fair complexion — as well as the same heart-shaped face. But Ruth saw Chad Hallston in her as well.

"Come on," Derek said, moving around them to lead the way up the walk.

Ruth smiled her welcome, hoping Brooklyn and Alycia would know it was genuine. Wanting to make sure, she held out her hands. "Brooklyn, my dear. How wonderful to see you again. I'm so glad you could come to stay with me until your house is ready to occupy."

A bit of the wariness departed Brooklyn's blue-gray eyes. "Thank you, Mrs. Johnson."

"Call me Ruth. Please." Her gaze dropped

51

to the little girl. "Alycia, welcome to Thunder Creek. I knew your mother when she was your age, and you're every bit as pretty now as she was then."

The child sidled a little closer to Brooklyn, but there was no look of fear in her eyes. Ruth thought that a good sign.

To Derek she said, "Will you bring in their things, dear, while I show them around?"

"Sure thing."

Ruth motioned toward Brooklyn. "Come inside, you two. You must be hungry after driving all day. As soon as I show you to your rooms, we'll get you something to eat." She turned and headed into the house.

Behind her, Brooklyn said, "We hate to be any bother. I can fix us some —"

"Bother? Not at all. It's a joy to have someone to cook for. I rattle around in this big old house all by myself most of the time."

On the second floor, she opened the door to her favorite guest room. It had once belonged to her eldest son, Ken. Derek's father. But it had long since lost all traces of his boyhood. These days the room was distinctly feminine, decorated in varying shades of teal — one of Ruth's favorite colors — including the floral bedspread on the queen-sized four-poster bed.

"This will be your room, Brooklyn, and Alycia can stay in the room across the hall."

"We could share this one, Mrs. Johnson."

"Ruth," she reminded.

"Ruth. We don't mind sharing. Really. We're used to —"

"But there's no need." Her gaze flicked to Alycia. "Unless you don't want a room of your own. Here." She stepped back into the hall. "Let me show you."

The room opposite had been her daughter Bianca's room. And years later, when Bianca's daughter Samantha had come to stay awhile after graduating from college, it had become her room. It delighted Ruth to think of another girl staying there, even for only a few days.

Alycia took one look at the canopy bed and the large bay window overlooking the creek and park, and her face broke into a grin. "I'll stay in here."

"Good." Ruth clapped her hands together. "That's settled."

Footsteps on the stairs told her Derek had arrived with her guests' belongings. "We'll leave you two alone to settle in. Just come to the kitchen when you're ready. I'll have sandwiches prepared and on the table." She gave mother and daughter a parting smile before leaving.

53

Derek wasn't long behind her.

"Would you like to stay and eat with us?" she asked him.

"No, thanks, Gran. I need to get going. I'm on duty for another hour." He kissed her cheek. "Tell Brooklyn I'll tow her car to the Hallston house as soon as my shift is over. She can decide what to do with it after that."

He was trying hard to be gracious, dear boy. It wasn't that he was selfish by nature, but letting go of the property he'd saved toward for nearly two years wasn't easy. She would have to pray for him, as well as for Brooklyn and her daughter. She sensed the days ahead wouldn't be easy for any of them as they adjusted to their new normals.

CHAPTER 4

After a night of tossing and turning, of debating whether or not to come to see her dad, Brooklyn stood on the sidewalk and stared at the two-bedroom bungalow where she'd grown up. The peach-colored rosebushes that fronted the house were in bloom, giving it a gentle, peaceful appearance. That was a facade. It always had been.

Her heart pinched. Hope and dread warred within. Hope that her dad had changed. Dread — no, more like certainty — that he would be the same man she'd run away from. But she wouldn't know until she saw him.

Steeling herself, she moved up the walkway, stepped onto the stoop, and rapped on the front door. Part of her wished he wouldn't be at home, that she could delay this meeting for a few more days.

Or forever.

But she couldn't put it off. The last thing

she wanted was to run into her dad by chance. She wanted no element of surprise. This first meeting in eleven years had to be on her own terms, by her own design. She wanted him to know that she wasn't afraid of him.

A sound from inside gave her a moment of warning before the door was yanked open. Her father's eyes revealed irritation at first, perhaps because of the early hour. Then came recognition, surprise, and anger in quick succession.

"Hello, Dad."

"What are you doing here?"

"I want to talk to you. May I come in? I won't stay long."

Brooklyn wouldn't have been surprised if he'd slammed the door in her face, but in the end all he did was grunt. Then he turned and walked to his favorite chair. She drew a steadying breath and stepped through the doorway. But she didn't go far.

Unpleasant memories assaulted her. Her stomach twisted, and again she had to resist the urge to run away. But she wouldn't. She was done running away. She'd done enough of that in her life. No more. Not anymore.

Beneath her breath, she whispered, " 'I can do all things through Him who strengthens me.' "

"What?" Her dad snarled the word.

She ignored him as her gaze swept the small living room. The sofa looked the same, except it was more worn. It was in exactly the same place it had always been. How many times had she sat there while her father railed at her about her many shortcomings and failures? Countless.

She shook off the memory, reminding herself once again that she wasn't that girl, that her dad couldn't make her become that girl again, no matter what he said or did.

"Why are you here, Brooklyn?"

"I needed to tell you that Alycia and I have come back to Thunder Creek to live."

He stiffened away from the back of the recliner. "You've *what*?"

"Chad . . . Chad passed away this spring, and he left us his parents' house in his will."

"I don't believe it. Why would he do that? He didn't want you. He didn't want either of you. You told me so yourself when you tried to come sniveling back with a brat in your belly."

Maybe he couldn't make her run away, but sadly, his words still had the power to sting, even after all this time.

"You're as worthless as your mother ever was." It was a familiar litany. "You should've had the good sense to stay away like she

57

did. Did you come back to embarrass me?"

As she'd feared, he hadn't changed. Or perhaps he had. Perhaps he'd grown angrier, more bitter, more hateful with the passage of time. She could almost feel the back of his hand colliding with her cheek.

She reached behind her for the door. "Think what you like, Dad. My daughter and I are here in Thunder Creek to stay. I . . . I'd hoped things could be different between you and me. But if not, fine." She squared her shoulders.

"You shamed me, Brooklyn. Do you hear me? You were a disobedient child, and then you became a tramp, like your mother. Were you pregnant when you ran away with Chad? Did you force him to marry you? Or maybe you tricked him into it. You must have. That boy and his family were too good for the likes of you."

Tears began to fill her eyes. Lest he see them, she hurried out of the door as fast as her weakening legs would carry her. She kept going until she'd turned a corner and her girlhood home was out of sight. Then she stopped to lean her back against the trunk of a tree.

"God," she whispered, eyes closed, "keep me strong." She drew in a slow, deep breath

58

through her nose and released it. Once, then again.

Feeling steadier, she opened her eyes and began to walk. On the way to her dad's house, she hadn't seen much of anything. Her thoughts had been too focused on that dreaded first confrontation. Now she took in her surroundings.

A few of the houses had new coats of paint. Some trees had grown taller and fuller. But mostly the town and the neighborhood she was in looked the same as they did in her memories. And to be fair, not all of her memories were sad or scary ones. For instance —

Her cell phone rang, startling her. She plucked the phone from the back pocket of her jeans. A smile lifted the corners of her mouth when she saw the caller ID, and she quickly punched the button to answer the call. "Esther."

"Hello, Brooklyn."

She stopped walking. "How are you?"

"I'm doing all right. I spent yesterday at the beach, and it was lovely. But I called to see how you are. I trust you arrived in Thunder Creek all right."

"Yes. We got here okay. My car conked out just as we got to town, but otherwise it was an uneventful trip."

59

"And?"

Brooklyn knew there was no point trying to hide the full truth from her friend. "And it isn't so bad being here. It doesn't feel as strange as I thought it would." She drew a quick breath. "I've just been to see my dad, to let him know Alycia and I are in town and plan to stay here." She looked back the way she'd come. "It went about the way I expected it to."

"Oh, I'm sorry, dear."

Not wanting to dwell on the negative, she faced forward and began walking again. "Our house is kind of a wreck. Well, not a wreck really. But plenty dirty from what I could tell. The power wasn't on yet when we got here, so there were no lights and no water. Plus the windows are all boarded over. We couldn't stay there, and we really couldn't afford to stay in the motel. But then we were invited to stay with Ruth Johnson." She quickly explained who Ruth was and detailed how staying with her had come about.

"Thank You, Jesus," Esther said softly when Brooklyn was finished.

That brought another smile to Brooklyn's lips.

"I was afraid you would be lonely your first few days back in Idaho, and I'm grate-

60

ful God made sure that didn't happen."

"I am lonely for you, Esther." Her voice caught at the end.

"My friend, I miss you too. And I'm praying for you and Alycia every single day."

Tears came to her eyes again, and this time she didn't bother to fight them.

"Brooklyn, I am so very proud of you — for the woman you are, for the woman Jesus is molding you to be. You remember that in the days ahead. Okay?"

"I will, Esther."

"Good." There was a pause, then Esther added, "I've got to hang up now. But we'll talk again soon. I promise."

Ruth's husband, Walter, had mostly read books that had to do with advancements in medicine. He'd never been much for novels, with the exception of murder mysteries. But their daughter Bianca had devoured all kinds of fiction from a young age. Most of Bianca's childhood favorites — anything to do with horses, dogs, or girl detectives — had been left in her parents' home when she'd left for college and had never been reclaimed. Instead, they'd stayed on the bookshelves for her own children to read whenever they came to Thunder Creek to visit Pappy and Gran.

61

Now Ruth watched Alycia as she sat on the floor in front of the den bookshelves. Time and again, the girl removed a book from the shelf, studied its cover, opened to the first page, read quickly, then closed and put it back before removing the next one. It had been too many years since a child had been eager to look through the selection of books available in Ruth's home. She enjoyed watching almost as much as she imagined Alycia enjoyed looking.

The sound of a closing door drew Ruth's attention toward the kitchen. "I think your mom is back from her walk. Do you want to stay here or come with me?"

Alycia didn't look up. "I'll stay here, please."

Ruth chuckled as she moved away. But in the kitchen, her smile vanished when she saw Brooklyn's tear-streaked face. "What's wrong?"

The young woman shook her head.

On a hunch, Ruth said, "You went to see your father, and he made you cry."

"Yes, I went to see him, and it wasn't pleasant. But that isn't why I'm crying." Brooklyn reached for the tissue box on the counter near the door.

"Do you want to tell me about it?" Ruth asked gently.

62

"Where is Alycia? I'd rather she didn't see me like this."

"She's in the den, going through our old collection of children's books."

"Then I should have plenty of time to compose myself." The hint of a smile curved the corners of Brooklyn's mouth. "She loves to read." She dried her cheeks with the tissue, then patted her eyes. "Sometimes it felt like we lived at the library in Reno on my days off."

"Reading's a good pastime for a child. Sparks the imagination." Ruth motioned toward the kitchen table. "Let me get you some coffee."

Brooklyn hesitated a moment before sinking onto one of the chairs. Silence fell over the room while Ruth filled two mugs. A short while later, she settled on a chair opposite the younger woman. Brooklyn held the proffered mug between both hands but didn't take a sip right away. Ruth had learned to be patient and let silence last as long as was needed.

Finally, Brooklyn said, "My good friend is dying."

"Oh, my dear. I'm so sorry."

Brooklyn's smile was bittersweet. "You sounded just like Esther right then."

Without any encouragement on Ruth's

part, Brooklyn told her about Esther Peterman. By the time she was finished, the tears were flowing down her cheeks again.

Ruth felt like crying herself. "She sounds like an amazing woman."

"She is." Brooklyn took more tissues from the box and blew her nose.

After another lengthy silence, Ruth decided a change of subject was called for. "So tell me. What are your plans now, Brooklyn?"

"My plans?"

"It couldn't have been easy, returning to your hometown after so long. Even with a house waiting for you. You must have some plans in mind."

Brooklyn gave Ruth a look that seemed to say she was glad to talk of something else. "Yes. Actually, I do. I plan to turn the house into a B&B." She sat straighter as she wiped her eyes with another tissue. "It will take time and money, of course. More than I have at present. But I'm going to do it. I did a lot of research while we were still in Reno, and I'm convinced it's a great location for what I want to do. Very scenic and right on the way to the fruit orchards and vineyards, not to mention the Snake River. Thunder Creek's small motel wouldn't be real competition for it. My B&B would serve a completely different kind of customer. I really think it can succeed."

The determination and courage Ruth saw in Brooklyn's eyes made her want to give a shout of joy. It had never been a secret in Thunder Creek how hard Reggie Myers had been on his daughter, both before and after his wife left him. The girl Ruth remembered had been fearful much of the time, even when she'd tried to hide it with rebellion and bravado. Ruth saw no remnant of that girl in the woman who sat opposite her.

"I don't want to be a waitress for the rest of my life, Mrs. Johnson. Although I'm a good waitress and I love serving people. But the B&B will allow me to do that while earning a better wage than waitressing, and it will allow me to spend more time with Alycia and give her a better life."

"Well, good for you," Ruth said with a firm nod. "I think it's a fine idea. And if I can be of help in some way, I hope you'll ask. I love to help the people of Thunder Creek whenever I can." She offered a smile. "And I hope I can be as good a friend to you as Esther Peterman has been all these years."

CHAPTER 5

Later that morning, with a trunk full of cleaning supplies provided by Ruth, Brooklyn drove to the Hallston home in a car also provided by Ruth. Now, standing in the middle of the living room, assessing its condition, sadness washed over her once again. She wasn't sad for herself. She wasn't afraid of the work it would take to put it right again. Her sadness was for Chad's mother. Marie Hallston had created a home that was warm and welcoming. Even Brooklyn had felt at home within these walls. But years of neglect had erased that feeling.

Someone — Derek and some of his friends, she assumed — had removed the boards from all of the windows, letting sunlight through the dirt-streaked glass. It touched the many dust motes floating in the air and highlighted the cobwebs hanging from the ceilings. How long would it take before she and Alycia could move in?

Longer than she wanted, no doubt. Not that she didn't feel welcome in Ruth's home. But she needed to be here. She needed every day to count. Tomorrow she would bring Alycia with her to make the initial cleanup go a little faster.

"One thing at a time," she reminded herself. "Take it one thing at a time, and it will get done."

She set the plastic caddy of supplies on the floor, then went to the wall switch, saying a quick prayer. With a flick, the lights came on. "Yes!"

She was thankful for the power, of course, but the glow of the lightbulbs revealed even more of the work ahead of her. She remembered the walls in the living room as pale yellow — Marie Hallston's favorite color — but they looked tan now. The sofa, chairs, end tables, and coffee table had been draped with sheets, which were covered in a layer of dust. The hardwood floor was as dusty as the protective sheets over the furniture.

Brooklyn drew a deep breath and moved into the formal dining room. The large table and chairs surrounding it were also covered with sheets. But the elegant buffet had been ignored, along with the knickknacks on it. She wondered why these items hadn't been protected as she lifted a Bo Peep figurine

67

and blew on it. Dust flew up in a cloud, making her sneeze.

In the kitchen, she found evidence of mice and was thankful none were scurrying around in the daylight. The refrigerator door had been braced open with a block of wood. No lights were on. No running sounds. She removed the block and closed the door. Still silent. Leaning to the side, she saw the cord was disconnected from the wall. A little maneuvering and she soon had the appliance plugged in. It began to softly whir. She smiled at the sound. It was a small miracle that it worked after so many idle years.

With her plans for the B&B in mind, she finished the tour of the lower level — the family room with its fireplace, the cozy den, the large master bedroom, plus one full bath and another half bath — then climbed the stairs for a quick look at the rest of the bedrooms and baths. Beds and dressers were draped with more dusty sheets, but at least mice hadn't made obvious nests in any of the mattresses. Another small miracle, no doubt.

As she retraced her steps to the kitchen, she wondered why Chad hadn't returned to Thunder Creek after leaving her. He hadn't had the same reasons to run away from this town. His parents had loved him. He'd had

68

friends aplenty. He could have come back and been welcomed with open arms. And even if not then, why not sell the house after his parents died? Why had he allowed it to sit like this, going to ruin? It made no sense to her. Worse yet, she would never get those answers. It was too late.

She closed her eyes, feeling a different kind of sadness wash over her. Chad Hallston had broken her heart when he'd abandoned her in Reno all those years ago. Time had healed the pain he'd left behind. Now all she felt when she thought of him was sorrow. For many reasons. But most of all she was sorry he'd never known his amazing little girl. By his own choice.

She shook her head, driving away the unwelcome memories. The past couldn't be changed, no matter how much she might wish it. Better to focus on today.

"Hey!" came Derek's voice from the living room. "Anybody in here?"

Startled at the unexpected sound in the silent house, her pulse skipped a beat or two. "I'm here." She left the kitchen and hurried to the front of the house.

Derek wasn't in his deputy's uniform today. Instead, he wore jeans and a black T-shirt with sleeves that hugged the well-developed muscles of his upper arms. It was

69

a good look on him.

"The place looks even worse with the boards off the windows," he said as his gaze swept the room.

Understatement, she thought. "Thanks for taking them off. I needed the extra light."

He nodded. "Some of my buddies pitched in. Didn't take us long." He took several strides into the room, stopped, turned in a slow circle. "Man, are you sure you can make it livable anytime soon?" He seemed to look everywhere but at her.

She wasn't sure why, but she felt insulted by his question. As if he'd judged her incapable. "I'm not afraid of hard work."

"That's a good thing." He reached up and swiped at a cobweb hanging just out of his reach. "Maybe tearing down the place *was* a good idea," he said softly.

Had she heard him right? "What did you say?"

Now he met her gaze. "Sorry. Nothing." He glanced away again and took a couple of steps toward the dining room. "I talked to another friend of mine about your car. He says he'll take a look at it, see if he can fix it for you."

"Is he a mechanic?"

Derek smiled at that. "Not exactly. Maybe you remember him. Justin Mathers."

70

"Justin? Yes, I remember him. Short. Glasses. Math and science whiz kid, wasn't he?"

Derek smiled. "That's him."

"And he's still around Thunder Creek? I pictured him as a university professor living in a big city. Or maybe working for the government in some high-level think tank."

"Your first idea was close to right. He is a professor. Just not in a big city. He teaches at Boise State, but he still lives in Thunder Creek and commutes back and forth. He married a gal he met in college, and they have four kids."

"Four? Already?" Nobody got older in memories, she realized. She still envisioned Justin Mathers as a socially awkward boy, even if he was a college professor.

"Yeah. And I wouldn't be surprised if they decide to have more kids. Justin and Carol seem to thrive on the chaos of a big family."

Brooklyn had once dreamed of having several children. She hadn't liked being an only child. Maybe if she'd had sisters or brothers, her dad wouldn't have focused all of his judgment, criticism, bitterness, and punishments on her. But that was another thought she needed to shove away.

She glanced over her shoulder toward the kitchen, then back at Derek. "I'd better get

71

to work. I left Alycia with your grandmother, and I don't want to impose on Ruth's kindness for too long."

"Trust me. You're not imposing. Gran loves to help a neighbor whenever she can." He motioned with his hand, taking in the room. "Give me a holler if you need help with heavy lifting. I live right next door."

She felt her eyes widen. How had she missed that bit of information yesterday? Had he mentioned it when they were here? She was certain he hadn't.

He must have seen her surprise. "I bought the old Kellogg property six years ago. I'm farming it. Well, more like what some folks call market gardening. I guess the place is too small to be considered a real farm. But the produce I grow is Certified Organic." He said the last words with pride. "I hope to expand the operation eventually."

"I never would have guessed you wanted to be a farmer."

"Caught me by surprise too. But once the idea took hold . . ." He shrugged.

She sensed he would have liked to add something, but when he didn't, she repeated, "I'd better get back to cleaning."

"Right." A different tone had entered his voice. Aloofness? Reluctance? Something. "Like I said, I'm right next door if you need something." He disappeared through the doorway without a backward glance.

She remained where she stood for a short while, pondering the brief conversation. Perhaps she wasn't being fair to Derek. While he hadn't seemed overly friendly, either yesterday or today, he had been more than a little helpful — taking them to his grandmother's, removing the boards from the windows, talking to Justin about her car. At present she was grateful for any kindness, even if it did sound reluctant. At the very least, she was thankful he didn't appear to outright dislike her, the way he had years ago.

She took a breath and squared her shoulders. "Okay, enough procrastinating. Time to hit it hard." She pushed away thoughts of her neighbor and of the past. "I am going to make this place sparkle."

As she grabbed the cleaning supplies, she couldn't help but feel a budding optimism in her heart.

Derek leaned the hoe against a wheelbarrow before wiping his forehead with the back of an arm. It was hot for June. All spring it had been unusually warm. The growing season was two or three weeks ahead of normal.

73

After taking a few long gulps from his stainless-steel water bottle, he let his gaze sweep over his land. Except where the house and outbuildings stood, all of the three acres had been pasture when he bought the property. His second summer here, he'd put two acres under the plow for the raising of produce. One acre had remained pasture for his two horses and the beef calf he raised each year.

It was a small beginning, but Derek had big dreams.

Or used to have.

His gaze shifted to the neighboring land. To the Hallston place. No, Brooklyn's place.

His plans to buy those additional ten acres had been in the works for a couple of years. If he'd been able to come up with the down payment at the start, it would have been a done deal. The property would have been his before Chad got his fatal diagnosis that then led him to change his mind about selling.

He sighed, knowing he needed to let go of his disappointment. Although, if he was honest with himself, it was more like resentment. Besides, there was always a chance Brooklyn would be willing to sell the land to him. He hadn't asked how long she intended to stay. What would a widow with

74

one child do with that big house and ten acres anyway? Maybe he should have brought it up yesterday, but something had made him want to wait for a better time. Maybe because she'd looked tired. Maybe because she'd been obviously worried about the expense of car repairs. Whatever the reason, he'd chosen not to make an offer to buy her out just yet.

Once again, he looked toward the neighboring property. Only this time his gaze settled on the house. He could see the nose of his grandmother's car peeking around the corner. Which meant Brooklyn was still inside.

She shouldn't have to do all that cleanup alone.

Another sigh escaped him.

"I helped her already," he muttered to himself. "I towed the car. I got Justin to look at it. I took the boards off the windows. Isn't that enough?"

No, his conscience told him. He needed to do more. He had a neighbor in need. A few moments of help here and there weren't enough. Only how much more could he do? Between his work with the sheriff's department and his farm, he didn't have a lot of hours to share with the widow next door.

Just an excuse, that persistent voice of his

75

conscience whispered. It sounded a great deal like Gran's voice.

"Okay, fine. I'm going. I'm going."

Brushing his hands across the thighs of his jeans, he headed once again across the fallow field separating the two properties. But when he rounded the corner of the house, he stopped, surprised to find two other cars — familiar cars, both of them — parked in the driveway. Female chatter and laughter carried to him through the open front door.

His feeling of surprise didn't last long. To be honest, he should have expected that Gran and her friends would pitch in. But still he had to step onto the porch and look inside. He didn't know when they'd arrived or how many were here, but what the women had accomplished in the four or five hours since he'd walked out this same front door amazed him. Sheets were gone from the furniture. Windows had been cleaned of years of dirt. Cobwebs had been swept from the ceilings. Floors had been dust mopped and rugs vacuumed. Even the walls seemed to be brighter.

"Hello!" he called out.

"Derek!" His grandmother appeared in the dining room archway a few seconds after he heard her voice. Her gray hair was

76

covered with a kerchief tied in a knot near her forehead. She wore a loose-fitting cotton shirt and a pair of denim trousers, and she held a mop in her right hand. "You've come just in time."

"I have?"

"We could use your help."

"And about time!" Camila Diaz's voice drew his eyes toward the hallway. A moment later, her head appeared in the den doorway. She grinned at him, then disappeared again.

Two or three more voices from upstairs called his name in unison, one of them — Millie Smith, his neighbor to the west — adding, "Isn't it great to see this place come alive again?"

Lying through his teeth, he called back, "It sure is, Millie."

"Derek."

He looked toward his grandmother again.

She motioned him forward. "Come with me."

"Right."

Gran turned and moved out of sight. Derek hesitated a moment, then followed after her.

The transformation in the kitchen was even more remarkable than in the living and dining rooms. Almost the way it had looked when Chad's parents were alive. Except,

77

that is, for the stove that had been pulled out beyond the cupboards, presumably so Tracy Vinton — who stood next to the appliance, scrub brush in hand — could clean the wall behind it and floor beneath it.

"We're having a whale of a time trying to get that back in its proper spot," Gran said. "It's a snug fit."

With a nod, Derek moved to the stove, eyed either side of it to judge the opening between the countertops. Tracy backed away to give him room. He gripped the front edges of the white appliance and began to maneuver it back into place. A bit of grunting, mumbling, and shoving were required before he accomplished the job.

Gran applauded as he straightened and turned around. "Thank you, r. That was a big help."

"No problem. Anything else I can do?"

"No, I think we've done as much as we can manage for one day. Most of the gals need to get home to their families now."

He gestured toward the other rooms. "You've done a lot."

"We have, indeed."

"How long have you been here?"

"A few hours. We couldn't leave Brooklyn to do it all herself."

78

"I thought you were helping by watching Alycia."

"I decided Brooklyn needed more elbow grease. So I took Alycia to the library. Helen is keeping an eye on her there."

The creak of the closing screen door drew Derek's gaze in the direction of the back porch. Brooklyn entered the kitchen a moment later, a metal bucket in hand.

Gran said, "Look who showed up in time to get the stove back in place."

Brooklyn looked from him to the stove and back again. "Thanks." Weariness filled the single word and was etched on her pretty face as well.

He shrugged. After everything Brooklyn and the ladies of the town had accomplished, his contribution seemed paltry — and he didn't care one bit for the twinge of guilt he felt because he hadn't done more.

"Brooklyn, dear," his grandmother said. "It's time you and I went back to town."

"But I thought I would —"

"Come along." Gran whipped the kerchief from her head. "We'll return tomorrow and keep at it until everything is ready for you to move in."

Brooklyn looked ready to protest a second time, then pressed her lips together as she nodded. Whether it was to honor Gran's

79

wishes or because she suddenly realized how tired she was, Derek couldn't be sure. Whatever the reason, he felt a small spark of respect spring to life.

CHAPTER 6

The next day, as Derek dropped the last of the hay into a feed box, he heard an excited, girlish squeal not too far behind him.

"Horses! You've got horses!"

Before he even turned, he knew who he would see: Alycia Hallston, her eyes big and round, a smile as wide as the western sky bowing her lips.

"Can I pet them?" she asked, moving closer.

Derek hadn't paid the girl much attention that first day, but he'd had time since then to think about her quite a bit. Her and her dad's dying request. Because now that Alycia was in Thunder Creek and would be living next door, Derek needed to figure out what his part in her life was supposed to look like. Right now he didn't have a clue.

"Can I?" she persisted.

He glanced over his shoulder. Blue Boy stood near the fence, muzzle buried in hay.

"Sure. Come on over."

Alycia arrived in an instant and poked her head between the rails of the fence.

"Whoa!" Derek put his hands on her shoulders and drew her back. "Wait a minute." He turned her to face him. "Let's set a few rules, shall we, kiddo?"

She scrunched up her nose, even while nodding.

"You don't go anywhere near these horses or any other livestock without an adult present. Got it?"

"Got it."

"You don't go into the pasture without my permission. Got it?"

"Got it."

"And you do exactly as you're told anytime you are on my property."

"Got it," she answered before he could pose the question a third time. Another smile tugged at the corners of her mouth.

One thing for certain, she wasn't intimidated by Derek.

"All right, then." He watched her clamor up to the middle rail of the fence. Her hands gripped the top one.

"He's so tall. Are all horses this tall?"

"Not all of them. Sunny, the mare over there, isn't nearly as tall. You haven't been around horses before, have you?"

82

"No." The word came out on a breath laced with wonder. "Nobody had a horse where we lived. No place for 'em. We lived right in the middle of town. We didn't even have a yard of our own."

That was hard for Derek to imagine. He'd never lived anywhere without plenty of wide-open spaces.

"But there's a park not too far from our apartment, and my school has a big playground."

"Well, maybe you can get a horse, now that you've got all that land behind your new home." The words came out without a hint of bitterness. He was glad of it. It meant he'd made some progress in adjusting his attitude.

The girl's eyes widened. "Do you think so? I asked Mom if I could get one, but she said they cost a lot."

"Well, she's right about that."

"We've never had any kind of pet, like a dog or a cat even." Alycia leaned forward. "Can I touch him now?"

"Sure. Just move slow and put your hand on Blue Boy's back."

"Blue Boy. That's his name?" She followed his instructions. "Hey, Blue Boy." She patted him. "How you doin'?"

The gelding huffed into the hay, never lift-

83

ing his head, and continued to chew.

Alycia didn't seem to care that Blue Boy was oblivious to her gentle touch. But at last she straightened and hopped down from the fence. "Thanks, Mr. Johnson."

"You're welcome. Going home now?"

As if in answer to his question, he heard Brooklyn call her daughter's name. He looked across the field to the Hallston house and watched as she hurried toward them. Her concern was obvious even before he could read her expression.

"Alycia Marie, what are you doing over here? Didn't I tell you not to go anywhere without asking me first? You were supposed to be in the backyard."

Marie was Alycia's middle name? Derek looked at the girl, and his respect for Brooklyn went up another notch. He liked knowing she'd honored Chad's mom that way, despite being separated from Chad by the time Alycia was born.

"Sorry, Mom." Alycia dipped her head. "I saw Mr. Johnson with his horses, and I came over for a closer look." She glanced up again, a smile blossoming. "Mr. Johnson let me pet the big gray one."

Brooklyn tried to maintain her stern expression, but even Derek could see her irritation with her daughter wane. "Just don't

84

do it again. I need to know where you are. You're new here. You could get lost." She looked up and met Derek's gaze. "And don't be pestering Mr. Johnson either. Just because we're neighbors doesn't mean he wants you dropping over uninvited."

"I don't mind," he said without thinking. Surprise followed an instant later at the realization there was truth in his words.

And judging by the look that flashed across Brooklyn's face, she was surprised too.

"As long as she gets your permission first," he added.

Her expression softened. "That's kind of you, Derek. Thank you."

Maybe it wouldn't be all that hard to honor Chad's wishes. Being a father figure didn't mean actually *being* a father. He could let her hang out with him now and then, maybe teach her a little about gardening or about the animals on his place. Poor kid said she hadn't owned a pet before. That was just wrong.

Brooklyn took hold of Alycia's hand. "We need to get back to the house."

Alycia said, "See you later, Mr. Johnson."

Then the pair of them walked away.

A new thought popped into his head as he watched them leave. Chad had written that

85

he wasn't going to tell Brooklyn about his request. What would she think if she did know? Would she be glad, or would she hate the idea? Would she think Derek worthy of such a responsibility?

And the crazy thing was, he wanted her to think him worthy of it.

The house was too quiet and empty, Brooklyn decided after Ruth and her friends departed. They'd shown up this morning for another work session, filling the house with chatter and soap. And what those women had accomplished on their second day of cleaning seemed even more miraculous than the first.

Now that the last of them had called it quits, packed up their supplies, and exited with cheery farewells, Brooklyn and Alycia were left exhausted. No, more than exhausted, at least on Brooklyn's part. She was amazed. Amazed that so many of them had come to help, not just one day but two. Amazed by their friendliness and their laughter and their smiles. The main reason they'd come, she was certain, was because they loved and admired Ruth Johnson. Ruth had asked them to help Brooklyn, and so they had. But it was more than that. Brooklyn had felt their genuine warmth. As if she belonged in their midst. Thunder Creek had never felt like home before. It had been a place to run from. But maybe she and Alycia would fit into this community after all. She hadn't allowed herself to hope for such a thing, but now she did.

"What would you think if we stayed in our house tonight?" Brooklyn asked Alycia as they reentered the house.

"Really? Cool."

"Not as nice as Mrs. Johnson's guest rooms but —"

"But it's ours."

Brooklyn stopped, leaned down, and kissed the top of her daughter's head. "Do you know how wonderful you are? And you're right. The house is ours. We have a home and acres and acres for you to play on."

Home. The word felt good in her heart. She hadn't expected it to feel that way. At least not this soon.

Looking at Alycia again, she said, "Let's go to the grocery store. What would you like to eat tonight? How about spaghetti? That would be fast and easy."

"Yeah. Spaghetti!"

It was lucky for Brooklyn that her daughter wasn't a picky eater. Because of their limited finances, they had often made do

87

with canned soup or a plate of pasta. Maybe now she would have a chance to improve her culinary skills. After all, if she was going to feed guests at her future B&B, she'd better be able to cook something more than grilled cheese sandwiches, tuna casseroles, or spaghetti.

But trying out new cuisine wasn't in their budget just yet. "Let's go." She grabbed for her purse. "After we're done shopping, we'll get our things from Mrs. Johnson's house."

An hour and a half later, Brooklyn and Alycia carried the last of the grocery bags into their house.

"I wish you would have stayed with me one more night," Ruth said from the front porch. "Your phone isn't working yet and you don't have a car to drive."

"I have a cell phone, Ruth. I don't need a landline. Not until I actually have a business to run." Brooklyn set down the plastic shopping bag in the middle of the living room and returned to the porch. "And I spoke with Justin Mathers earlier. He says he'll have my car up and running by tonight. It wasn't anything too serious after all."

"But there is still so much that needs done here in the house. So many repairs to make. It's cleaner, of course, but —"

88

"All the more reason for us to stay here. We'll be more aware of what needs work, and we can accomplish things a little at a time."

Ruth looked unconvinced.

Brooklyn hesitated, then gave in to her impulse and gave the older woman a hug. "Thank you for making us feel so welcome. You've been so kind, and we appreciate all you've done for us. Truly."

"Oh *pish*. Don't mention it." Ruth stepped back and lightly patted Brooklyn's cheek. "You've got my number. You call if there's anything I can do for you. Anything at all." She motioned to the neighboring property. "And don't forget that Derek is right next door if you need him."

Brooklyn nodded.

Ruth leaned to one side, looking into the house, and called, "Good-bye, Alycia. Come see me again soon."

Alycia ran out of the house a few seconds later. "I will, Mrs. Johnson." The two exchanged a hug. "Bye."

Brooklyn and Alycia stayed on the front porch, waving at Ruth Johnson as she pulled out of the driveway. Then, with a grin at each other, they turned and went inside.

Late afternoon sunlight spilled through the clean windows into the living room, and

89

a memory, unbidden, washed over Brooklyn. A memory so strong it didn't seem like a memory so much as that she'd fallen back in time.

She'd been terrified the summer afternoon Chad had brought her home to meet his parents. She'd been certain she would be rejected, as she'd been rejected by others. And yet Marie Hallston had greeted her — a girl from the proverbial wrong side of the tracks — with a smile as warm as the sunlight that had spilled into the living room, painting everything with a buttery golden glow. Brooklyn had soaked in the acceptance like a dry sponge in a bathtub. That day and every time after that.

"Mom?"

The past dissolved around her.

"Are we gonna eat now?"

Brooklyn blinked, glanced toward her daughter, and nodded. "Sure. Let's eat. Spaghetti still sound good?"

"Yup."

She picked up the grocery bag she'd left on the floor earlier, and the pair headed to the kitchen.

90

CHAPTER 7

Saturday mornings were the busiest day of the week at Sips and Scentimentals. Ruth's regular customers knew that was the day she made her extraspecial sticky buns. The gift shop always did well then, too, although those customers were mostly visitors to the area — folks driving over to visit the wineries to the west of town or to buy fresh produce in season at one of the farmers' markets or roadside stands.

On this particular Saturday morning, the shop was abuzz with conversation. While Ruth's longtime employee and dearest friend, Camila Diaz, helped customers in the gift shop, Ruth observed her new part-time waitress as the girl delivered pastries and coffee or tea to the tables. Gina was young and inexperienced, but she was also very willing to learn. And she would get better with practice.

As was true of most things in life.

91

The jingle of a bell announced the arrival of another customer, drawing Ruth's gaze toward the entrance. Surprise widened her eyes as she watched Mac Tompkins escort his wife toward a newly vacated table in the rear corner. To the best of her knowledge, this was Mac's first visit to her shop. Not his kind of establishment, she was certain. And judging by the expressions on both his and Fran's faces — his angry, hers tense — neither of them had arrived in the best of moods.

"I'll take care of them, Gina," Ruth said as she picked up an order pad.

She prayed silently as she walked toward the table and greeted them. "Welcome to Sips and Scentimentals."

Mac grunted something.

Fran whispered, "Thank you."

Ruth hovered her pencil over the order pad. "Would either of you care for a sticky bun? They're fresh out of the oven."

"Just coffee for me," Mac answered. "Black. She'll have the same."

Ruth knew from a few church gatherings that Fran didn't drink her coffee black. "I'll bring some cream, just in case."

Fran glanced up. Some attempt had been made to hide her black eye with makeup, but the bruise was still obvious to Ruth. It

92

made her blood boil, seeing the purple-rose shadow beneath the concealer.

Drawing a quick breath first, she forced a pleasant smile. "I'll have your coffee to you straightaway."

Camila met her behind the counter. "You look like you could chew nails," she said softly.

"Is it *that* obvious?"

Her friend nodded. "Uh-huh."

"About as obvious as her black eye." Ruth drew another breath — a slow, deep one this time. "Why does she stay with him?"

"I don't know. If Emilio ever hit me, he would get the same with a skillet two seconds before I was out the door for good."

This made Ruth's temper cool, and she smiled at her friend. First, because she knew Camila's husband was one of the gentlest men ever born; Emilio Diaz wouldn't hurt anything or anybody, not for any reason. Second, because she knew he adored Camila with every breath in his body. And third, because she knew Camila would indeed take a frying pan to the person who threatened her or anybody she loved.

"I wish Fran had some of your fire." Ruth poured coffee into a couple of mugs.

Her friend glanced across the shop. "We never understand the choices a person

93

makes without walking a mile in their shoes."

"I know." She sighed. "I know. I just wish I could help her."

"Ruthie, you would pull every chick in this town under your protective wings if you could. But I believe that's God's role, not yours."

"Ouch."

Camila cocked an eyebrow, as if to say, *You know I speak the truth.*

With a nod of agreement, Ruth set the coffee mugs on a tray, along with a small pitcher of cream, and carried it all to the table.

Brooklyn sat at the kitchen table, a notebook and calculator before her. Off to the side were her checkbook and several sealed and stamped envelopes. These were the last of the bills she'd brought with her from Reno. Her old life was truly and completely a thing of the past now.

Still, she had to wonder what Chad had been thinking when he left this house to his widow and daughter without also leaving plenty of funds for its upkeep. He should have known what little finances she had. He must have known. If he'd been able to track them down after all those years, if he'd been

94

able to learn what he needed to know in order to leave this place to them in his will, surely he'd known it would be a struggle for Brooklyn to make the necessary repairs and improvements to the house he'd boarded over and left behind. Couldn't he have left her some necessary funds too?

That sounded ungrateful, even inside her own head.

She rubbed her forehead with her fingertips, rose from the chair, and walked out to the back porch. A soft breeze carried Alycia's voice to her. Her daughter sang something to herself as she swung from the thick rope tied to a large tree branch. Seeing Alycia as she leaned back and stretched her feet toward the sky — happy and carefree — made Brooklyn smile.

How I love her.

After Chad had walked out, leaving his seventeen-year-old wife pregnant and alone in a strange city, Brooklyn had briefly considered having an abortion. Thank God she hadn't been able to go through with it. A life without Alycia was unimaginable. She had to blink away tears at the mere idea of it.

Her happiness is all that matters.

In the city, surrounded by concrete and bricks more than anything else — not to

95

mention countless strangers — Alycia had been required to stay close to their apartment, except for when the two of them had gone somewhere together. Until this week, Alycia hadn't known the freedom of a makeshift swing in a big backyard. She had never lived next door to horses, a calf, and a coop full of chickens. She'd never seen the stars when they weren't competing with the bright lights of the city.

Perhaps all of that was what Chad had been thinking about when he left the house to them, with or without the proper funds for its upkeep.

"Hey, Mr. Johnson!" Alycia threw herself off the seat in midswing.

Brooklyn followed her daughter's gaze until she found Derek striding across the field, carrying a small basket in one hand. Alycia ran to meet him. They exchanged a few words, Alycia grinning all the while. Then they started toward the house. They looked surprisingly natural together. Almost like —

Tears sprang back into Brooklyn's eyes, this time tears of sorrow. For the love she'd never known from her own father. For the love her daughter had never known from Chad.

Derek held up the basket as they drew

96

closer. "Thought you might enjoy some strawberries."

"I don't know how much cash I have." She pushed open the screened-porch door. "But I'll have a look."

He shook his head. "No. I didn't mean for you to buy them. They're yours. These are about the last of the strawberries for the season. They came on early this year." He stopped at the bottom of the steps.

"You grew them?"

"That's what I do. Remember? Organic farming."

She shrugged, then took the basket from his outstretched arm. "I guess you seem more like a deputy to me than a farmer."

"Can't a man be both?" He grinned. He'd always had a nice smile.

Disturbed by that thought, Brooklyn motioned with her head for him to follow her inside. In the kitchen she set the basket on the counter near the sink before getting a large bowl from a cupboard.

"Bill paying, huh?" Derek said.

She glanced toward the table, not liking the idea that he might discover more about her situation than she chose to tell him. But there was nothing to worry about. Her notebook was closed, as was her checkbook. "Yes." She dumped the strawberries from

97

basket to bowl.

"Never seems to end, does it?"

"I'm sorry?" She looked up.

"Paying bills." He shrugged. "Right when you think you're getting ahead, something comes up. Least that's how it's been for me. I do well with a crop, and then an animal gets sick or a piece of machinery breaks down." He paused before adding, "That's life, I guess."

"I guess."

Derek glanced out the doorway. A muscle ticked in his jaw. Then he looked at her again. "Brooklyn, I was wondering what you plan to do with all this property."

"Do with it?"

"Ten acres is a lot of land."

Brooklyn looked out the kitchen window. "I haven't given it any thought. The house is plenty to cope with right now."

"Yeah. I guess you're right. Maybe —" He broke off the sentence, looking suddenly impatient.

With himself or with her?

Wariness niggled at her insides, and she tried to push the feeling away. In recent months, she'd realized that distrust was her default reaction toward men, especially when they seemed to want to say something but didn't. Her instant mistrust was a trait she didn't like about herself and wanted to change. And yet mistrust him she did in that moment.

Still staring out the window, she repeated words of encouragement in her head. *Remember what Esther said. I don't have to let old hurts and insecurities run my life.*

Had she forgotten Derek was right there in the room? It seemed like it to him. And maybe it was just as well. He needed to give her a little space before broaching the subject of the land a second time. He didn't want to bungle it. Next time he wouldn't beat around the bush and hope she caught his meaning. He would be better prepared.

"Well," he said, keeping his voice light, "enjoy the strawberries."

"We will," Alycia chimed in for the first time since they'd all entered the house.

Without thinking, he reached out and ruffled the hair on the top of her head. The girl pulled slightly away, giving him a look that said she was too old for that particular gesture. Then, just as suddenly, she grinned back at him, and he caught a glimpse of his old friend in her smile. So much like Chad that it almost hurt. His throat tightened. "See ya later, kiddo."

Moments later, walking across the field

99

that separated the two properties, Derek continued to think about Chad. In the past, he'd figured his friend had had good reasons for moving far from Reno and his only child. But now he wondered. What *would* be a good reason to abandon a child? Even if Brooklyn had done something terrible to drive Chad away from his wife, would it justify leaving his daughter too?

It shamed Derek that he'd never asked his friend why he'd left Brooklyn. In fact, he'd never asked any hard questions. He'd simply assumed Chad had to be in the right, which meant his wife had to be in the wrong.

Derek remembered a time, a couple of years after Chad and Brooklyn eloped, when he'd walked into his grandparents' kitchen and found Marie Hallston seated at the table, face in hands, weeping. Weeping for the son she hadn't heard from in over two years. Weeping because she hadn't known what became of him.

Or had she known?

Derek stopped and looked back at the house with its faded yellow paint. Had Chad's parents learned they had a grandchild before they passed? Was *that* why Marie Hallston had cried in his grandparents' kitchen? Was *that* why they'd been on the highway, somewhere in Nevada, in treacher-

100

ous February weather when their vehicle slid off the ice-covered road?

With a shake of his head, he started toward home again. Near the back porch, he set the empty strawberry basket inside a small shed and went inside. As he reached to open the refrigerator door, thoughts turning to dinner, the phone rang.

"Hello," he answered.

"Derek? It's Millie."

Millie Smith, his neighbor.

"Hey, Millie."

"Are you free at the moment? I hate to ask, but Tommy is hiking with some friends down along the river, and they've found a dog that's hurt but won't let anybody help it. The boys are still there. They called me because they didn't know what to do. Glen's not home yet. I could call the sheriff, but —"

"No, that's all right, Millie. I'll be glad to help. Are you at the house? I'll pick you up and you can show me where to find them."

As a deputy, he'd been involved in more than one animal rescue, and when they ended successfully and a beloved pet was returned to the owner, everyone was happy. But sometimes the circumstances were hard — a puppy farm or starving horses in an overgrazed pasture.

101

He grabbed the keys to his truck, patted his pocket to make sure he had his cell phone, and then headed out the door. Ten minutes later, he and Millie Smith were driving toward the river. They found the bikes Tommy and his friends had left at the side of a parking lot near a trailhead. Another fifteen minutes of walking, and they heard voices above the soft sounds of the smooth-flowing river.

"Tommy," Millie called.

"Over here, Mom."

An outcropping of dark-gray rocks came into view. The boys stood near a small cave-like opening, one of them leaning over and peering into the dark recesses.

"Mom." Tommy waved when he saw her.

As they drew closer, Derek thought he heard whimpers.

"I don't know what happened to it," Tommy said, looking from his mom to Derek. "But there was a lot of blood coming up the trail from the river. We followed it up here 'cause we knew it had to be in trouble, but we can't see it very good in there. We don't have a flashlight with us."

"I've got one." As Derek stepped closer to the opening, the boys moved aside. He went down on one knee. Blood had left dark smears on the rocks at the entrance. He

102

pointed the flashlight into the dark interior. A pair of eyes reflected the light back at him.

It was a small dog — he could tell that much — and it was frightened, cowering as far back as it could go, whimpering softly, sounding as if it didn't have the energy for much more than that. Should he use the catch pole he'd brought with him? Not knowing where the dog was injured or how severely, he wasn't sure that was the best option. But judging by the blood he'd seen already, he feared it could bleed to death before they could coax it out in the open. *If* they could coax it out.

He pulled back from the opening and took his phone from his pocket. The local vet, Ethan Walker, was in his contact list. He pressed the button and waited for Ethan to answer. Unfortunately, all Derek got was voice mail. He left a message and hung up.

This rescue was up to him.

He glanced over his shoulder. "Tommy, I'll need you to hold the flashlight for me."

"Sure."

"The rest of you better move farther off the trail. The dog's scared already. We don't want to make it worse as we bring it out."

Millie and the other three boys obediently moved out of view.

In the end, the dog didn't resist the rescue

103

effort. Once the loop of the catch pole was around its neck, it hobbled toward the opening. The toy-sized dog wasn't a breed Derek could name right off hand. Its coat was brown and white — where it wasn't stained by blood, some of it still bright red.

Derek unbuttoned his cotton shirt and removed it, then used it to wrap the dog. Holding her — he knew now the dog was female — close to his chest, uncaring if he got blood on his T-shirt, he stood. "Millie, can you call Ethan again? Tell him I've got the dog and am taking her to my place. Looks like she might have been shot. Maybe she has a broken front leg too. I'll do what I can for her, but he should get there as fast as he can."

His neighbor made the call as they hurried back to the parking lot. The boys were on their bikes and racing toward Thunder Creek before Millie, now behind the wheel of Derek's truck, had started the engine.

104

CHAPTER 8

Guilt was a great motivator, Brooklyn decided as she carried the hot casserole dish across the field to Derek's house. She knew he was inside. His truck was parked in the drive, and she'd seen him enter through his back door no more than fifteen minutes ago.

Alycia rang the doorbell while Brooklyn waited behind her.

It had been five days since Derek brought over the basket of fresh strawberries. Strawberries that had sweetened breakfast for several mornings in a row. And each time she'd taken a bite of one, it had reminded her how less than gracious she'd been for his thoughtfulness. Not just over the strawberries but for other things he'd done since he found them stranded on the side of the road.

Time to give him a proper thanks.

The door opened, revealing Derek in a dark T-shirt, jeans, bare feet, and wet hair.

Fresh out of the shower, if she wasn't mistaken. For some reason, that realization made her blush.

"We brought you dinner, Mr. Johnson," Alycia said with her usual enthusiasm.

His eyes widened, no doubt surprised by the gesture, but before he could say anything, he looked down and to the side, brushing at something with his right foot. "Back," he said in a commanding voice.

"You've got a dog?" Alycia leaned forward, trying to see. "Mom, look! He's got a dog! I didn't know you had a dog, Mr. Johnson. I didn't see one when I was over the other day."

Brooklyn didn't know what she expected to see, but it wasn't the tiny canine Derek lifted into view. The dog sported one of those protective cones around its neck and head, and its right front leg was in a cast.

"Come on in." Derek stepped back and opened the door wide. "I don't want Miss Trouble to get outside."

"Miss Trouble?" Brooklyn almost laughed aloud. How much trouble could a dog that size be? The animal couldn't weigh more than five or six pounds, tops.

"How'd she get hurt, Mr. Johnson? Is she gonna be okay?"

Ignoring the girl's questions, Derek kept

106

his gaze on Brooklyn and the hot dish in her hands. "Come on in," he repeated. Then he led the way to the back of the house.

In the kitchen, Brooklyn set the casserole dish on the stovetop.

Almost in unison, Derek put the dog on the floor. "Whatever you made, it smells good."

Brooklyn didn't have a chance to answer.

"What'd you say her name is?" Alycia dropped to her knees beside the dog.

"Miss Trouble. Trouble, for short."

"How come?"

"Because she isn't my dog, and I didn't plan on taking care of her. But somehow the vet talked me into keeping her here while she recovers from her injuries." He shrugged. "That's the trouble."

"Poor thing." Alycia stroked the dog's back. "What happened to her?"

"Somebody shot her."

Alycia gasped. "No! Why would anybody do that?"

Derek's expression turned dark. "I've never figured out why anybody is cruel to animals, but if I ever find out who did this to Trouble, I'll —" He stopped, perhaps realizing he shouldn't express his full sentiments to the child.

"Are you gonna keep her, Mr. Johnson?"

107

Derek squatted on the opposite side of the dog, bringing himself to Alycia's level. "I doubt it. She won't make much of a farm dog. I mean, she's so small. What would she do around here? And look at all that long hair on her tail. It'll get full of foxtails and thistles and other weeds."

"What breed is she?" Brooklyn asked.

"Ethan — he's the local vet — says she's a papillon."

Alycia frowned. "A what?"

"A papillon. It means 'butterfly' in French. Or so I'm told. I don't remember seeing one before. She's not exactly a farmer's breed of dog. Bigger dogs are better suited to the country. My last dog was an Irish setter."

Brooklyn smiled at once. "Do you mean Ben? I remember him. He was gorgeous. Followed you and Chad everywhere." She regretted the words at once. She didn't like to bring up Chad in front of Alycia, but now that she was back in Thunder Creek, reminders were everywhere and his name came easily to her lips.

"Yeah, Ben did follow us everywhere." Derek stood again. "He was a great dog. Ben and I more or less grew up together." Sadness flickered in his eyes. "He died right about the time I bought this place, and I've

108

never gotten around to getting a dog to replace him."

"He must have been really old."

Derek moved to the oven, took a dish towel, and lifted the lid off the casserole. "He was twelve. Almost thirteen. Old enough for a setter."

Alycia gave Trouble's back one more stroke, then got to her feet. "Wish Mom would let me have a dog." She didn't whine the words, but a ten-year-old's effort to manipulate her mother was there, all the same.

Brooklyn reached out to tap her daughter's head with the tips of her fingers. A light touch, but strong enough to get the message across.

Derek met her gaze again. He seemed to weigh his thoughts for a long while before saying, "Why don't you let Alycia help me take care of Miss Trouble?"

Immediately, Brooklyn felt boxed into a corner. "I don't know, Derek. I —"

"Yes, Mom. *Please* say yes."

That made the trapped feeling worsen. As if it were two against one.

Oblivious, Derek continued, "Maybe you'd find out that she's responsible enough to have a dog of her own."

It was Derek's head she would like to

109

thump now. Hard. Didn't he have enough sense not to say that in front of Alycia?

"And to be honest," he added, "I really could use the help. She could come over a few times a day to let her out and maybe feed her sometimes. No big deal."

Brooklyn reminded herself that he didn't have kids of his own. She shouldn't blame him for not knowing he should have talked to her privately before making his suggestions. "I suppose we could give it a try."

"Thanks, Mom!" Her daughter hugged her. "I'll do everything Mr. Johnson tells me. I promise. And I'll be . . . responsible, like he said. You'll see."

Derek knew he'd put his foot in it. He could tell by the expression on Brooklyn's face. Or more precisely, the look in her expressive eyes. Well, like Gran often said, in for a penny, in for a pound.

"Brooklyn, can you spare a moment? I'd like to talk to you about something else."

She lifted an eyebrow, seeming to give him permission to continue.

"But first, let me show Alycia what Trouble's going to need. Is that all right?"

Brooklyn nodded. "It's your dinner that's growing cold."

He laughed, hoping to lighten her mood,

before turning toward the girl. "First thing I'll do, kiddo, is write up a schedule for you. Two copies. One to post on the wall in the mudroom and one for you to take home with you. Then you and your mom will both know what's expected. Okay?"

"Sure," Alycia answered.

"Great. Now let me show you where I've got the dog's food and water and how I carry her outside. She gets around well enough in the house in that cast and cone, but she can't manage the steps on the back porch yet."

"So I don't need to carry her in here. Just when we go out. Right?"

"That's right."

It surprised him, how much he liked this girl already. How comfortable he was around her. It was more than the way she reminded him of her dad, although he supposed that was part of it. There was an inner glow about her that even a bachelor like him would be hard-pressed to miss. He might not have kids of his own, but he understood a kid didn't grow up this happy, good natured, and obedient without a decent parent in the picture. He had to give Brooklyn credit where credit was due.

As he put Miss Trouble into Alycia's arms so she could carry the dog outside, a mem-

111

ory of Brooklyn at about the same age popped into his head. It had been summer, the Fourth of July town celebration in the park. He remembered her standing beside an ancient tree. All alone. There'd been something so . . . forlorn about her.

Forlorn. Not a word he used often. Not a word he'd thought of back then either. What thirteen-year-old boy would? But now that the word had entered his head, he couldn't shake it. It made him feel almost guilty for the way he'd ignored her back then. After all, even as a kid he'd been somewhat aware of her difficult home life. A life bordering on poverty. No mother. A harsh, unsmiling, perhaps unloving father.

Perhaps even worse than all of that.

He scowled. *Had* it been something worse? He didn't want to think so. Thunder Creek was a warm, welcoming community, full of good people, but no town was free of the sins that so easily entangled. He'd learned that in his years in law enforcement.

And for the first time, he wondered if her elopement had come about for reasons besides teenage passions. Had there been other reasons that had caused her to flee her hometown?

He gave his head a shake. It wasn't his business, and it had happened a long time ago. Better not to complicate things more than they were.

To Alycia he said, "Why don't you sit under the tree there and let Trouble move around a bit if she's willing? I'm going to talk to your mom."

"Sure."

He pointed at her, stressing his instructions. "Don't go anywhere else. Agreed?"

"Agreed."

Derek turned and went back inside. In front of the oven, Brooklyn straightened as he entered the kitchen. The casserole was missing from the stovetop.

"I couldn't let your dinner get cold after all," she said.

"Thanks." He motioned toward the table. "Let's sit down."

He'd seen wariness in Brooklyn's eyes before, and he saw it again now. Still, she complied with his request.

He raked the fingers of one hand through his hair as he sat opposite her. "I'm not quite sure where to begin."

"Might as well be at the beginning."

Her wariness remained, but Derek saw courage too. As a teenager, she'd tried to appear brave through reckless behavior. What he saw now was the real deal.

He drew a deep breath and puffed it out.

"Chad wrote to me before he died. The attorney forwarded the letter to me back in April." The room was so quiet he heard the ticking of the clock in the living room. "Did he write to you too?" Derek thought he knew the answer but still needed to ask.

Although her eyes seemed to say it was none of his business, she shook her head. "I only got a letter from the attorney. Along with a lot of papers to do with the house."

"Did the lawyer mention that Chad agreed to sell his parents' property to me a couple of years ago? I've been saving to make the down payment ever since."

"No," she answered softly. "He didn't mention that."

"No reason he should have, I guess." He paused to clear his throat. "I understand why Chad left the place to you and Alycia. It was the right thing to do. And I don't know what all went on between you two that caused you to break up years ago. Whatever it was, I believe that Chad felt he'd been in the wrong. I know leaving you the house was his way of trying to make up for some of that."

"Derek . . ."

He held up a hand. "Let me finish. Please."

Another nod.

114

"I understand about the house, like I said. But what about the land? What do you plan to do with it?"

"I told you the other day. I haven't thought about it."

"The thing is, Brooklyn, I want to expand my farm. Having a couple of acres of crops is never going to be enough to do what I hope to do." He drew another quick breath. "I'd like you to think about selling the land to me."

Disappointment swirled in Brooklyn's belly. Had Derek been kind and neighborly only because he wanted the land? It appeared so. And, if true, it shouldn't surprise her. On the other hand, if Chad had truly agreed to sell the property to him, Derek had a right to be disappointed as well.

She met his gaze. "I'm sorry, Derek. I don't have an answer for you. It's too soon. I . . . I have plans of my own, but I don't know if those plans will need to include all ten acres."

"Fair enough."

She could tell it was hard for him to say those two words. And despite their meaning, she also heard how very much he wanted her land.

"But think about it," he added. "Will you?"

"Yes. I'll think about it. Just don't expect an answer anytime soon. It could be a long wait."

In his eyes, she saw his internal struggle to accept what she'd said. For a moment, she thought he might offer a persuading argument or two. But he didn't. Instead, he stood. "I'll get Alycia and Trouble. I imagine you want to get back home for your own supper."

Again, she couldn't blame him for his reaction. She was an obstacle to the plans he'd had, and whether or not he would believe her, she was sorry for that. But being sorry didn't mean she would change her mind. As she'd told him, she had plans of her own.

CHAPTER 9

Nerves tumbled in Brooklyn's stomach as she pulled into a space in the church parking lot the following Sunday.

There were two churches in Thunder Creek — St. John Catholic Church on the east end of town and Thunder Creek Christian Fellowship at the corner of Lewis and Sharp Streets. The latter was where Brooklyn had attended Sunday school until rebellion trumped obedience. Once that set in, even fear of her father's wrath hadn't been enough to make her go to church.

It felt more than a little strange to walk through the front doors of the building again after so many years. It also felt good. Because she was a different person now. God was no longer a remote judge somewhere high in the sky, waiting to punish her whenever she misbehaved, the way her dad had punished her time and again. God loved her. He loved her lavishly just as she was,

117

but He wasn't content to leave her that way. He'd changed her on the inside. He was changing her still.

Glancing down, she squeezed her daughter's hand. "Sit with me or go to Sunday school?"

"Sunday school, I think."

Brooklyn almost asked if Alycia was sure, but managed to swallow the words in time. Her daughter needed and wanted to make friends with other kids her age. With school out for the summer, church was the best place for that to happen. Especially since their new home was out in the country rather than in a neighborhood full of kids.

"Brooklyn. Alycia."

They turned to see Ruth Johnson coming toward them, smiling a greeting.

"I'm so glad to see you here this morning." Ruth stopped, leaned forward, and lightly kissed Brooklyn's left cheek. Drawing back, she asked Alycia, "Do you need me to show you where your Sunday school class is?"

Brooklyn couldn't help but smile at the question. The church wasn't large, and there was only one hallway to follow. Even if Brooklyn hadn't already been familiar with the building, Alycia could have found it on her own without trouble.

"Sure," Alycia responded. She released her mother's hand.

How, Brooklyn wondered, had her daughter become so fearless about meeting new people and going new places? Brooklyn had been just the opposite so much of her life. She thanked God she hadn't made Alycia afraid of her own shadow.

"Come along with us, Brooklyn." Ruth motioned with her head. "I'll introduce you around before the service starts. Of course you'll know many of us already, but there are some newcomers in our midst."

On their way to and from the Sunday school rooms, Ruth didn't miss a single opportunity to introduce — or reintroduce — Brooklyn to others they met in the hallway and narthex. There were quite a few familiar faces among them. A couple of Brooklyn's former teachers, one from elementary school and the other from high school. Several of the women who'd answered Ruth's call to clean the Hallston house. Even a number of former classmates, although none she could have called a friend. She hadn't been very good at making friends when she was younger.

Maybe I'm not much better at it now. At the thought, she felt a sharp wish to see Esther again.

119

If Brooklyn had had her own way, she would have slipped into the last pew in the sanctuary. But Ruth hooked arms with her as they entered and led her almost to the front. And there, waiting in the second pew on the right, was Derek. He stood, welcomed his grandmother with a kiss, then nodded a greeting in Brooklyn's direction before making room for them both. Brooklyn soon found herself seated between Ruth and Derek, not quite sure how that had happened.

After a period of silence, Derek asked, "Does it feel good to be back here? In church, I mean." If he held a grudge against her for not agreeing at once to sell him her land, he hid it well.

She shrugged. "A little strange, to tell you the truth."

"Strange?"

"I quit coming to church that last year I was in town. Chad and I, we would go for long drives, or in the summer we'd go swimming. Sometimes we'd —" She broke off, ending with another shrug.

"Yeah. I remember how it was."

"Even Dad couldn't force me to come." She glanced over her shoulder.

As if reading her mind, Derek said, "You won't see him here. He doesn't come to

120

church anymore."

That bit of news surprised her. Her dad had cared about appearances, even when he hadn't cared about people or God. He hadn't come to church to worship. Church attendance had been a way to make himself look like a good person to those around him. Perhaps even to play up the role of abandoned husband.

Of course, Brooklyn hadn't understood that as a teenager. It had taken years — and coming to know God herself — for her to begin to make sense of it all.

"Your dad had a disagreement with Pastor Vinton not long after he and his wife came to pastor the church," Derek continued. "Don't know what it was about. But whatever it was, it was serious. He's never been back."

"I'm sorry for him." Her heart seemed to skip a beat at the words, at her own surprise. Because it wasn't a platitude. She spoke truth: she *did* feel sorry for her dad. Sorry that he'd never experienced the forgiveness of a Savior. Sorry that he'd never allowed the Holy Spirit to change him on the inside. Sorry that he couldn't seem to love his daughter and even refused to know his granddaughter.

A line from a recent reading in the book

121

of Hebrews repeated in her memory: *"See to it that no one comes short of the grace of God; that no root of bitterness springing up causes trouble."*

A "root of bitterness." What a perfect description for what had happened to her father after her mother left him. After she left them both. Or perhaps that root of bitterness in his heart was the very reason her mother had gone away. Perhaps —

Mrs. Salmon — the town's piano teacher for the past fifty years — began playing the organ, intruding on Brooklyn's thoughts. She was thankful for a reason to push the memories away, instead rising to join the rest of the congregation in song.

It was difficult for Derek to focus on Pastor Vinton's sermon. He kept remembering the way Brooklyn had said she was sorry for her dad. There had been something in her voice, something he'd heard despite how softly she'd spoken. What was it? What did it mean? He didn't know, but he wanted to. And even why he wanted to know was a mystery to him.

When the service ended, Derek slipped by Brooklyn and kissed his grandmother's cheek one more time. "I'd better get home and take care of the dog." He stepped into

122

the aisle.

"Aren't you coming to my place for Sunday dinner?"

"I don't know, Gran. I've got lots to do."

"But you still have to eat, and it wouldn't hurt you to rest a bit either."

"Well . . ."

It was hard to refuse Gran anything, whatever she asked of him. The bond between them had always been strong. But in the years after Gran had been widowed and his parents, as well as Derek's married sister, had moved away, the bond between grandmother and grandson had grown even stronger.

He grinned at her. "All right. I'll take care of Trouble and a few other chores. Then I'll be over."

"Bring the dog back with you. Then you won't have to worry about leaving earlier than you want."

"I'll think about it." Remembering Brooklyn, he looked beyond Gran's shoulder. "See you later."

She nodded as she offered the hint of a smile. He found himself relieved not to see any sadness in her eyes.

Once at home, Derek sped through his most pressing chores. When his stomach rumbled, it made him glad he'd promised

123

to return to Gran's. She was amazing in the kitchen and was guaranteed to serve something much better than he would have whipped up for himself on the fly.

As he prepared to depart about thirty minutes later, he considered leaving Miss Trouble behind, despite his grandmother's invitation. But the little dog looked up at him with pleading eyes, and he gave in. "All right, all right. You win." He scooped her into one arm, holding her against his side. "I guess Alycia won't have to take care of you this afternoon."

But he was wrong about that.

He should have known, given they'd shared a pew that morning, that he would find Brooklyn and her daughter at his grandmother's home, along with four other guests — Pastor Adrian Vinton and his wife, Tracy, as well as Camila Diaz and her husband, Emilio. Just enough people to fill every chair around the long dining-room table. Ruth Johnson was a consummate hostess, and her Sunday dinners were all but legendary in Thunder Creek.

"Oh good," Gran said when she saw him enter through the front door. "Dinner is about ready to go on the table. Come ahead, everyone, and be seated."

Alycia took Miss Trouble from Derek, a

124

smile curving her mouth and a twinkle in her eyes, and he knew he wouldn't have to give the injured pet another thought until it was time to leave. The girl put the dog in a blanket-lined box next to the sofa — his grandmother was nothing if not prepared — and said, "Stay, girl." Before anyone else could sit down, Alycia took a chair at the table that gave her a clear view of the box on the living-room floor.

Adrian Vinton blessed the meal, and then platters and bowls were passed clockwise around the table. For a while, all attention was focused on the food as hostess and guests moved the feast from serving dishes to plates. But soon conversation came to life, often interspersed with laughter.

Derek found his gaze turned on Brooklyn more often than not. She didn't participate much. Not at first. But he didn't think it was due to nerves. Instead, she seemed to enjoy learning more about the individuals around the table. A reminder to him that, although she'd been born and raised in Thunder Creek, she was more of a stranger to the town than the Vintons, who had arrived four years earlier. Still, it couldn't have been a surprise to Brooklyn when Tracy Vinton asked her a question, perhaps worried that she didn't feel included or perhaps just to be friendly.

"What will you do, Brooklyn, now that you're back in Thunder Creek?"

Brooklyn didn't hesitate to answer. "First thing I've got to do is look for a job."

"And what sort of work do you do?" Adrian asked.

"I'm a waitress." Brooklyn shrugged. "That's what I did the whole time I was in Reno." Her gaze swept the table, stopping on Gran. "I managed the wait staff at a restaurant in Reno before we left to come here, so I shouldn't have a problem getting a job. The question is, how far will I have to go to get one?"

Derek hadn't known any of that, but he suspected his grandmother had. Gran had probably learned everything about Brooklyn's life in Nevada the very first night she and Alycia stayed with her.

"And eventually I plan to turn our house into a B&B."

She did? A bed-and-breakfast? That was news to him.

But his grandmother had already known that bit of information as well. "I told Brooklyn that I think it's a wonderful idea. It will make such a nice addition to our town. A homey B&B will be a far better place to stay than at the motel."

126

"But what a lot of hard work it's going to be," Camila said. "Getting a new business up and running. Remodeling that big old house. It makes me tired just to think of it."

Brooklyn looked around the table a second time. Her gaze lingered a moment on Derek, then stopped for a good while on her daughter. "I'm not afraid of hard work, and it doesn't have to be done overnight. We've got time. When it's ready, it's ready. We can do this. Can't we, Alycia?"

"You bet, Mom."

"Tell them some of your plans, dear," Gran encouraged with a smile.

"Well, it's early yet. There are so many things that will need done. First of all, I'll have to talk to a contractor, because I'd like to add a second bedroom on the main floor for Alycia. That way she and I can stay downstairs and the upstairs bedrooms can all be for guests." Enthusiasm entered her voice and put a sparkle in her eyes as she looked around the table. "And I thought I would try to work out some sort of package deals with one or two of the vineyards and maybe with one of the excursion companies that do boat trips on the river. I also thought about buying some bicycles for guests who would like to explore the area that way."

Derek didn't think he'd ever seen Brooklyn Myers this animated.

"Oh," she went on, "and I thought about creating a special garden area that would be used for weddings and anniversaries and other special occasions. They do weddings at several of the vineyards, but not everybody wants to be married in that kind of setting. I have lots of space I can use and so many wonderful, big trees that would shade the spot I'm thinking of."

Tracy smiled. "You *have* given this lots of thought, Brooklyn. That all sounds wonderful. I can envision it already."

Other words of encouragement and congratulations were repeated around the table, but all Derek envisioned was his purchase of those additional ten acres fading into obscurity.

Brooklyn couldn't recall ever feeling this way. Almost euphoric. She belonged at this table, with these people. They had accepted her as one of their own, and they liked her ideas for the B&B. It felt so good.

When the meal was over, Brooklyn insisted that Ruth allow her to do the dishes. Camila and Tracy tried to join her, but she shooed them out of the kitchen as well. "Please. Go join the others. I can do this by myself. I want to."

128

"But that isn't right, for you to do it alone," Tracy said.

"I don't mind. Really, I don't. Please go join your husbands." How could she explain that she wanted just a short while alone so she could bask in the unfamiliar sense of well-being, of approval?

"Don't worry, ladies." Derek stood in the doorway, more dirty dishes in his hands. "Brooklyn can wash, and I'll dry."

Some of her pleasant feelings drained away. She wouldn't be able to savor her emotions with him in the room. It wasn't that she disliked him, but neither was she at ease in his presence, despite his neighborly efforts.

Tracy glanced from Derek to Brooklyn and back again. Instead of further argument, she smiled. "Come on, Camila. We'll leave them to it."

"It's all right, Derek." Brooklyn frowned at him. "I don't mind doing this alone."

"I know. But I'm going to help anyway."

Suspecting that nothing she could say would make him leave, she turned toward the sink. He brought the rest of the dishes to the counter, then stepped back out of the way while she scraped off food and loaded the dishwasher. Afterward, she filled the sink with hot soapy water and began to

129

hand wash the remainder of the dishes and cookware.

She had grown used to the silence when Derek stepped to her left side, dish towel in hand. "Why didn't you tell me about your plans for a B&B?"

"I don't know." She shrugged. "It didn't come up."

"But you told me you didn't know what you were going to do with the rest of the land." His tone and words were accusatory.

"That's what I said." She let the skillet slide back under the suds and turned to look at him. "And it's true. I still don't know what I'm going to do with it."

"Really?"

He might as well have called her a liar. "Really." Her voice was low, but it didn't disguise the anger she felt.

"Didn't sound like it from where I was sitting at the table." He sounded angry too. "You've got all kinds of plans. A wedding venue. Gardens. Guests to entertain. That takes space."

"Derek —"

"You know what?" He dropped the dish towel on the counter. "Maybe it would be better if one of the ladies gave you a hand. I've got chores to do back home." And just like that, he strode out of the kitchen.

130

Her anger vanished almost as quickly as it arrived, replaced by a searing disappointment and the conviction that any kindnesses Derek had shown her were related to the land she'd inherited and nothing more.

CHAPTER 10

Late on Monday morning, Brooklyn was balancing on a step stool, hammering a nail into the wall in an upstairs bathroom, when the doorbell rang. "Alycia!" she called before remembering her daughter was at Derek's house, taking care of Miss Trouble.

At the thought of Derek, she wanted to grit her teeth. She'd waffled between anger and disillusionment ever since the exchange between them yesterday. Maybe she would ignore the bell. There wasn't anybody she needed to see. Especially not in her current mood.

The doorbell rang again.

"All right. All right." She stepped off the stool. A glance in the mirror over the sink showed a woman with a dark bird's nest for hair and a smudge of dirt on her right cheek. To say nothing of the faded, loose cotton top she wore over yoga pants. Not a great look.

The doorbell rang a third time.

"I'm coming," she called as she hurried down the stairs. If it was a salesman out here in the boonies, she would give him a piece of her — "Oh! Mrs. Johnson. Ruth." She pulled the door all the way open. "I'm sorry I kept you waiting. I was upstairs."

"Heavens, I know you're busy, dear." The woman wore her usual cheery expression. "No need to apologize. Waiting didn't hurt me a bit."

"Come in. Please." Brooklyn rubbed her dirty cheek with her fingertips, then wondered if she was making it better or worse. She lowered her hand.

Ruth entered the house and walked to the middle of the living room before stopping and turning to face Brooklyn, her smile still in place. "I wouldn't have intruded, but I have what I think is good news for you."

"Good news for me?" Brooklyn took a few steps forward.

"I ran into Zach Mason at the drugstore this morning. Do you remember Mr. Mason?"

She shook her head.

"He owns the diner on Main Street."

Brooklyn might not remember the owner, but she *did* remember the Moonlight Diner. When she was a teenager, it had been the

133

only place to eat in Thunder Creek, other than a drive-in burger joint. As far as she knew, that was still true, not counting Ruth's shop, which sold pastries and other desserts to go with the tea and coffee.

"Zach is in need of a waitress. One of his gals quit last night. No notice or anything. So he needs an experienced waitress as soon as possible. I told him about you. He promised not to give the job to anyone else until you meet with him. But you'll have to go in today. Can you do that?"

"Today?" She touched a hand to her hair. "I'm a mess."

But this was an opportunity she couldn't pass up. She'd expected to have to go into Caldwell or Nampa to find employment. All of that driving in her old car would burn gas, which in turn would burn up her wages. And it would also mean more time away from Alycia. A job right there in Thunder Creek would be a godsend.

"Not to worry." Ruth waved her toward the stairs. "You go shower and do whatever else you need to do. I'll look after Alycia until you get back."

"Thank you, Ruth. You're an angel."

"Hardly." The older woman laughed. "Now, where's your daughter?"

"Over at Derek's, taking care of the dog."

134

"I should have known. I'll walk over there. Good luck to you, dear. Alycia and I will be waiting when you get home."

Last Saturday's mail had brought Derek a couple new books on organic gardening to add to his growing library, and he'd finally found a few minutes to flip through them. He hoped to find a few more ideas on how to turn a larger profit from a smaller property.

He also hoped looking through the books would take his mind off the words he'd exchanged with Brooklyn in Gran's kitchen. He'd been less than gracious. He knew that. Yet it didn't take away the resentment he felt. Brooklyn could have told him about her plans. She shouldn't have led him on, let him think she *might* sell the land.

He looked up from the book on the table, staring out a window without really seeing.

Maybe not being able to buy the land was God's way of slowing him down. Maybe he'd been trying to move too fast. Maybe God didn't want him going into debt. It wouldn't be the first time he'd gotten an idea in his head and rushed to fulfill it without considering every detail.

There was a psalm that said a man's steps were directed by the Lord. He believed it.

He also believed Gran, who'd told him once that God's stops were just as important as His directions to move ahead. "Waiting is more difficult than walking," she'd said, "because waiting takes patience. But when God delays us, there is a purpose."

It might be good if he took that lesson to heart for a change.

He looked down again and closed the book before him. He'd ordered it because of an excerpt he'd read on the Internet about starting a one-acre self-sustaining farm. Another chapter was about starting a five-acre farm. Although not directly related to raising and selling organic produce, the chapter had lots of important information. Maybe that's where God wanted him to focus for now.

Derek longed to be a good steward of the earth. He wanted to "live simply and love extravagantly," as he'd heard a visiting pastor put it a couple of years before he bought this farm. In fact, those words had planted the desire that had led to what he was doing now.

Still mulling his thoughts, he rose and walked to the back porch. He heard Alycia's laughter before he saw her, seated in the shade of a tree. Miss Trouble hobbled around on the lawn, trying to sniff the ground, but the protective cone stopped the dog before her tiny black nose could quite reach the grass. It made an amusing sight, and he grinned.

"You never learn." The girl giggled again, her words carrying to Derek.

"What doesn't she learn?"

Gran? Derek hadn't heard the closing of a car door. But there she was, nonetheless, walking toward Alycia.

"Hey, Gran." He pushed open the porch's screen door. "Didn't expect to see you so soon."

"I didn't expect it either."

"Hi, Mrs. Johnson." Alycia hopped to her feet and picked up Miss Trouble.

"Hello, Alycia. How's your little charge?"

"She's doing really good." The girl looked toward Derek. "Isn't she, Mr. Johnson?"

"Yeah, she is." He motioned with his head. "Come inside, Gran. I'll get you something cool to drink. It's getting hot out there."

"I can only come in for a moment. I'm here for Alycia. Brooklyn has an errand to run, and I volunteered to stay with Alycia until she got back."

The instant Gran spoke Brooklyn's name, he knew he was going to have to apologize to her for what he'd said. Right or wrong, justified or not, he needed to tell her he was

137

sorry for his behavior.

"Come on, Alycia," Gran said to the girl, arm outstretched. "Let's go with Derek. See what he has to cool us off."

There was no denying that his grandmother had taken Brooklyn and Alycia under her wing, becoming their only family. Reggie Myers notwithstanding.

It must have been tough, having him for a father.

God had blessed Derek with the best of childhoods. Parents who'd supported, encouraged, and loved him — and his younger sister, Cara — in every possible way. Grandparents who'd been his greatest cheerleaders and had spoiled him to no small degree. Funny, noisy, rambunctious aunts, uncles, and cousins who'd enlivened every family gathering. What had it been like for Brooklyn, with no mother, no siblings, no extended family that he knew of?

"Lonely," he softly answered himself. Which only made the need to apologize seem stronger. Blast it.

In the kitchen he moved the books from the table to the counter, then went to the refrigerator to get the pitcher of iced tea. "Alycia, what would you like? I've got apple juice, if that's okay."

"Sure. That'd be good."

138

He glanced over his shoulder. "Sugar in your tea, Gran?" He always asked, even though he knew the answer.

"Thank you, dear. Just a little."

After dropping ice cubes into three glasses, he poured tea into two of them and juice into the third. He added some sugar to one of the teas and stirred with the spoon, then carried all three glasses to the table.

Gran took a sip from her glass. "Oh, that's so good."

He smiled but said nothing. After all, his grandmother ran a coffee and tea shop. She served far fancier brews than what he'd made with tea bags, water, and sliced lemons. Of course, she would never say her beverages were better, no matter what he set before her. She simply wasn't wired that way.

"You know," he said, "I could have kept an eye on Alycia for a short while. She was over here anyway." He sat opposite his grandmother. "No need for Brooklyn to call you and make you drive all the way out here."

Was he trying to ramp up his resentment with that comment? It felt like it.

"She didn't call me. I came to see her. There's an opening for a waitress at the Moonlight that I wanted her to know about.

139

It's perfect for her. It's local, and the hours are somewhat flexible. Zach's always paid a fair wage, which makes it even better. It's an answer to prayer. Truly. So I drove straight over and offered to stay with Alycia while Brooklyn goes in for an interview."

Derek stared into his glass of iced tea. "She's lucky to have you as a friend, Gran."

"And you, dear?"

He knew what she meant, although she was careful not to ask the real question outright because of Alycia. She wanted to know if he could become Brooklyn's friend as well as her neighbor. Maybe. If he tried hard enough. But he wasn't sure he was ready to try. He'd like to stay angry with her a little bit longer.

Only how could he stay angry and ask for forgiveness at the same time?

He glanced up, meeting his grandmother's gaze. She offered a tender smile, and he shrugged in reply. It was the only answer he had for now.

CHAPTER 11

At a few minutes after four o'clock — closing time — on Wednesday, Ruth sank onto a chair at a table next to the large front window for a few moments' rest. It had been an unusually busy afternoon at Sips and Scentimentals. Camila had left an hour earlier for a doctor's appointment, and Gina had the day off. Which meant closing the shop was up to Ruth.

She closed her eyes. On days like this, when her feet hurt and she longed for nothing so much as a soak in the tub, she wondered if she was crazy to run a business at her age. After all, Walter had left her financially stable. Even if she lived well into her nineties, as her mother and grandmother had before her, she wouldn't have to worry about money.

Then again, she hadn't opened her shop because she needed the income. She'd opened it because she'd needed something

141

to fill her days. Days that had seemed impossibly empty after her husband passed.

She opened her eyes and looked around, memories flooding in.

The gift shop area was where Walter's private office had once been. He'd had a large oak desk and a creaky old swivel chair that they'd bought at an auction soon after they'd moved to Thunder Creek to begin his practice. Nearly every spare inch of wall space had been lined with bookshelves. The shelves were still there, but now they held merchandise rather than medical books.

What had once been the reception area, front office, and exam rooms was now the tea shop, the floor space filled with tables and chairs. No trace of a doctor's office remained. Instead, feminine touches in her favorite pastel colors were everywhere. New plate-glass windows had been installed to let in the sunlight, making everything inside more inviting.

With a smile, she remembered the way their three children used to come visit their father when they got home from school. Walter had always made time for them, and his receptionist had known better than to book appointments during that half hour. How precious those years had been, she thought now. And how brief. Overnight, it

142

seemed, they'd grown up. Just as quickly, Ruth and Walter's grandchildren had grown up too. And finally everyone except Derek and Ruth had scattered in the wind.

"Time and tide wait for no man," she whispered to herself.

The shop door opened, drawing Ruth's thoughts to the present. She was prepared to announce that the shop was closed, but seeing Sandra Dooley in the open doorway, she caught herself. "Come in, Sandra."

"I know it's after closing time. If you're busy . . ."

"Don't be silly. I'm not busy at all. Come on in. What can I get you?"

Sandra shook her head. "I'm not here for that. I'm here for advice." She closed the door behind her.

"Nothing serious, I hope."

"Serious to me." Sandra sank onto a chair opposite Ruth and hooked strands of auburn hair behind her ears.

Ruth thought it beautiful hair too. Even now with a smattering of gray around the temples. The town's postmaster for over two decades, Sandra was both pretty and intelligent. Of course, Sandra's sense of humor could be slightly off kilter at times, but that was something else Ruth loved about her. She was amazed that no man had managed

143

to entice the attractive woman into marriage. Not that there hadn't been offers. Sandra simply loved her independence — or so she said. However, unless Ruth missed her guess, romance was heating up between Sandra and the owner of a bookshop in Caldwell.

"How can I help?" she asked when Sandra didn't begin on her own.

Her friend tapped the tips of her polished fingernails on the table. "You know I've been seeing Lou Connolly for several months."

"Mmm." It seemed her suspicions were about to be confirmed. "You've mentioned that a time or two."

"Well, what I didn't mention is . . . I've been seeing another man too." She stopped tapping her nails. "For about the same length of time."

"Good heavens. Who?"

Sandra gave her head a small shake. "No one you'd know. He lives in Ontario. His name is Forrest. Forrest Blanchard."

"I see." Although she wasn't certain she did.

"He's the spitting image of Richard Armitage. You know. The actor."

Ruth had no idea who that was. She rarely went to movies, and she watched almost no television. But she chose to nod in silence.

"The thing is . . ." Sandra drew in a deep breath and let it out on a sigh. "The thing is I like both Lou and Forrest quite a lot. I love them, really. Each in their own way. And they . . . they both love me. They've asked me to marry them. I mean, Lou wants me to marry him, and Forrest wants me to marry him."

"Good heavens," Ruth said again, this time in a whisper.

"And for the first time ever, I don't want to say no."

Afraid she knew the answer this time, Ruth asked, "Not say no to which one?"

"That's just it. I can't decide. I need your help."

Ruth Johnson was not one to shy away from giving advice when asked for it, but this was one of those rare moments when a loss for words was greater than the desire to provide wisdom. Especially since Sandra didn't profess faith in God, so suggesting prayer or looking for an answer in the Bible weren't meaningful options.

"How did you know Walter was the one?" Sandra asked. "I mean, really absolutely positively know for certain that you wanted to spend your life with him."

This brought a smile at last to Ruth, as

thoughts of Walter always did. It hadn't been like that the first year or so after his passing. Back then, thoughts of him had brought tears and longing and loneliness. But now that he'd been gone a few years, grief had softened into sweet memories and an ever-increasing awareness of eternity.

Sandra's nail tapping resumed, harder this time, translating impatience instead of nerves.

"I loved him," Ruth answered softly. "And he loved me. It was as simple as that."

"Love doesn't guarantee happiness in marriage. You know that, Ruth. All you have to do is look at the number of divorced people we know right here in town to realize that truth. Most of those people started out in love." Sandra shrugged. "Maybe they all started out in love. But it didn't last. How do you know it will last?"

Ruth heard familiar words replay in her memory. *"Love is patient. Love is kind."* Words from the Bible that had been spoken in countless wedding ceremonies for decades, perhaps centuries, including at her own. But how many people lived up to them? *"Love is not jealous. Love does not seek its own way. Love doesn't take into account a wrong suffered."* Even she and Walter hadn't lived up to them. Not without

146

the help of the Holy Spirit, and even then not all the time. There had been countless opportunities during their marriage to ask each other for forgiveness and to learn humility in the bargain.

"You're right, Sandra. Love isn't enough. Not if what you mean by love is that butterflies-in-your-stomach sensation. It takes ever so much more than that."

Sandra closed her eyes for a moment. "You're going to get all Christian on me, aren't you?"

"Probably." Ruth smiled. "But you knew that when you walked through that door."

Sandra met her gaze. "All right. Let me have it."

Hank McLean often asked Derek to join him for dinner on nights when his wife worked late and their kids were with his in-laws. Most of the time, Derek declined. He always had a lot of chores awaiting him at home, and spending money on dining out when there was food in the fridge seemed foolish. But today when Hank asked him, Derek accepted. Maybe that unexpected answer came easy because he no longer felt the same urgency to save money. For now, the Hallston property was out of reach.

Hank was a twenty-year veteran of the

sheriff's department, and Derek had cause to admire the man on multiple fronts. Hank put God, wife, and children before anything or anyone else. He was honest and steadfast, never rushing to make a decision before considering all sides. He was a lot like Derek's dad, which might be another reason Derek liked him so much.

The two men entered the Moonlight Diner a little after six o'clock. About three quarters of the booths and tables in the L-shaped room were occupied. After a quick glance around, Hank led the way to the empty booth at the far end. Derek would have selected the same table — the one with a view of the entire diner as well as the door.

The waitress arrived with eating utensils wrapped in paper napkins, two glasses of ice water, and menus. As she placed everything on the table, Derek glanced up to say thanks. The word stuck in his throat when he saw Brooklyn in white shirt and black skirt, the uniform of the female wait staff at the Moonlight.

Hank didn't have the same problem. "Thanks."

That loosened Derek's tongue. "You got the job."

"I got the job." She didn't look at him as she positioned her pencil over her order pad. "Do you want something to drink while you decide?"

Her tone was cool. In fact, Derek thought icicles could form in the air.

"Water for me," Hank answered.

"Water's fine for me too."

"Okay." Still not looking at Derek, Brooklyn slid the pencil behind her ear. "I'll give you a few minutes to decide what you want to eat, and I'll be back."

After she walked away, Hank said, "I take it you know her."

"Brooklyn Myers. Chad Hallston's widow. And my new neighbor."

"I see."

Of course his friend understood. Derek had talked often to Hank about his plans for those ten extra acres. Hank also knew that Chad's will had changed things. But Derek hadn't shared the most recent events, including how he'd felt Brooklyn misled him.

"Did I perceive a bit of frost between you two?"

Derek released a short, humorless laugh. "Just a bit." Quickly he caught his friend up on the details about Brooklyn's plans for the land and the words they'd exchanged the previous Sunday and the way he'd felt about them since.

149

"But you still haven't apologized."

"No. We haven't run into each other until now."

"Maybe you need to take the initiative. You think?"

Derek hesitated before answering, "Yeah. I know you're right."

"Is your problem only about the land?"

He frowned as he mulled over the question. "Probably not. I didn't like her when we were younger, and I expected to feel the same way about her when she came back. But I've realized that my feelings were because she came between Chad and me. Our friendship was never the same after he took up with her, and I blamed her for it." He looked at Hank. "Truth is she isn't at all what I expected. She's never had it easy, from what I can tell. But she hasn't let it knock her down and keep her there. She's got what Gran would call *gumption*."

The object of his comments returned to their booth. Pencil once again in hand, she asked, "Are you ready to order?" There was a little less frost in her voice this time.

Derek nodded. "I am."

"Me too."

Brooklyn's gaze went to Hank first. "What can I get you?"

A short while later, orders taken, Brooklyn headed for the kitchen at the back of the diner. Derek watched her go. She moved easily, in a way that said she was comfortable in her job. When Derek looked back at Hank, he found his friend smiling, as if he'd discovered a secret. He felt his own eyes widen when he realized what the look meant. "Don't even think it, Hank. You know I've sworn off women for the time being."

His friend nodded, but amusement remained in his eyes.

Derek didn't feel the same way. His last relationship had ended on a bad note, his former girlfriend accusing him of being more interested in his tomatoes and carrots than in her. Sadly, that was probably the truth. If he'd been serious about her, it wouldn't have been that way. He was sure of that. And since he had no time to get serious, he had no intention of dating anybody. Especially not his new neighbor. That would be a big mistake, he was sure.

"All right," Hank said. "Have it your way. But one day you're going to meet the right girl, and everything will change."

"Maybe. But it's not going to be now."

For a short while, as they waited for their dinners to arrive, Hank and Derek talked about recent changes within the Thunder

151

Creek Sheriff's Department. Nothing earth shattering, but there were some employees who resisted any kind of change, even in a department as small as theirs.

Derek's stomach growled right as Brooklyn arrived, balancing a large round tray that held their dinners. Derek suspected the smile hovering at the corners of her mouth was because she'd heard the growl too. He also couldn't help noticing that she looked dwarfed beneath the tray. She'd always been a slight thing — narrow shoulders, not an overabundance of curves — yet still undoubtedly feminine.

"Here you go, gentlemen." Moments later, the plates were on the table. "Anything else I can get you?"

Both men shook their heads.

"Okay, then. Enjoy."

With a quick smile, she turned and walked toward a nearby booth with a new customer. Before she got very far, however, she stopped in her tracks. Even though she faced away from him, Derek could tell something was wrong. Everything about her body posture screamed tension.

His gaze shifted to the customer, and alarm bells went off. It was Reggie Myers. How had he missed him coming in? As he watched, Brooklyn squared her shoulders and took the last few steps to her dad's table.

Reggie looked up and scowled. "I'd like a different waitress." His voice carried to the diners in nearby booths.

"I'm sorry, Dad," Brooklyn answered, her voice lower but still audible. "Lucca's busy with her own tables. What can I get for you?"

"Send her anyway. Anybody can wait on me but you. I don't want you."

"That's unfortunate, because I'm the waitress you're stuck with."

There was strength in her voice rather than anger or hurt, and Derek felt a spark of pride in her.

Then Reggie called her a foul name. The diner went dead silent.

In an instant Derek pushed up from the booth and strode to Brooklyn's side. "Mr. Myers, maybe you should leave."

"You can't throw me out. I've as much right to be here as anybody." Reggie sneered at Derek, challenging him. "Are you going to arrest me if I don't go?"

"You do have a right to be here, sir, unless you cause a public disturbance. Swearing at your daughter loud enough for the entire dining room to hear qualifies as a disturbance, in my opinion."

153

Reggie cursed.

Derek drew himself up to his full height. "Don't make me tell you again, Mr. Myers."

For a moment, Reggie stared up at him, and Derek could see the calculating going on behind his eyes. In the end, Reggie held his tongue. Instead, he shot an angry glare at Brooklyn, rose, and marched out, shoving the door hard enough to make it shudder against the frame.

Silence returned, uncomfortable, almost anxious. Then, one by one, the other customers turned their gazes upon their plates. A few tried to resume normal conversations. But it was all a pretense. The air was thick with embarrassment, curiosity, questions, and more. Not only that. Brooklyn had begun to tremble.

Derek took hold of her arm near the elbow. "Come with me," he said softly. His gaze swept the room. Heads ducked again. They took a couple of steps, then Brooklyn seemed to crumple into herself. He caught her with an arm around her waist. "Easy does it." He escorted her outside into the warm summer evening and away from staring eyes and listening ears. Thankfully, her father was already out of sight. Still, Derek turned her away from the parking lot and guided her toward a bench beneath a neigh-

154

boring shop awning.

"Thank you," she whispered.

He sat beside her. "No problem."

They were silent for a short while before Brooklyn said, "Your dinner's getting cold. You should go back in."

"Not yet. Not until I know you're okay."

"I'm fine. It's just . . . It's just that I didn't expect that to happen. Dad used to . . . He used to hide his anger better than that. He could be gruff, even rude, but he rarely made scenes in public."

"But he was like that with you? In private."

The silence was longer this time. So long he didn't think she would answer. But finally she whispered a reply. "Yes."

He heard acceptance, resignation, perhaps even forgiveness in that one little word. And it tugged at his heart. "I'm sorry, Brooklyn."

She shook her head, as if to tell him she didn't want his pity.

"I'm sorry about the other day too. I shouldn't have taken my frustration out on you. It wasn't fair of me."

She studied him, no doubt wondering if he meant what he said.

"Maybe we can start over." He offered a hint of a smile. "Okay, neighbor?"

She inhaled and let the air out slowly.

155

"Okay, neighbor." Then she stood. "I need to get back to work. I don't want to lose my job the very first week."

"Zach won't fire you over this. He knows Reggie. We all do."

"Maybe he won't fire me, but he would have the right to." She took a couple of steps away, then looked back at him. "Thanks, Derek, for trying to help with my dad. I owe you."

"You owe me nothing."

A half smile curved her mouth, although sadness remained in her blue-gray eyes. "You'd have done the same for anybody, right?" she stated. "It's your job as a deputy."

He hesitated, then shrugged. Although he wouldn't admit it to her, he wasn't sure if what she'd said was true. Helping her had felt more . . . personal than that.

Brooklyn managed to finish her shift with a modicum of efficiency. But always she was aware of eyes watching her. Lucca, the other waitress. Peter, the cook. Zach, her boss. The customers. Even the ones who came in long after her dad had left, no doubt having heard the gossip from others.

It wasn't that what he'd done or said in the diner had surprised her. Not really. The

156

surprise had been how much his words had unexpectedly hurt. Shouldn't that have changed by now? Shouldn't her visit the day after she got back to town have somehow made it easier to deal with his rejection? It had been crystal clear then that the relationship was not going to get better.

She wasn't afraid of her dad. Not like she'd once been. He wouldn't physically hurt her anymore. But that ache in her heart for the loving dad she'd never had . . . That pain never seemed to go away. It lingered in the far corners of her heart. Maybe it was worse because her daughter had never had a loving dad either. Her own situation was beyond her control, but Alycia's? That was Brooklyn's fault. She hadn't chosen wisely. Still a child herself, she'd rushed into marriage without any idea of how immature and selfish Chad was, without any clue that he would leave as soon as the novelty of an elopement wore off.

As she drove home after work, she remembered Derek's arm around her back as he'd escorted her outside. There'd been a moment when she'd wanted to sink into his support. She had felt sudden and complete exhaustion, emotionally and physically, and it would have been nice to allow someone

157

else to carry the burden, at least for a short while.

That she would have allowed that "someone" to be Derek Johnson either horrified or amazed her. She wasn't sure which. Perhaps both. Still, it was nice that he'd apologized. She would much rather be on friendly terms with her next-door neighbor. And, to be fair, maybe her distrust of men had kept her from telling him the whole truth when he'd asked about the land. Maybe it had appeared to him as if she'd lied to his face, giving him the right to be a little angry.

The front porch light welcomed Brooklyn as she pulled into the driveway. She stopped the car at the side of the house and turned off the engine, then sat still, allowing the night air to settle around her.

"God," she whispered. "Help me not to distrust without reason. Don't allow my past with my dad and with Chad to color my future relationships with other men." She drew a deep breath. "And help me forgive my father. Even if he never changes. Even if he can never love me or treat me kindly, don't let me become like him. Don't let bitterness take hold in my heart."

Crickets chirped and frogs croaked. Leaves rustled softly in the nearby trees.

158

Tears filled her eyes.

"Lord, You're my heavenly Father, but I'm not sure I know how to experience You that way. I don't always know how to respond to You as a beloved daughter. I struggle with it all the time, and I know that's because of my earthly father." A tear splattered onto the back of her hand. "Please don't let it be that way for Alycia. Please, God, help her know how loved she is by You."

She opened her eyes and reached for the car door, feeling a sudden need to hold her daughter in her arms.

CHAPTER 12

After a difficult night of lying awake — heart aching, thoughts roiling — Brooklyn was in the midst of a deep, dreamless sleep the following morning when her daughter burst into the bedroom and hopped onto the bed.

"Morning, Mom."

Brooklyn groaned and tried to cover her face with a pillow.

Alycia stole it from her. "What're we doin' today?"

Alycia was one of those kids who was ready for full-on conversation the instant she opened her eyes in the morning. Brooklyn preferred a little more time — and at least one cup of coffee — before being expected to converse. However, mothers didn't always get to choose how or when their days began. She'd learned that soon after the birth of her daughter.

"Mom?"

160

Opening her eyes, Brooklyn released a soft sigh. "How about we paint your bedroom?"

"Really? And can we do drawings on it too? You know. Like I showed you in that magazine at Mrs. Johnson's."

Brooklyn wondered how expensive stencils were. Would decals cost less, or would they be more? "We'll see."

"Please, Mom."

"We'll see what they cost at the hardware store. Okay?"

It was Alycia's turn to sigh, but hers was louder and much more dramatic.

Fully awake now, Brooklyn laughed and drew her daughter into a tight embrace. "You know that won't make a difference. Right?"

"Yeah." Alycia giggled. "I know. But I gotta try."

A twinge of sadness tightened Brooklyn's heart, an unwelcome memory of her own childhood and how she'd never dared ask her dad for anything. Thankfulness immediately followed. She was thankful that Alycia had grown up fearless, despite everything. She was thankful that even though poverty had dogged them and made so many material things beyond their reach, her daughter had remained cheerful. When Alycia asked for something and was denied, she accepted the way it was, albeit sometimes with one of her dramatic sighs.

Brooklyn smiled as she whispered into Alycia's ear, "How did I get lucky enough to have you for a daughter?"

" 'Cause God loves you that much."

Joy over the truth of that statement burst in her heart, driving out the momentary sadness, and she laughed along with Alycia all over again.

A few hours later, Brooklyn and Alycia stood in the paint aisle of Snake River Hardware. The air was heavy with a mixture of smells that were hard to identify but seemed fitting for such an establishment. A little paint. A touch of grease. A bit of mustiness. The tiled floor could have used a good scrubbing, as could the large plate-glass windows at the front of the store. And yet even those things seemed as they should be.

"What color for the walls?" Brooklyn asked her daughter as she reached toward the paint chips on display.

"Blue!"

No surprise there. Blue was Alycia's favorite color. Sky-blue and turquoise in particular. Brooklyn moved her hand above the row of paint chips until she found an

162

appropriate strip. Pulling it out, she handed it to her daughter.

"That one." Alycia squinted at the name beneath the bottom color. "*Waterside*. That's the one I want."

Brooklyn grinned. "Don't you need to think about it first?"

"Nope. That's the one."

"Okay, then. Now let's see if they have any wall stencils you like. But remember: it can't be expensive."

"Horses." Alycia clapped her hands together twice. "I want some horses. And a dog too. One that looks like Trouble. Do you suppose they've got one of those?"

"I don't know, honey. We might not have that many choices."

"Can I be of help?" a man's voice asked from behind her.

Brooklyn glanced over her shoulder. "Yes, we —" She stopped abruptly. "Vic?"

"Well, I'll be. Brooklyn Myers. I heard you were back."

"You work here?"

Silly question. Victor Cottrell — a former classmate — wore a dark-green apron stamped with the name of the hardware store.

"Yeah. I've been working here since I was a teenager. Shoot. I got the job before you

163

and Chad left Thunder Creek." He paused a moment, then added, "I was sorry to hear about him, by the way. Hadn't seen him since his folks died. He was way too young to go like that."

Brooklyn gave a brief nod, not quite sure how to respond to expressed sympathies. She was Chad's widow almost without having been his wife.

"This your daughter?" Vic looked down at Alycia.

"Yes. Alycia, this is Mr. Cottrell."

"Hello," she answered with a polite nod.

"Hey, there, young lady. You look a lot like your daddy, don't you?"

Alycia shrugged.

"Yes, she does," Brooklyn answered for her.

Vic looked up. "So what brought you into Snake River Hardware?"

"We need paint and some stencils for Alycia's bedroom walls."

"Horses!" Alycia chimed in quickly. "And blue paint." She held out the paint chip, her index finger on the shade she wanted. "Waterside."

"Knows what she likes. Makes my job easier." Vic motioned with his head. "Stencils are at the end of aisle four. Let's see what we can find." He led the way, Alycia

164

right behind.

Brooklyn stayed put, thoughts drifting back in time once again. She'd known Vic since the first day of kindergarten, but it wasn't until she'd begun to develop a figure that he'd shown interest in her as a girl. She'd gone out with him a few times. Well, *snuck out* was a more accurate description. Her dad hadn't allowed her to date yet, so she'd waited until he fell asleep before slipping out her bedroom window. By the standards of many, she hadn't been a truly "bad" girl. But she'd made plenty of stupid choices. Choices she regretted now.

"Mom, come here and look at this."

She shook off the memories and hurried to the end of the aisle.

Brooklyn had been in Derek's thoughts a lot since the previous night. So when he entered the hardware store, intent on buying a new hammer and a pound of two-inch nails, it didn't seem surprising to find her and Alycia there.

When Alycia saw him, she hurried over with a large stencil wrapped in cellophane packaging. "Look what Mom's gonna paint on the wall of my bedroom. A horse. Isn't it cool? It looks like Blue Boy, kinda, doesn't it? But I think we're gonna have to do a dif-

165

ferent color than Blue Boy 'cause my walls are gonna be blue already, and gray won't show up good. That's what Mom says." She stopped talking to draw a breath.

He grinned.

"I was hoping to get a dog stencil, too," she continued, "but they don't have one that looks like Miss Trouble."

"Not surprised about that." He looked toward Brooklyn, who watched as Vic Cottrell put a gallon can in the paint shaker.

"And besides, Mom says we can only afford to buy one. Wanna see what color my room's gonna be?"

"Sure." He followed the girl toward the far right corner of the store.

Brooklyn glanced his way. A wisp of a smile appeared on her lips.

"Morning," he said.

"Good morning."

"How are you?" he asked, thinking of what had happened at the diner.

"I'm fine."

She looked fine too. None of the sadness or disappointment he'd witnessed yesterday. And no more frost either. She really had forgiven him.

He pointed at the can of paint. "Looks like you're planning a busy day or two."

"Longer than that. The whole house needs

166

painting. But we're starting with Alycia's bedroom and will work our way through the other rooms over the summer."

Grabbing a paint chip from the counter beside Vic, Alycia held it toward Derek. "That's the color I chose. Isn't it pretty?"

"Sure is."

To her mom, Alycia said, "Mr. Johnson likes the horse I picked too."

"I'm not surprised he likes it." She gave him another of her brief smiles. "He seems to like lots of things you like."

Her words made Derek feel good for some reason. After all, he was as yet clueless how he was supposed to go about this father-figure thing. Maybe just being a pal would be enough. Or at least the right place to start. Perhaps that's why he offered, "I could give you some help with the painting. I'm pretty handy with a brush and a roller."

Brooklyn's face immediately got that wary expression he'd seen more than once. "I couldn't ask you to do that."

"You must be nuts, Brooklyn," Vic piped in as he switched off the paint shaker, plunging the air into silence. "Never turn down help with painting."

Derek's jaw tightened. He didn't need or want Vic's input. "You didn't ask me. I offered."

167

"But you're so busy," Brooklyn said. "You —"

"Having Alycia's help with Trouble has freed up a lot of my time."

That was an exaggeration, and they both knew it.

Her smile returned. Only this time it lingered on her lips and even managed to reach her eyes. What a difference from yesterday. She was resilient; he'd give her that.

He cleared his throat, aware that the silence had grown long. "What time do you want me to come over?"

"In an hour? But only if it's truly convenient for you."

It wasn't convenient, but he realized he didn't care. "I'll be there." With a final smile, he turned and went in search of hammer and nails.

When Derek arrived at Brooklyn's house a little after eleven o'clock, carrying a stepladder with him, he found her back-porch door open.

Stopping in the entrance, he called a hello.

"Come on in. We're upstairs."

He followed her voice.

The furniture in Alycia's bedroom had been moved to the center of the room and

168

covered with a couple of drop cloths. The windows were naked except for the protective tape Brooklyn had begun to apply to the glass. Both Brooklyn and Alycia had changed into old clothes, apparently ready for paint spatter, and both had caught back their dark hair into ponytails.

Derek leaned his ladder against the wall, his gaze taking in the paint cans and other supplies set on another drop cloth. "I brought a ladder, just in case. Looks like you've got everything else we'll need."

"I hope so. I'm an amateur at this." Her eyes swept the room. "We weren't allowed to change paint colors in our apartment in Reno. The walls were never anything but white all the years that we lived there, and it was the landlord who took care of the painting when the time came."

That didn't sound so bad to Derek, having somebody else choose colors and do the painting. But then, he'd never given much thought to interior design, or whatever women called it. He cared more about functionality than aesthetics.

"Which do you want, Mr. Johnson?"

He lowered his gaze to Alycia, who stood before him, a paintbrush in one hand and a roller in the other.

"Roller, please." He reached for it, grin-

169

ning at the girl and not stopping to wonder why he felt so lighthearted at the idea of spending the afternoon painting a little girl's bedroom.

"You do the high stuff, Mr. Johnson. I'll paint down here."

He gave her a quick salute. "Yes, ma'am." He wasn't sure what the look Alycia gave him meant. Maybe that she thought adults — or more specifically he — could be weird. And he couldn't argue with that. He'd been ten himself once.

It didn't take long to get to work. Derek pried off the lid from a can, stirred, and poured paint into a couple of trays. One tray for him and Alycia, who planned to start on the wall in the corner where her stencil would eventually be applied. The other for Brooklyn, who chose to paint the wall around the two windows.

"Do you like to paint?" Alycia asked as she swiped her brush in the tray.

"I can take it or leave it. But I've done my share of it." He set the roller against the wall and applied the paint.

"What's your favorite color?"

"Never really thought about it." He got another one of those looks but pretended he didn't see it.

"Mom's favorites are peach and pink."

170

"I've noticed."

Surprised by the truth of his own words, he cast a glance over his shoulder. Brooklyn was on her knees, concentrating on her brush as it followed the line of wall along the molding. She didn't appear to have heard him. Just as well. He wouldn't want her to get the wrong idea.

Wrong idea? What did that thought even mean?

He looked back at the wall before him, added more paint to his roller, and returned to work. But the silence, brief as it had been, bothered him. "My grandmother told me you like to read, Alycia. What's your favorite book?"

The girl rattled off a few titles, none of which meant anything to him. He didn't let on.

"Do you like to read?" she asked, glancing up at him.

"Yeah, when I can find the time. Mostly I read books about organic farming."

She wrinkled her nose. "That's not very fun."

He laughed. "You might be surprised, kiddo."

"You're like Mom. She likes . . . What kind of books are they, Mom?"

"Biographies and memoirs," Brooklyn

171

answered, fast enough that Derek knew she'd been listening to them. Perhaps even before they were talking about books.

Curious, he glanced over his shoulder again. This time she was looking at him, her paintbrush idle in her hand. She smiled, and it felt as if they shared a secret. Pleasure spread through him, warmed him, seemed to make the bedroom glow.

Brooklyn saw something change in Derek's eyes. She wasn't quite sure what it was, but once it was there, she felt a sudden need to get up and move around, to draw a deep breath, and to slow her quickening heartbeat.

"How about some music?" she asked before hurrying out of Alycia's room.

In her own bedroom, she stopped to lean against the wall. She touched her cheeks with her fingertips. Was she flushed? She felt flushed. Perhaps she needed to turn down the air-conditioning a degree or two. It was growing much too warm in the house.

She took another deep breath before she pushed off the wall with her backside. She grabbed the small CD boom box from her dresser and a few CDs to go with it, not caring which ones. Whatever was on top of her music collection was fine with her. Then she walked back to Alycia's room.

Smiling, she stepped through the doorway. "Here we go. This should make the work go a little faster." She glanced at the jewel case. "Do you like Josh Turner?"

"Yes!" Alycia answered.

Brooklyn's gaze rose to meet Derek's.

"Sure do," he said with a slow grin.

She felt warm again. What was odd, she realized, was that she didn't seem to mind.

CHAPTER 13

" 'Me and my gang,' " Brooklyn sang loudly, drowning out the music of Rascal Flatts coming from the boom box. They'd all sung along to lots of songs as they'd worked for the last few hours, but this time the paintbrush in her hand had become a miniature guitar that she pretended to play.

Alycia twirled in circles, her hands in the air, singing lyrics that were a mix of right and wrong. Mostly wrong.

Even Derek had joined in the crazy celebration that had begun with the final stroke of Waterside blue paint. But his instrument was an upended bucket and a couple of paint paddles.

When the song ended, Brooklyn bent over in laughter. She'd laughed so hard her sides hurt. Who knew painting a bedroom could be this much fun? And the time had flown by.

Straightening, she found Derek smiling at

her, his eyes sparkling with humor. A frisson of pleasure shivered up her spine. Something in her expression must have caught his attention, because she saw a new awareness color his own.

"Maybe we're not ready to take this act on the road just yet," he said, his gaze still locked with hers.

"Probably not." The words came out a whisper.

Alycia asked, "What act?"

"Nothing, honey. Mr. Johnson was teasing us."

"I don't get it."

What Brooklyn didn't get was the odd tumble in her stomach and the quickened beat of her heart that had been happening all afternoon.

It was Derek who looked away first, his gaze lowering to Alycia. "Glad to know you like country music, kiddo. Shows you've got good taste."

"Sure," she answered.

He glanced up again and held up his paint paddles with a wry smile. "I need to take care of the chores I've got waiting at home."

"Of course." Masking a sudden nervousness, she moved briskly to take the paddles and set them with the rest of the tools. "We never would have gotten this far this fast

175

without your help, Derek. Thanks so much."

"I was glad to do it." His smile was still in place, making her believe he meant it.

She followed him down the stairs and to the back porch. "Come back and have dinner with us," she said impulsively as he pushed open the screen door. "We'll order pizza."

"That's not necessary."

"But it is. We've been at it for hours. You've worked hard and must be starving. We're hungry too. Please. Come back when you've finished your chores."

He hesitated only a moment. "Okay. You talked me into it. I'll be back in half an hour or so."

With a last nod and smile, he headed out. She remained in the doorway and watched him go, wondering about the strange feelings that still whirled inside of her.

"Hey, Mom," Alycia called. "Are we gonna do the horse now?"

She shook her head as she reentered the house and climbed the stairs.

"No. That has to wait until tomorrow." She began to gather up the paint supplies. "Remember what the man at the hardware store told us? We have to wait until the paint on the walls has had lots of time to dry. We can't do it until tomorrow at the earliest.

But we can order pizza."

"Yeah!"

After carrying the supplies downstairs and washing off the paint in the sink, she retrieved her cell phone from the nightstand in her bedroom. It only took a few minutes to find the number for the Pizza Hut that delivered to Thunder Creek. She splurged for the largest size, half meat lovers — hoping that's what Derek would want — and half Canadian bacon and pineapple, Alycia's favorite.

That done, she went into her bathroom to clean up. When she saw her reflection in the mirror, she snorted. No wonder Derek had grinned. Her appearance was worse than she'd imagined. Paint smudged one cheek as well as the tip of her nose. And her hair looked like an appaloosa's blue-speckled rump. Why hadn't Derek looked as bad? Other than a few sprinkles on his right hand, there hadn't been any paint on him.

She glanced out of the bathroom to check the clock on the wall. She should have time enough to shower.

"Alycia?"

"Yeah?"

"I'm going to take a quick shower. I should be ready before the pizza gets here. But if the delivery guy comes, you can get the money to pay him from my purse. Okay?"

"Okay."

Brooklyn managed to get showered in record time, even with taking care to get rid of all paint evidence. As good as her word, she was finished, dressed, and coming down the stairs just as the doorbell rang.

"Can I still get the money?" Alycia asked.

"Sure." Brooklyn barely had time to open the front door before Alycia had returned with her wallet.

The teenager who stood on her porch looked bored to death. He rattled off the price in a monotone voice. She paid him, including a nice tip that she could ill afford, but it didn't gain her a change of expression. She understood better than he could know. She'd worked her share of boring, low-paying jobs. So she smiled and thanked him again as she took the pizza box from his hand, then closed the door and headed toward the kitchen.

"Mmm. That smells good." Alycia followed hard on her mother's heels. "I'm starved."

"I'm hungry too. Derek better hurry or he might not get any."

As if summoned by her words, a knock sounded on the screened-porch door. "It's me," Derek called.

"Come on in. The pizza just got here."

He appeared through the doorway. "Mom said I always had perfect timing when it came to food."

That odd tumbling sensation returned to her stomach at the sight of him. He had showered too. She could see the sheen of dampness in his hair. Freshly showered . . . and much too handsome. She turned toward the counter, not liking this new awareness of him, and set the pizza box on it.

"How can I help?" Derek had moved to stand close behind her.

She swallowed a gasp of surprise and managed to say in a normal voice, "Why don't you help Alycia set the table?"

"Sure. The kitchen table or in the dining room?"

"The kitchen is fine."

What wasn't fine was the way she felt with him standing so close.

Derek didn't move, his gaze fastened on Brooklyn's nape where short dark hairs formed little fishhook curls against her pale skin. It would be so easy, he realized, to reach out and brush the tendrils there. To lean in and . . . kiss that spot.

Except he had no business thinking such

179

things. No, more than that — he had no *need* to be thinking such things.

No romantic involvements wanted, he reminded himself.

He turned. "Hey, kiddo," he said to Alycia, glad for any distraction. "Where do I find the plates? Let's get this show on the road."

Before long they were seated at the table, each of them with slices of pizza on their plates. There was no conversation at first. Derek was okay with that. It gave him a little more time to get a better grip on himself. Because he really didn't want to get into another relationship. And even if that weren't true, he definitely wouldn't want to get involved with Brooklyn. It would be much too complicated and almost certainly doomed from the start.

True, she wasn't the girl he remembered, the one he hadn't liked very much. And he couldn't deny that he liked the woman she'd become. The devoted mother. The hard worker. He liked her determination and her smile and the sound of her laughter. They could probably be friends. Maybe they'd become friends already.

She caught him watching her. "What?" She touched her cheek where the paint had been earlier, as if worried she'd missed a spot.

"Nothing," he answered. "Just . . . this is nice. Thanks for inviting me to join you."

"You're the one who needs thanking. We'd still be painting if you hadn't helped us."

"To tell you the truth, it feels kind of good to see this house come alive again."

A month ago he would have sworn he felt the exact opposite. A month ago he wouldn't have cared if the house was torn down and the trees cleared to make room for planting. Amazing the difference a few weeks could make.

Brooklyn's gaze swept the kitchen. "It feels good to me too. Far better than I expected. I mean, I always liked this house, and I'm thankful to have it. I'm excited about what we can do with it. But I didn't expect it to feel like home. At least not this soon." She gave a little shrug. "I was away from Thunder Creek a long time, and my memories aren't hap —" She broke off abruptly.

Derek wished she'd finished her thought. He knew her better than he used to, but it didn't seem to be enough.

"Mr. Johnson?"

It took a moment before he turned his gaze toward Alycia.

"Do I need to go let Miss Trouble out?"

181

"No." He shook his head. "I took care of her when I was at home. She'll be fine for a while."

Alycia looked disappointed.

"Well . . . I guess she wouldn't mind your company. She has been shut up and alone a good portion of the day."

The girl's face brightened.

Derek glanced in Brooklyn's direction. "Is that okay with you?"

"I guess." To Alycia she said, "Bring her over here to our backyard."

"Great!" Alycia hopped up from her chair and was out the back door in no time.

"You know what you've done, don't you?" Brooklyn cast a frown in his direction, although she didn't quite carry off the look of irritation. She wasn't as upset with him as she tried to appear. "She's going to want a dog of her own."

"I could give her Trouble."

Now Brooklyn's expression — almost horrified — was in earnest. "No, you cannot!"

Derek laughed as he lifted both hands in a sign of surrender. "Okay. Okay. Sorry. Won't mention that again. I promise."

"You'd better not." She released a sigh, her look softening. "There isn't room in our lives to get a pet." As if wanting to change the subject, she pointed at his plate. "An-

182

other slice?"

"Sure." He pushed back his chair. "You?"

She shook her head, and he took his plate to the counter to grab another piece. "Did you have any pets when you were growing up?"

"No. Dad wouldn't have them."

She spoke matter-of-factly, but her words made him feel sorry for her.

"I can't imagine a life without animals in it." He returned to the table and dug in. After swallowing, he added, "When I was little, we always had dogs and cats around the house."

"Your cousin Samantha loved horses. I remember that."

"She sure did. Still does."

"Where is Sam now? I think your grandmother told me when we stayed with her, but I've forgotten."

"She's got a job in Oregon."

"What's she doing?"

"I'm not sure exactly. Some kind of accounting for a really big firm. I would go mad, shut up like that, working with numbers all day, but it seems to suit her. She likes a calm and steady ship."

Brooklyn nodded without comment.

The topic seemed spent, but before Derek could think of another one, Alycia's voice

183

drifted through the doorway. "Me and Trouble are back, Mom."

Amusement flickered across Brooklyn's face. "Me and Trouble," she repeated. "They do sort of go together." Then she laughed.

Derek joined in the laughter. How could he help it? The sound was infectious.

The silence came as quickly as the laughter. Brooklyn blushed and lowered her gaze. "I suppose I'd better get my act together. I work tomorrow."

He took his cue and made quick work of finishing his last slice of pizza. "Did you find a permanent babysitter for Alycia?" He wiped his mouth with a paper napkin.

From outside: "I'm not a baby."

That brought a smile back to Brooklyn's lips.

"Sorry," Derek called to Alycia. Lowering his voice, he said, "I didn't know she could hear us. What do you call them if not a babysitter?"

"A sitter. Leave off the 'baby' part. And yes, I found someone, thanks to your grandmother. Mrs. Nims. Do you know her?" As she spoke, she reached for the empty plates.

"Yeah. Nice lady."

"That's what I thought when I met her." She stood and walked into the kitchen, set-

184

ting the dishes in the sink. "And she's able to work whenever I do. It's nice to have someone who can be that flexible. A waitress's schedule isn't always ideal, even with an accommodating boss like Zach."

She tried to stifle a yawn. Derek saw it anyway. "I'd better get out of your hair. Thanks for the dinner."

"Thanks again for the help, Derek."

"I was glad to do it." He hoped she knew that he meant it.

Outside, he said good-bye to Alycia, apologizing a second time for the babysitter remark, then carried Miss Trouble toward home. He yawned, thought of Brooklyn, and smiled again.

Yeah, they were becoming friends, and that was a good thing.

CHAPTER 14

Derek had exchanged his deputy uniform for a pair of jeans and a colored T-shirt when he heard a rap on the door. Before he could leave the bedroom, he heard Alycia call out, "Are you home, Mr. Johnson?"

"I'm here."

"I came over to take care of Trouble. Is that okay since you're home?"

"Sure. Go ahead." Barefooted, he walked down the hall to the kitchen.

Alycia stood inside the doorway to the mudroom. "She's been out a couple of times already, and I fed her this morning, right on time."

"Good to know." Derek raked the fingers of one hand through his hair. "Is your mom still at work?"

"Uh-huh. She told me she won't be home until after dinner. Mrs. Nims is gonna fix us fried chicken and biscuits."

"Lucky you."

"Wanna come over like you did for pizza?"

He flashed the girl a grin. "No, but thanks for asking."

"Sure." She lifted Miss Trouble into her arms and carried the dog outside.

Derek went to the refrigerator, where he filled a glass with cold water from the dispenser in the door. Tipping back his head, he drained it with big, long gulps. He hadn't known how thirsty he was until the water touched his lips. After filling it a second time, he went to the back door and looked out to where Alycia waited for the papillon to do her business.

"Chad," he said softly, "you really missed out. You made a big mistake, buddy."

Alycia looked up, as if she'd heard him. When she found Derek watching her, she waved.

"Kiddo," he continued in the same soft voice, "I'm going to do whatever it takes to fill in where your dad left a hole. I don't know exactly how, or even what that means for sure, but I'll do my level best. That's my promise to you. And to your mom too."

He drank the last of the water in the glass before heading outside.

The first thing he did was to refill the water tank for the livestock. The calf ignored him, but the two horses crowded in, enjoy-

187

ing the fresh water but also hoping for a carrot or bit of apple or some other treat.

"I spoil you two." Derek patted Blue Boy on the neck, then repeated the action with Sunny. "Sorry. That's all the treat you get right now."

He slipped through the pasture railing and headed out to the fields. After changing the settings on his sprinkler system, he opened the valve to start the flow of water. A few more adjustments to accommodate for the breeze, and he had the spray right where he wanted it.

Finished with that, he went to a section of the farm that wasn't being watered, walking up and down the rows, checking the progress of the vegetables, pulling weeds when he saw them. The work didn't require much in the way of concentration, so it was easy to let his thoughts drift. First to yesterday and the fun he'd had, painting and later eating with Brooklyn and Alycia. Then further back, to the day Chad first brought Brooklyn to a gathering of friends. Not really a party. Just a bunch of kids hanging out at a friend's house, swimming in the pool, dancing to music on the patio.

Chad had brought a bottle of something. Vodka, probably. He'd liked vodka. Liked it a little too much, in Derek's opinion. Chad

had always been reckless, a thrill seeker, a rule breaker. He'd liked to drink and party and he'd had more girlfriends than Derek could remember. Brooklyn Myers had been one of the prettiest girls in Thunder Creek. Maybe *the* prettiest. And once Chad took her out, he'd decided she was his girl and nobody else's. Derek had done his best to discourage the relationship. He'd thought she had a wild streak in her to match Chad's.

But he had to wonder now: was that true? It didn't add up with the girl who had raised a daughter on her own. And done such a good job of it too. Made him wish that he knew more about —

A shrill cry broke into his thoughts. He stiffened and turned, then heard another one. *Alycia!* He broke into a run toward the barnyard. As he drew closer, he hollered her name.

"I'm here, Mr. Johnson! I'm here!" The words were tinged with fear.

When he caught sight of her, his heart almost stopped beating. She was dangling off the side of the six-foot-tall fence near the shed. Her left foot and ankle were tangled in the rope that had been looped around the corner post. The top of her head was about a foot or more above the ground.

189

Blue Boy stood close to her, nuzzling her side. The rope slipped, and she dropped another inch or two, startling both girl and horse. Alycia cried out again.

"Hold on," Derek shouted. "I'm almost there."

He half stepped, half dove between the fence rails. But then he made himself slow down for fear he would startle Blue Boy. The horse was far too close to the girl for Derek's comfort. He clucked his tongue, drawing the gelding's attention. Blue Boy, greedy as always, headed toward Derek in hopes of some sort of reward. All the horse received was a quick pat before his master hurried once more toward Alycia.

Relief rushed through Derek the instant he had a hold of her and there was no more danger. With her arms around his neck and the tension off the rope, he was able to untangle her ankle and foot. But he kept a tight grip on her until they were both through the gate and all the way to his back porch.

"Are you hurt?" he asked as he set her on the top step.

She shook her head, but he tested her ankle anyway, gently moving it from side to side. She stiffened and sucked in a startled breath.

190

"You've got a good sprain, I'll bet. How on earth did you get caught in that rope?" He narrowed his eyes. "You were up on the fence, weren't you? Didn't I tell you not to get near the horses without permission and without an adult with you?"

She nodded, tears welling in her eyes.

"Do you know how much worse that could've been? What if I hadn't heard you? What if that rope had tangled around your neck instead of your ankle? What if one of the horses had spooked and kicked you?" Even as he snapped the words at her, he knew he wasn't as angry as he sounded. But for some reason he couldn't keep from scolding her. "You shouldn't have done that, Alycia. You shouldn't have disobeyed me that way."

"Derek? What's happened?"

He straightened and turned. Eunice Nims hurried toward him, a worried expression knitting her brows. It was all he could do not to turn his irritation on her. Why hadn't she kept an eye on Alycia? Wasn't that what Brooklyn paid her to do?

"I couldn't find her anywhere." Eunice patted her breast, as if mimicking her rapid heartbeat.

The adrenaline that had propelled Derek across his acreage drained away as suddenly

191

as it had come, taking his anger with it. "She's all right, Mrs. Nims. She hurt her ankle, but otherwise, she's okay."

"I called her mother at the diner."

Derek didn't have to ask if Brooklyn was on her way. He knew she was.

"I should take Alycia home," the older woman said.

"Let's not move her just yet." He looked down at the girl on the steps. "But you'd better call Brooklyn again and let her know you found her and she's okay."

As Brooklyn drove toward home — faster than the posted speed limit — a long list of possible disasters raced just as fast through her mind. Various ways that Alycia could be hurt or trapped or in trouble.

Her cell phone rang as she pulled into the driveway. She slammed on the brakes at the same time she answered it. "Hello."

"We found her," Eunice Nims said. "She's all right."

Brooklyn reached for the door. "Where are you?"

"At Derek Johnson's."

Brooklyn took off at a run. Whether from instinct or habit, she raced toward the barnyard and back entrance. Words couldn't describe the emotions that shot through her

192

when she saw her daughter, seated on the steps, head bowed, crying softly. Eunice Nims sat beside her on the steps. Derek stood nearby.

When he saw Brooklyn, he echoed Eunice's words on the phone. "She's all right."

"What happened?"

"Looks like she sprained her ankle."

Eunice rose and moved off to one side. Brooklyn quickly took her place. "What happened?" she repeated, this time to her daughter.

Alycia sniffed as she wiped tears from her cheeks. "I fell off the fence and got my foot caught in a rope." She pointed toward the pasture.

"A rope. How did that happen?" She glanced up at Derek.

Before he could answer, Alycia said, "I'm sorry, Mr. Johnson. I'm real sorry. I won't ever do anything like that again."

Derek leaned toward Alycia. "You'd better not, kiddo. I have to be able to trust you to mind me."

"I know. I'm real sorry." Alycia sniffed again as she bowed her head.

"Maybe now isn't the time —" Brooklyn began.

"I think now is exactly the time." Derek's gaze snapped to meet hers. "She'll get over

193

a sprain fast enough. But she could have been hurt a lot worse because she didn't follow the rules I set down."

Brooklyn knew he was right, but she still didn't like him trying to take charge. *She* was Alycia's mom. *She* was the one who would correct her child. Nobody else. Rising from the step, she said, "I need to get Alycia home so I can call the doctor."

"I'll carry her." Derek leaned down and lifted her daughter in his arms. After a moment, Alycia clasped her hands behind his neck and leaned a cheek against his shoulder.

For some reason, it infuriated Brooklyn, the way he suddenly took charge. But even in her anger she knew she couldn't have carried Alycia all the way across that open field. She might have been able to handle a shorter distance, but she couldn't have managed all that way. Not across an overgrown field with such hard, uneven ground. And so she let him go. She allowed him to lead the way — something she hadn't done with a man for better than a decade.

At the house, Derek carried Alycia up the stairs and into her bedroom. All the furniture was back in place now, although the wall opposite the bed still awaited the promised stencil of the horse. Brooklyn had

194

planned to do that when she got home from work.

At the thought, she stifled a groan. First her dad had made that scene in the diner. Now her daughter had made Brooklyn miss the remainder of her shift. Rather than entering Alycia's room, Brooklyn turned and went into her own room to make the necessary phone call.

"Moonlight Diner."

"Zach, it's Brooklyn."

"Did you find Alycia?"

She drew a quick breath. "Yes. She was over at Derek's place. Just next door. But Mrs. Nims couldn't find her before she called me. Alycia got hurt somehow. A sprained ankle, we think, but she hasn't seen a doctor yet, so I don't know for certain."

"Well, don't you worry about us. You get her to the doctor, and we'll see you tomorrow."

"I'm so sorry about this, Zach. You should be able to depend on me and —"

"Don't you give it no nevermind. Being a parent's never easy. Being a single parent's twice as hard 'cause you're trying to fill two spots."

"But I'm so new there. I promise this won't be a habit."

"You take care of your little girl. I've got

195

the diner covered. Now, go on with you."

"Thanks, Zach," she said softly before ending the call.

She sat on the edge of the bed, feeling drained, exhausted. Her mind had gone blank.

"Brooklyn?"

She looked toward the bedroom door. Derek's broad shoulders seemed to fill the opening. He watched her with concern in his eyes.

"Are you all right?" he asked.

"I'm fine. It's Alycia who got hurt. And if that wasn't enough, you hurt her feelings. You made her cry."

"It's a sprain, Brooklyn. That's all."

She stiffened, her worry changing to anger, and the nearest person was about to catch the brunt of it. "Where did you get that medical degree, Dr. Johnson?"

A frown skated across his face at her words. "Don't need to be a doctor to tell it isn't that serious. And I didn't make her cry. She didn't listen and she got hurt — and in case you didn't notice, I had to make a lesson out of it."

"Not just a doctor, then." She jutted her chin toward him. "Now you know everything about parenting too."

"Not everything. But even I understand

196

that much." There was now a touch of exasperation in both his expression and his tone.

She rose from the edge of the bed. "I'd better see to her. And I still need to call the doctor."

He stared at her a moment, then took a breath. "Brooklyn, I need to tell you something. Something that —"

"Not now. Whatever it is, it can wait."

"All right." He took a step back into the hallway. "Later, then." He glanced toward Alycia's bedroom. "Let me know how she's doing." Then he disappeared from view.

Brooklyn waited a few moments, then sank onto the bed again, trying to make sense of her feelings and reactions. She understood that, irrational though it might be, fear for her child's safety had been replaced by anger once the danger was over. But her response to Derek's words of correction to Alycia confused her.

Or maybe it didn't. Perhaps in her mind she had turned Derek's mild rebuke into the harsher chastisements of her own father.

She straightened and allowed the thought to linger. Was that what she'd done? Was she so quick to allow her past, the memories of her dad, to color so much of her present? If so, she wasn't being fair. Not to Derek and not to Alycia either.

"God," she whispered, "I've come so far. Most of the time I feel strong and sure of myself. But will the day ever come when I'm completely free of negative reactions?"

She felt a sudden desire to hear Esther's voice, to listen to her friend's sound advice. But that would have to wait. For now, she needed to get back to her daughter.

CHAPTER 15

Ruth had heard about Alycia Hallston's mishap before Derek sat down in her kitchen the next morning.

"You'd think Brooklyn never got into any scrapes when she was a kid," he muttered as he stared into his coffee mug. "And I don't know why she was mad at me anyway. I wasn't the one who broke the rules. Alycia did, and the kid was sorry for it. Like she should be."

"Brooklyn was frightened."

"*She* was frightened? I was the one who found Alycia hanging over the fence, about to fall on her head or get it kicked in by a horse. It took a half dozen years off my life. But I had enough good sense to know all she got was a sprained ankle out of it."

He'd been scared the way a parent would have been. Ruth could have told him so, but she supposed it was better for him to figure that out on his own.

199

It didn't take him long. "I guess I scared a few years off Mom's and Dad's lives when I was a kid."

She answered with a soft chuckle.

"I'll apologize the next time I talk to them."

"Just don't confess to misdeeds they don't already know about. All that does is give them nightmares about what *could* have happened to you in the past."

He frowned. "Huh?"

"Never mind. Someday you'll understand, once you have adult children of your own."

They were silent for a while, both of them sipping the dark brew in their mugs.

Finally, Derek said, "Did I tell you I asked if Brooklyn would sell me some of her land? That was before I knew about her B&B plans."

"No. You didn't mention it."

"Yeah, well, I did. And she said she'd think about it." He shrugged. "Then when I heard about the B&B, it felt like she'd led me on." He paused for a moment. "I didn't react well to her news, and we exchanged a few words over it."

"Oh." That explained why he'd left so abruptly after that Sunday dinner.

He took a drink of coffee. "I apologized to her. I knew I wasn't being fair, the way I reacted. And we seemed to be getting along. It felt like we were becoming friends even. And now this."

"Sounds like you need to earn back her trust."

A humorless laugh escaped him. "Not sure I'd made that much progress with her in the first place. She's a skittish filly."

"Then earn her trust now," Ruth replied softly.

"That might be easier said than done."

"Anything worthwhile is rarely easy to obtain."

He drew in a deep, slow breath. He seemed to know she had more to say. He was right.

"Seriously, Derek, you should remember something: we are all products of our pasts. The good and the bad. You're the man you are because of your environment. Because of your parents and your friends and your education." Ruth gave her grandson a firm look. "Brooklyn is too. Take the time to understand why she responded the way she did. I believe it goes deeper than concern for her daughter's health or even because she was being overprotective. And be patient with her."

"Okay, Gran. I'll try." He rose from the chair. "Time I was on my way."

201

Derek's arm around Ruth's shoulders, they walked to the back door. It made Ruth remember a hundred different times when they'd walked together this same way. Through this house. Across the park. Lots of places. And even though he'd towered over her since before his fifteenth birthday, her memories were filled with the days when it was her arm that had rested comfortably on his shoulders instead of the way it was now. She remembered his little boy face turned up at her with a grin, freckles from the summer sun smattering his cheeks and the bridge of his nose.

Thankfulness washed over her. She understood why her two sons and only daughter, along with their spouses, had moved away from Thunder Creek, relocating to locations where better jobs awaited them. But she was endlessly grateful that Derek had chosen to remain, that his roots in this small town had gone as deep as her own.

They stopped at the doorway, and he leaned low to kiss her cheek. "Thanks for the advice, Gran. I'll do my best to follow it."

"I know, dear. I have faith in you."

"You always did."

"Grandmother's prerogative."

He pulled a pair of sunglasses from the

202

pocket of his gray T-shirt and slipped them on. It was a good look on him with his short-cropped hair and his sun-burnished skin. Every bit as handsome as his grandfather had been, although taller and more muscular.

"I'll see you at church in the morning," Derek said, catching her before her thoughts could wander too far into the past.

"Yes, dear. See you there."

On her break, Brooklyn stepped out behind the diner to call home. Alycia answered on the second ring.

"Hi, Mom."

She envisioned her daughter the way she'd left her that morning, on the sofa in the living room, her leg propped up on a couple of pillows. "Hi, honey. How are you feeling?"

"I'm *fine*. Just like I was when you left." Alycia sighed for dramatic effect.

"I get to worry if I want to. I'm the mom."

"I know." There was a moment or two of silence, then Alycia added, "It wasn't Mr. Johnson's fault that I got hurt, you know. Don't be mad at him, Mom."

"I'm not mad, honey. Really I'm not."

"Will you tell him you're not mad?"

She hesitated a moment before answer-

203

ing, "Yes, I'll tell him."

"Thanks! 'Cause I don't want him to say I can't help with Trouble anymore."

Brooklyn smiled. She should have known the dog was of major concern in her daughter's mind.

After telling Alycia she would call again later, Brooklyn went back inside. In a narrow room off the kitchen, she left her phone in the small locker assigned to her. She'd barely turned around when Zach entered.

"Brooklyn, I keep forgetting to ask you: will you be able to work our food booth on the Fourth? I only need you for a few hours in the afternoon. I've got the evening hours covered."

After how tolerant and kind Zach Mason had been to her, she couldn't refuse him. And it wasn't as if she and Alycia hadn't planned to go to the town's annual celebration in the park. "Sure," she answered her boss. "Whatever you need."

"One to four sound all right? After the parade."

She nodded. "One to four. I'll be there."

When she was a girl, the same age Alycia was now, Brooklyn had longed to be able to spend the entire day at the park on the Fourth of July, sampling the food, listening to the music, enjoying the fireworks with a few friends. But her dad had said it was a celebration that invited drunkenness and reckless behavior, and no daughter of his was going to be tempted to be like her mother. The words had stung, even though she hadn't completely understood them.

As a teenager, Brooklyn had simply slipped out of her bedroom window and gone to the park anyway. Those last two summers in Thunder Creek, Chad had met her there. They'd held hands and danced and kissed. And once he'd brought a bottle of tequila with him. She'd gotten sick, throwing up in the bushes. That was the last time she'd drunk any liquor with Chad. If her dad had found out . . . A shudder passed through her, and she shook her head, driving away the unpleasant memory — as was becoming a habit now. Then she headed out to continue her shift.

The Moonlight Diner was always popular. True, that was partly because they were the only sit-down full-menu restaurant within the town limits. But it was also because they had good food at good prices. Tough to beat that.

Saturdays were especially busy. Brooklyn had always preferred those kinds of shifts. It made the hours fly by. She didn't notice her tired feet or tired back as long as she rushed

205

from table to table, taking orders, delivering food, and offering smiles. While it wasn't her intention to remain a waitress any longer than necessary, she was good at it. God willing, she would be just as good at running a B&B — although that day was still far in the future.

Around four o'clock, a group of teenaged girls — dressed in cheerleading attire — entered the diner, laughing and talking and laughing some more. Brooklyn guessed they'd been rehearsing for the upcoming Fourth of July parade, since there was no other reason to be in those outfits in the summer. All six of them piled into a booth meant for four. They hardly glanced at her when she delivered their menus.

"I'll be back with your water," she said to no one in particular.

They weren't paying attention to her anyway. They were laughing again, and a few scattered words made it clear that boys were the focus of their conversation. No surprise there. Brooklyn wondered what it would be like to be their age and popular, confident, carefree. Unafraid to go home. But it was pointless to wonder such things.

When she stepped behind the counter a few moments later, Lucca leaned close and said, "I wouldn't be that age again for a million bucks."

"I was *never* that age." She hoped that didn't sound like self-pity.

If it did, Lucca didn't let on. She simply turned to pick up some plates of hot food.

Brooklyn filled six tumblers with water and ice, dropped drinking straws onto the tray, and returned to the booth. At the moment she reached it, one of girls said, "He's a hottie for sure."

Brooklyn looked up as she set the tumblers on the table. All of the girls were staring out the window.

A different one said, "I suppose. For a guy his age."

Brooklyn's gaze followed theirs. Across the street, outside Kitchner's Sweet Shop — oh, the amazing fudge that had come out of that little store since the First World War, as their sign proudly stated — was Derek, talking to an elderly woman with a walker. The short sleeves of his gray T-shirt revealed his suntanned biceps, and the dark glasses he wore made him look more like a movie star than a farmer.

One of the girls said, "I don't care how old he is. He's definitely Deputy Mc-Dreamy."

Agreement made her pulse quicken. *He* is *a hottie.*

207

Horrified by the thought, she glanced down and finished setting the water glasses on the table. Then, tray now tucked under one arm, she asked, "Are you ready to order?"

After escorting Mrs. Holtzman to her car and putting her walker behind the driver seat, Derek returned to Kitchner's. He paused at the door, glancing over his shoulder in the direction of the diner. Brooklyn had been in his thoughts for most of the day. Maybe because Gran had encouraged him to earn his neighbor's trust.

Or maybe it was something more than that.

He entered the candy store.

"Be right with you."

Owen Kitchner, the fourth-generation owner — or was he the fifth by now? — of Kitchner's Sweet Shop, was a small man. No taller than five foot four. And he weighed no more than a hundred and thirty pounds by Derek's estimate. He had thick gray hair and a wide smile, and his temperament was as sweet as the candy he made. But it was that deep voice coming from such a slight body that always made Derek want to grin.

"Hey, Derek." Owen walked through a doorway from the back of the building where the candy was made, wiping his hands on a towel. "Haven't seen you in here in a month of Sundays."

"You know me, Owen. I've never had much of a sweet tooth."

"Ouch." The man pressed a hand to his chest. "You know how to hurt a guy."

"Sorry." Derek laughed. "But I am here to buy, if that's any consolation."

"Could be. Just could be." Owen dropped the towel on the counter and moved to stand behind the lighted display. "What can I get for you?"

Derek didn't have to think long and hard. He remembered what Brooklyn's favorite candy had been back in high school. Chad used to come in here to buy it a piece or two at a time, and more often than not, Derek had tagged along with him. "I'll take a pound of the Idaho Dreams fudge."

"A pound." Owen grinned. "She must be special." He winked before reaching for a box.

"She's ten," Derek countered. But of course that was a half-truth. If the candy had been only for Alycia, he would have bought an assortment instead of an entire pound of her mother's favorite.

"Plain or with nuts?"

"Plain." Odd, wasn't it, that he remem-

209

bered that detail as well.

Owen hummed to himself as he took fudge from the tray in the display and arranged pieces in the fancy-paper-lined box. When he finished, he settled the gold-foiled cover over the top. "Want a gift card?" He carried the box to the register.

"No, thanks. She's *ten.*" This time it felt like a full-out lie rather than a half-truth.

Owen chuckled. "Suit yourself." He punched in some numbers. "That'll be sixteen dollars and ninety-five cents."

Derek took a credit card from his wallet and held it out to the proprietor, all the while wondering why he was spending seventeen dollars on a box of candy. For what? Would a box of fudge earn Brooklyn's trust? Would it make her want to sell him some of those ten acres? Not likely. And was that even what he wanted it to do? He wasn't sure. But he bought the pound of fudge anyway.

A few minutes later, the transaction completed, Derek stepped through the door of the candy store and headed down the street toward where he'd parked his truck. As he walked, he heard Gran's words in his head: *"We are all products of our pasts."*

He hadn't thought of it when sitting in Gran's kitchen, but now the words reminded him of something. Earlier this year, a friend had sent him an article about daughters without dads. Michael had thought it was good information for an officer of the law to have. Derek had skimmed the article, then filed it away. Now the little he remembered nagged at him. Maybe because even that little bit seemed to describe both Brooklyn and her daughter.

Arriving at his truck, he tossed the box of candy onto the passenger seat as he climbed into the cab. When he got home, he was going to look for that article. Maybe it would help him figure out what he was supposed to do next.

An hour later, Derek sat in front of his laptop, reviewing for the third or fourth time the information contained in the article. What an eye opener. He hadn't known that twenty-seven percent of children in the United States lived apart from their fathers. He hadn't known that many girls who grew up without fathers in the home, according to multiple studies, became sexually active at a younger age than girls with whole families. He hadn't known that girls without dads were fifty-three percent more likely to marry as teenagers and twenty percent less likely to attend college.

211

How could he have read this, even just skimming, and not taken in what it meant for society as a whole? And now for his neighbors in particular.

Sure, Brooklyn had had a physically present dad while she was growing up, but Reggie Myers had emotionally abandoned her. He'd been, at the very least, verbally cruel. No wonder she'd run away with the first guy who'd been nice to her. She'd married young and missed college and who knew what else. As for Alycia, Chad had completely abandoned her. Before she'd even been born. Would these dour statistics prove true for her?

"Not if I can help it," he promised aloud.

He no longer wanted to be a father figure for Alycia as a way of honoring the request of a dying friend. Now he wanted to do it for Alycia's sake alone.

And perhaps for Brooklyn's sake too.

212

CHAPTER 16

Brooklyn and Alycia stayed home from church the following Sunday. Brooklyn's excuse for the decision was her daughter's ankle, even though Alycia was mobile by then. Only the trace of a limp remained, most noticeable when she hurried down the stairs.

The real reason for staying home, Brooklyn acknowledged midmorning, had hazel eyes, close-cropped brown hair, chiseled features, and broad shoulders.

She groaned.

"What's wrong, Mom?"

Brooklyn glanced toward her daughter, lying on the sofa with the Kindle held between her hands.

"Nothing, honey. I just thought about something. It isn't . . . anything important."

"Oh." Alycia's attention went back to the book on the device.

213

Now she was telling lies to her daughter. Great.

Brooklyn set aside the crossword puzzle she'd been working on and rose from the chair. She walked to the large living-room window and looked outside. Despite the intense summer heat, the lawn was a deep emerald green, thanks to the irrigation canals and rivers that channeled water to communities and farmers throughout the Treasure Valley.

Farmers . . .

She wondered if Derek would return to his place after church let out or if he'd go to his grandmother's for Sunday dinner as he so often did.

Giving her head a shake, she turned from the window. "I'm going to get lunch started."

"Okay," Alycia answered without looking up.

"What book are you reading?"

"The City of Ember."

"Again?"

"It's *so* good, Mom. You should read it."

"I did read it. Before you did. But once was enough for me."

Alycia made a dismissive sound in her throat — a sound that said her mother was too old to understand so there was no point

214

trying to explain.

Brooklyn managed not to chuckle as she walked toward the kitchen. She was thankful, of course, that her daughter would rather read than play video games. Alycia was bright and inquisitive, which made her a good student, but she wasn't a shy homebody. She liked adventure, which undoubtedly had played a part in her mishap over at Derek's.

Derek. Again. Why couldn't he stay out of her thoughts?

With another shake of her head, she opened the refrigerator door and pulled open the vegetable drawer. She withdrew the yellow, green, and red peppers, followed by a large purple onion and a container of mushrooms. Next she looked in the deli drawer for the boneless chicken breasts she'd bought two days before. After slicing and dicing the vegetables and sautéing the chicken until it was cooked through — while somehow managing to keep a particular sheriff's deputy from reentering her thoughts — Brooklyn put it all together in a skillet, seasoned it, and left it to simmer until the peppers and onions were tender.

That's when a knock sounded on the back door. Her heart quickened, knowing who it had to be. As if her refusal to think about

215

Derek had conjured him up for real. He knocked again, louder this time. She drew a breath, straightened her shoulders, and headed to the door.

Derek stood on the other side of the screen, dressed for church rather than farm chores. Which meant he'd come straight to her house after this morning's service. Why did that make her heart quicken a second time?

He gave her a smile.

She attempted a small one of her own, although she couldn't be sure she'd been successful.

Finally, he asked, "May I talk to you? And with Alycia?"

Conflicting desires warred in Brooklyn's chest. She wanted him to go, and she wanted him to stay. How was it possible to want both?

"Come in." Apparently she'd decided which she wanted most. She pushed open the screen door, then turned away. To give herself a moment, she went to the stove and turned down the burner.

"I'm sorry," he said, having followed her into the kitchen. "I came at a bad time. I didn't mean to interrupt your Sunday dinner."

She faced him. "You're not interrupting

216

it. It has to simmer awhile."

"If you're sure."

"I'm sure. You said you wanted to talk to Alycia."

"Yes. To you both. But to you first."

She crossed her arms over her chest, aware of how defensive she looked, although not for the reasons he would probably think. "Okay."

He looked toward the front of the house. "Where is she?"

"In the living room reading."

He nodded. Gathering his thoughts, she supposed.

"Remember I told you Chad wrote to me before he died?" He spoke in a soft voice, one that wouldn't carry to the living room.

She didn't know what she'd expected him to say, but bringing up Chad hadn't been it.

"It wasn't just to tell me that he wasn't selling the land to me. He also asked something of me. And he said it was up to me to tell you when and if I thought the time was right. That he didn't intend to write to you about it himself."

Nerves began to whirl in her belly.

Derek set a canvas bag on the table before he took a couple of steps toward her. "Chad asked me to be . . . to be a kind of father figure to Alycia."

217

Brooklyn sucked in a breath. "What?"

"What he said was he wanted me to be the father to her that he'd never been."

"I don't believe you," she whispered. She didn't mean to call him a liar. But what he'd said sounded impossible.

"I thought you might not believe it." He reached into his shirt pocket and withdrew a piece of paper. He unfolded it before holding it toward her. "Go on. Read it."

She wasn't sure she wanted to.

His gaze was kind and a little uncertain. "I don't know, Brooklyn. Maybe I should have told you about Chad's note the day I picked you up by the side of the highway. It just all caught me by surprise. And to tell you the truth, I didn't know how I was supposed to go about honoring his request anyway." He kept his arm outstretched, silently urging her to take the note-paper from his hand.

Somehow she made herself take a step toward him. Then another step. And another. Until she could reach out and take the paper as requested. She recognized the handwriting, even after so many years. Tears welled, blurring the words on the page.

"He should have written to Alycia," she said.

"Yeah, he should have. But one day, when

218

you think she's ready, you'll show her this. She'll know her dad thought about her in the end. That he wanted even more than to leave a house for her to grow up in."

Brooklyn moved away from Derek, found the box of tissues on the built-in kitchen desk, and wiped her eyes. The hurt over Chad's leaving was nothing but a dull memory, but the pain she felt for Alycia had never dimmed. Not one iota.

Finally, control restored and eyes free of tears, she read the handwritten note Derek had given her. It was brief. But at least it was something. Why had Chad written to Derek but not to her? Why hadn't he provided explanations along with a house? So many answers to so many questions had gone with him to his grave. She didn't understand. She would never understand.

"You are not Alycia's father, Derek," she finally managed to say. "No one expects you to try to be."

"I expect it of myself."

Once again she faced him.

He continued, his expression intense. "I don't know why Chad did the things he did. He never explained anything to me and . . . to my shame . . . I never asked him the hard questions that I should have asked. Not even when he was here for his parents' funeral and definitely not after he agreed to sell me this property. But at the end" — he motioned toward the note in her hand — "Chad wanted to do right by his daughter. That's what matters now. And he asked me to help him do that. So now I'm asking you to let me try."

"Derek —"

"Look, I didn't go about things right when Alycia got hurt. Once you were there, I shouldn't have been the one to try to teach her a lesson, even if the accident did happen at my place. I overstepped, and I'm sorry. I'm the first to admit I'm new at this sort of thing. I'll need your help if I'm to . . . to be someone important in Alycia's life."

What was she to say to that? To any of it?

Derek pointed at the stove. "Maybe you'd better turn that down a bit more."

She whirled around. Steam rose around the lid of the skillet. She quickly moved to the stove and turned the dial, lowering the heat. Then she stopped and closed her eyes, trying to quiet the ping-ponging thoughts and questions in her head.

"Brooklyn."

She drew another deep breath and slowly turned.

"One more thing. I . . ." He paused, cleared his throat. "I brought this for you

220

and Alycia." He took up the canvas bag from the table and offered it to her. "To say I'm sorry to you both."

Derek figured it was a good sign when Brooklyn reached out and took the bag from his hand. She watched him with those pretty eyes of hers for what seemed an age before she lowered them to see what was inside. They widened when she recognized the box.

"Kitchner's," she said, almost too softly for him to hear.

"Yeah. I . . . I remembered you liked their fudge."

Her gaze lifted again, and she passed the canvas bag back to him. "You should give this to Alycia yourself."

The tension inside his chest eased. Unless he'd misread her, Brooklyn hadn't rejected Chad's request. Maybe she hadn't accepted it either, but at least she'd left the door open to the possibility of letting Derek be there in some capacity for Alycia.

"Come on. You can give it to her now." She turned and walked toward the living room. Derek followed right behind.

Alycia, reclining on the sofa, looked up when he entered the room. "Hey, Mr. Johnson." She grinned as she sat up and put aside the tablet that had been in her hand.

"How're you doing, kiddo? Your ankle getting better?"

"Sure. It's fine."

"All better?"

"Almost." She stuck out her leg and moved her foot in a circle, first clockwise, then counterclockwise. "See? Only hurts a little now."

"That's great." Derek drew a quick breath. "Listen. I wanted to say I'm sorry for the way I scolded you."

The girl raised her eyebrows.

"You shouldn't have broken the rules, but I should have handled it differently too. Think we can be friends again?"

"We never stopped being friends. And I told Mom it wasn't your fault."

"You did? Thanks." He glanced toward Brooklyn and back again. "Here. This is for you and your mom." He handed her the bag.

Unlike her mother, Alycia didn't just peer into it. She had the box out of the bag and the lid off in mere seconds.

"Hold it right there," Brooklyn said before her daughter could grab a piece and pop it in her mouth. "Not until after lunch."

"Aw, Mom."

222

"Lunch first."

Alycia sighed. "Okay." She put the lid back on the box.

"Would you like to eat with us, Derek?" Brooklyn sounded as if she meant the invitation. "It's kind of a stir-fry, only not really."

As always, Derek had plenty of chores awaiting him, but he wasn't about to leave when things were going better than he'd expected. Looking at Brooklyn, he answered, "I won't turn it down. It's starting to smell really good, by the way."

Brooklyn smiled.

Derek liked that he'd been able to make that happen again. Another step forward. An apology plus fudge was the right combination. Good thing to know for the future.

The future . . . As neighbors? As a father figure for Alycia? Or as something more? As he wondered about what it was he wanted, Brooklyn returned to the kitchen.

"How's Trouble doing?" Alycia asked.

Derek made himself focus on the here and now. "We're managing, but we'll be glad when you're ready to help out again." He settled onto a nearby chair. "You playing a video game?" He pointed at the device beside her.

"No. Reading a book."

223

"That's right. You told me some of the books you like to read when we painted your room."

"Yeah."

"So what're you reading now?"

She picked up the tablet, and excitement filled her voice. "*The City of Ember.* I've read it three times already."

"Wow. It must be good. I've never read any book more than once. Not counting my farming books when I'm looking to remember information." He tried to appear serious as he asked, "Would you like to borrow one of them? You could learn all about when to plant tomatoes and peas and —"

"Uh . . . no thanks, Mr. Johnson."

He laughed. "Want to tell me about your book, then?"

Alycia's face lit up. "Well, there's this girl named Lina and she lives in a place called Ember. And she's got a friend named Doon . . ."

Derek wasn't all that interested in the plot — but then, he rarely read novels, let alone what sounded like science fiction. He was more of a facts and dates kind of guy. However, he did enjoy watching Alycia as she explained the plot to him. It struck him again how well adjusted Alycia seemed. Maybe those statistics he'd read about girls

224

who grew up without dads didn't apply to her. Maybe she didn't need Derek in her life as much as he'd thought she might. Maybe Brooklyn had already filled that spot where Chad should have been better than Derek ever could.

But the truth was he *wanted* Alycia to need him. Crazy, wasn't it?

Even crazier, he was beginning to see himself answering that need. Maybe he could teach her to ride horses and to fish. Maybe he could help out when it was time for her to learn to drive. Maybe he could be the one who explained boys to her, from a guy's point of view, when she got her first crush. He smiled as he envisioned himself standing on the front porch, his posture slightly threatening, when a date came to pick her up.

"What's funny, Mr. Johnson?"

"Nothing, kiddo. I'm just glad you're feeling better."

Before Alycia could respond, Brooklyn called to them from the kitchen. "All right, you two. Lunch is ready."

225

CHAPTER 17

Derek was driving through town in the sheriff's SUV when Ethan Walker waved him down. He pulled his vehicle to the curb, and Ethan stepped to the passenger-side window, leaning down after Derek lowered it.

The vet leaned his forearms in the opening. "How's your little charge doing? Have you taken the cone off?"

"She's good. Removed the cone this morning, as instructed."

"Thought you'd like to know that I've come up empty on trying to find either her owner or the breeder she came from. She wasn't microchipped." He repositioned his sunglasses. "Probably not from around here. My guess is someone brought the dog out to the river to get rid of her. And if it was her owner who shot her and broke her leg, maybe it's just as well I can't locate him."

Derek cocked an eyebrow. "Why? Because

226

I'd want to do the same or worse to him if I knew who he was?"

"You'd have to get in line." Ethan's smile was grim. "Have you decided what you're going to do with her once the cast is off?"

"No." He looked down Main Street, then returned his gaze to Ethan. "I'm sure between the two of us we can find her a good home."

It was Ethan's turn to look away, then back again. "I've got somebody in mind."

"I'm sure you do," Derek answered dryly, reading the vet's mind.

Ethan patted the door frame. "Well, I won't keep you from your appointed rounds. Or does that only apply to the mailman?"

Derek put the SUV in gear. "You're a regular riot, Ethan."

"That's what my wife tells me." Ethan stepped back onto the sidewalk. "See you tomorrow."

Derek gave a brief wave. "See you tomorrow." Then he pulled back onto the street and continued on his way.

Once on the highway, his thoughts turned to Brooklyn and Alycia, as they so often did anymore. Maybe this time was because he soon drove past the spot where he'd found them and their broken-down car. Surprising how his attitude about Brooklyn had

227

changed in under a month.

Had her attitude toward him changed too? He thought so. He hoped so. A man could never have too many friends. Right? He grinned but didn't let himself take the thought any further than that.

Smoke smudged the sky today. A range fire to the south in Owyhee County had been burning for a couple of days, and he'd heard a new fire had started in the Boise National Forest to the northeast of them. The valley would be affected by the sooty skies for a while unless the predicted winds blew in during the night. Hopefully the weatherman was right. It would make for a more pleasant Fourth of July celebration if the air was free of smoke.

He arrived at a bend in the road. To the left, he would have been on his way out of the county and toward Oregon and Nevada. He turned right, the highway carrying him north past a number of the area vineyards.

Derek wasn't fond of wine. He had simply never cared for the taste. But there was something about the vineyards that appealed to him. Perhaps it was the stories from the Bible, first learned in Sunday school, about God's vineyard and about Christ as the vine and His people as the branches. Or maybe it was simply the look

228

of those grapevines in the summer, all of those neat rows following slopes and hillsides. Or the way those vines, carefully tended and pruned, produced fruit year after year.

As he passed Dubois Vineyards, he remembered Brooklyn mentioning the weddings often held at various vineyards in the area. Dubois was perhaps the most well known for such events. He'd attended several weddings there himself over the years. They also held concerts during the summer.

"Might be fun to go to one of those concerts again," he said to himself before slowing to make a turn and continue his circle back toward Thunder Creek. "Just might be."

Tracy Vinton smiled a warm greeting when she opened the door and saw Brooklyn and Alycia on the stoop. "You're a lifesaver," the pastor's wife said, drawing the new arrivals into the house.

Brooklyn looked around the living and dining rooms. Women were everywhere, sewing and beading. One sat on the floor making a sign of some sort. They all looked up. *Hello*s echoed from around the rooms before the women returned to their tasks.

"We're running so far behind," Tracy said. "Thanks for answering my call for more help."

"I'm glad I could come. After all the help you were to me when we got here . . ."

Tracy waved her hand as if to say her help had been nothing. Then she looked down at Alycia. "The other children are playing in the backyard if you want to join them."

"Sure. Here, Mom." She handed Brooklyn the book she'd brought along.

Tracy motioned with her head. "Come with me, and I'll introduce you. You probably met most of them at Sunday school when you came to church, but I'll make sure. And I'm glad your ankle is better."

"Me too."

Brooklyn felt more than a little awkward after Alycia was led away. She didn't know what she should do. Stand there and wait?

The feeling wasn't allowed to last long. From the dining-room table, Lucca Phillips called, "Brooklyn, come and help me with this bunting."

With a nod, she hurried to fill the chair beside her fellow waitress from the diner.

"Did Tracy tell you a bunch of our decorations were lost in a storage-shed fire?" Lucca pushed a needle and spool of thread in Brooklyn's direction. "And we didn't find

230

out about it until Saturday." She lowered her voice. "Don't ask what I think of that oversight. I might tell you."

Brooklyn offered a quick smile before turning her attention to threading the needle.

Pauline Salmon, seated at the end of the table, said, "Everyone's been working hard on the floats and never gave a thought to the other decorations. I mean, we've had the same ones for years and years."

Pauline would know. She'd been around Thunder Creek even longer than Ruth Johnson.

Speaking of whom . . . "Isn't Ruth here?" Brooklyn glanced quickly around the two rooms.

Lucca answered, "She was here earlier but had to leave. Her part-time waitress called in sick, so Ruth went back to help Camila in the shop." She slid some red-white-and-blue material in Brooklyn's direction. "Glad you and I weren't scheduled to work today."

"Me too."

Tracy returned and sat on the only remaining available chair. "I've got the kids playing Lawn Twister. That should keep them busy until they're all hungry again."

"Lawn Twister?"

Tracy laughed. "It's something Adrian saw

231

on the Internet. He spray-painted big colored dots on the grass to use instead of the plastic mat. Everything else is the same as the regular board game."

Brooklyn was tempted to rise and have a look for herself. Maybe it was something she could put to use at her B&B, especially for guests with kids. Instead, she made a mental note to look it up on the Internet herself.

Lucca shoved more material and thread in Tracy's direction. "We'll never have everything ready for the review stand if we don't get with it."

Tracy threw a small scrap of fabric back at Lucca. It didn't have enough weight to carry across the table, but it made both women laugh.

Brooklyn felt something warm and pleasant coil inside of her. Not just because of the banter between Tracy and Lucca but because of the feeling that she was part of it. That she fit in. That she belonged.

All those years in Reno, she realized, she'd never felt that way. Not really. Not even after she'd found the Lord and become involved in a church. It wasn't that other women hadn't been kind to her. Certainly Esther had been a dear friend. But she'd always felt like someone on the outside looking in. Never a part.

As surprising as it sounded, maybe she'd needed to come home.

"Brooklyn, before I forget to mention it," Tracy said, her needle and thread busy again, "our Wednesday night women's Bible study doesn't meet weekly during the summer, but we do have one potluck a month. We hope you'll join us for the next one."

That pleasant warmth in Brooklyn's chest intensified. "I'd love to, if I'm not working. When is it?"

"The twenty-sixth. In the church fellowship hall at six o'clock."

Smiling, her eyes on the fabric in her hand, she said, "I'll ask Zach to schedule me for the early shift that day."

CHAPTER 18

The downside to being a farmer, Derek had learned, was that he didn't have the same kind of freedom to do as he pleased on his days off from the sheriff's department. There was always work to do. Which made it surprising to find nothing that would keep him from spending the better part of the day at the town's annual Fourth of July festivities.

And even better, the weatherman's prediction had been spot on. A westerly breeze had cleared the air of smoke during the night. The skies were a cloudless blue, promising a picture-perfect day.

Around noon, his chores completed until evening, Derek swept Miss Trouble into the crook of one arm and got into his pickup. He knew beforehand that the little dog would bring plenty of ribbing from his male friends. Especially since he would spend most of the time carrying her around. Miss

234

Trouble was surprisingly mobile now. She'd learned how to compensate for the cast, especially now that the cone was off her neck. Still, he wouldn't want her getting hurt in the crowd.

Gran's property was surrounded on three sides by the town park. As a kid, Derek had thought it great that Gran and Pappy had a park for a backyard. The creek for which the town was named flowed through the middle of that park. Two footbridges allowed visitors easy access to both north and south sides. Tall trees provided shade from the hot summer sun, except for the playground area, where children could run from slides to swings to merry-go-round to teeter-totters, and the west end, which had a large area great for throwing a ball or a Frisbee.

When he arrived in town, Derek parked in his grandmother's private driveway. He didn't bother to knock on her door. He knew that by now she was on Main Street with a group of her friends, waiting for the start of the parade.

Dog in arm, he walked into the backyard. From there he could see the food booths that had been set up at the northeast corner of the park. People hustled about, taking care of last-minute things before the rush of

235

hungry citizens arrived. It was the same every year. The moment the parade was over, just about everyone came to the food booths. Brooklyn would be kept plenty busy for the three hours of her shift.

With thoughts of Brooklyn planted once again in his mind, he turned and strode toward Main Street. It wasn't difficult to find his grandmother, even with people lining both sides of the street. She and her friends set their lawn chairs in the same place year after year.

"Oh look," Gran said as she moved her umbrella from left shoulder to right. "Derek brought his new dog."

He opened his mouth to insist that Miss Trouble wasn't his dog, that as soon as the cast was removed, he planned to find her a new home. But the protest got caught in his throat. He grinned as he realized he had no intention of finding Miss Trouble a new home. Blast Ethan Walker's sneaky heart! He'd known the dainty little canine would wiggle and hop her injured way into Derek's heart. Someday Derek would have to get even.

"Hey, Gran." He passed Miss Trouble onto her lap as he leaned down to kiss her cheek, avoiding the rim of the umbrella. "Looks like I made it into town in time."

236

Gran checked her watch. "With a few minutes to spare."

Derek straightened and greeted by name each of the women seated near his grandmother.

"I brought an extra lawn chair if you want it," Gran said when he looked at her again.

"No, thanks. I'm good."

Music reached their ears from the opposite end of town. Conversations quieted as a feeling of anticipation settled over the crowd.

Although what was exciting about a Thunder Creek parade escaped Derek. First would come the flags carried by veterans. Next would be the high school marching band and the cheerleaders, the latter kicking their legs and shaking their pom-poms and every so often forming a pyramid, the smallest girl on top. The mayor would roll by in a black, new-model convertible, waving as if it were an election year, followed by the queen of the parade on horseback. More horses and riders representing the county rodeo would be right behind her. Usually there were a couple of floats put together by local service organizations right before the men's group from church appeared in go-carts, driving them in crazy circles while hooting and hollering. Men

237

acting like boys. Finally, Millie Smith would bring up the rear in a cart pulled by one of her miniature horses, harness covered in bells.

The parade never changed much year to year.

"Look," Gran said. "There's Brooklyn and Alycia."

He followed her gaze. It didn't take long to find them. Both of them were wearing sunshine yellow.

"Go ask them to join us, Derek."

It no longer surprised him how eager he was to do that.

Brooklyn saw Derek step off the curb as if he meant to cross the street. But then someone spoke to him and he stopped and turned to exchange a few words. It happened again, then again, and it was easy for her to see how admired and respected he was. As if she hadn't known it already. The Johnsons were pillars of the community, while Brooklyn had always felt like an outsider. But remembering her time with the women at the Vinton home yesterday, she knew that was changing. Had already changed, in fact.

Music growing louder, Brooklyn turned her gaze in the opposite direction. The

238

honor guard drew closer, the marching band right behind them.

"Here they come," she said, placing a hand on Alycia's shoulder.

Her daughter leaned forward to look around the man next to them. "I can see the flags."

"Hey, you two."

Brooklyn's head whipped to the right at the sound of Derek's voice. He'd made it across the street at last, and her heart gave a small flutter.

He grinned at her. "Gran wants you to join her and her friends." He pointed in Ruth's direction. "She's got an extra chair for you."

Brooklyn felt a sting of disappointment. Had he only come to issue his grandmother's invitation?

"Come on." He spoke louder to be heard over the approaching horns, clarinets, and drums. "Before the band gets here."

"Let's go, Mom."

Alycia was already crossing the street. No sprained ankle slowed her down today. Derek reached out with his left arm, not quite touching Brooklyn, yet gently, subtly encouraging her to go with him. The honor guard was almost upon them. Releasing a quick breath, she hurried after her daughter,

Derek right behind.

Ruth smiled as she motioned to the lawn chair next to her. "You'll want to sit down while you can, dear. You'll be on your feet all afternoon."

Brooklyn nodded, but before she could turn, the flag bearers arrived. Those who were seated in chairs stood. The women nearby, including Ruth, all put their umbrellas on the ground. Men removed hats and pressed them to their chests. Most everyone else put hands over their hearts. A blanket of reverence settled over the crowd for a few seconds. And then, with the flags gone by, a cheer rose to mix with the music of the marching band.

"Mom, look!"

The cheerleaders had stopped in the middle of the street and were forming a pyramid. Three girls on the bottom, two girls on their shoulders, and one girl climbing to the top. Brooklyn recognized all of them from the restaurant, especially the one who thought Derek was a hottie.

She felt her face grow warm — and it had nothing to do with the July sun beating down on them.

"I wanna be a cheerleader when I'm older," Alycia said. "Can I, Mom?"

"Sure, if you really want to." Brooklyn sat

on the lawn chair.

"You look flushed, dear." Ruth switched the umbrella to her near hand, giving some shade to Brooklyn. "Be careful. You don't want to have heatstroke. Derek, get something for her to drink."

"Don't fuss," Brooklyn insisted. "I'm fine."

Derek said, "No problem. They're selling bottles of water over there. Be right back."

The smiling cheerleaders kicked and spun by them, followed by the marching band. It wasn't a large band, but they were loud and played with great enthusiasm.

A short while later, Alycia gasped. "Mom, look!"

It was the parade queen on a prancing palomino. The girl's outfit and the horse's tack were rhinestone studded and sparkled with every prancing step the palomino took. The queen wore turquoise, from the cowboy hat on her head to the fancy boots on her feet.

"She's gor-r-r-r-geous," Alycia said, stretching out the last word.

Ruth leaned forward on her chair. "That's Reba Maxwell, Georgia's granddaughter. Reba's studying to become a doctor. Walter would be so pleased."

Was there anything Ruth didn't know

241

about the citizens of Thunder Creek? Brooklyn wondered.

Does she know that I like her grandson?

Liked him? Of course she liked him. He was a nice guy. Everybody in town liked Derek Johnson. There wasn't anything unusual or unexpected in that.

Only that isn't what you mean. Is it?

Her stomach fluttered nervously. She didn't know what she meant. She didn't *want* to know what she meant.

As if summoned by her thoughts, Derek arrived with the promised bottle of water, condensation dripping down its sides. "Here you go." He squatted beside her chair, looking much too friendly and handsome for his own good.

Heat surged through her a second time. She took the bottle from him, removed the plastic top, and took several long drinks of the cold water.

Awhile later, well after the end of the parade and now seated in the shade of a tall elm tree, Ruth let her gaze roam over the people milling around the park. No matter where she looked, she saw familiar faces. She recognized dozens of men and women, from their twenties to their sixties, along with teens and little children, whom Walter had treated in his clinic. Over the years, he'd set their broken limbs. He'd treated their fevers and their allergies. He'd sent some off to serve in Vietnam. Others to serve in subsequent wars like Desert Storm and Afghanistan. He'd given them good reports and bad. A baby was coming. The tumor was cancerous. Such was life. And she and Walter had been a part of it.

Over fifty-three years before, she and Walter had arrived in Thunder Creek. They hadn't known a soul in the town, but he'd believed he was called there to practice medicine, to serve the people of the community. And Ruth, of course, had been called to serve at his side as best she could.

She'd never admitted to him how afraid she'd been at the start. Afraid she would fail him. Afraid she wouldn't be liked by their neighbors. Afraid she would never belong in Thunder Creek. Walter would belong. Walter fit in wherever he went. It had been his nature. Men had liked him. Women had liked him. Children had liked him.

Their first weeks in town had passed in a blur of activity as they put their new house and his medical office in order. Glad for the hard work, glad that she could fall into bed exhausted every night, nineteen-year-old

Ruth had been content to spend every moment with her husband. But then the Fourth of July had arrived. In her memories, that was the day when she'd become a part of this community, the day when Thunder Creek had truly become her home. Suddenly she'd realized people knew her by name, were including her in the festivities, were doing their best to make her feel as if she belonged. If anybody had guessed how unsure of herself she was, they hadn't let on. And she'd loved them all for it. Still loved them for it to this day.

Maybe that was why the Fourth of July remained one of Ruth's favorite holidays. Different from Thanksgiving, Christmas, and Easter, which were favorites as well. But those holidays were about family and faith. The Fourth was about community and patriotism.

She smiled to herself as her gaze moved toward the food booths. The sign saying *Moonlight Diner* was a foot or two above all the other signs, making it easy to find. Of course she couldn't make out Brooklyn waiting on customers. Not through the throng of people.

But she did, a moment later, spy her grandson. His gaze was also directed toward the Moonlight's food booth. And something in his expression told her that he had a better view, that he was watching Brooklyn as she worked. It told her something more besides.

He felt something beyond friendship toward that young woman, whether or not he'd realized it.

"Well, I'll be."

From the day Derek was born, Ruth had prayed for his future, just as she had prayed for every one of her children and grandchildren. Those prayers for the future had included the people her loved ones would eventually marry.

As for her eldest grandson, he had seldom been without a girlfriend. Ruth had been fond of several of them through the years, but *the* girl had never appeared on the horizon. In fact, earlier this year Derek had announced he was done with dating for a while. That he had no time for emotional attachments.

From where Ruth sat, it appeared his opinion might have been changed by Brooklyn Myers.

Her smile grew, and she repeated to herself, "Well, I'll be."

"Penny for your thoughts." Camila unfolded a chair next to Ruth and sat on it.

"I'm plotting Derek's future."

"Oh dear. Poor boy."

Ruth laughed. "The danger of being the only grandchild living nearby."

Her friend laughed, too, before asking, "And just what are you plotting for him?"

"I believe he needs a wife."

"Have you got one in mind?"

"As a matter of fact, I think I do."

Sweat trickled down the back of Brooklyn's neck as she delivered an order to a young couple seated at one of the dozen tables forming a half circle around the sides and back of the diner's booth. She'd worked some busy shifts in her life as a waitress, but never anything like this. The whole town seemed to want Zach's food. The instant a table was emptied, someone else arrived to sit there.

At least she didn't have to worry about her daughter. Ruth and several of her friends had volunteered to keep an eye on the girl, and Alycia had kept her word, checking in with Brooklyn every half hour. The last two times she'd appeared, she'd had Miss Trouble in her arms.

The dog drew everyone's attention. Especially other kids. Whether it was Miss Trouble's cute face, pretty ears, petite size, the cast on the front leg, or a combination

246

of all of those things, Brooklyn didn't know. But the canine was introducing Alycia to even more children her own age.

"I'll be done in half an hour," she told her daughter, who had another girl with her this time, as well as the dog. "So be here on time."

"Okay."

"And check in with Mrs. Johnson again."

"I will."

The girl with Alycia reached out to stroke Miss Trouble's head.

"Who's your friend?" Brooklyn asked.

"This is Wendy."

"Hi, Wendy. Nice to meet you."

The girl didn't look away from the dog. "You too."

"Do I know you from church?"

The girl shrugged. "Maybe."

"What's your last name?"

"Royal." Wendy's eyes still didn't leave Miss Trouble.

Brooklyn smiled, knowing she might as well give up. She couldn't compete with the small dog in her daughter's arms. "All right. Off with you. I've got orders to take. But don't go too far and be back at four o'clock."

She watched for only a few moments as the two girls slipped away through the

247

crowd. Then she headed for a nearby table and three new customers. "What can I bring you?" she asked as she readied her pad and pencil.

Half an hour later, Brooklyn happily whipped off the dark-green apron she'd worn for the afternoon and started watching for her daughter's return. It was only a few minutes before she caught sight of her. Only this time it wasn't Wendy Royal who was with Alycia. It was Derek, and now he held the dog in the crook of his arm. The two of them looked so natural together that it made her heart squeeze.

"Hey, Mom. You done?"

She walked toward them. "Yes, I'm done for the day. So what do you want to do now?" Her question, though not intentional, was directed at both of them.

"The ball game!" Alycia said.

"Aren't you hungry?"

"Not yet. I want to see the ball game. Please."

Brooklyn remembered the impromptu softball games that had taken place on the Fourth when she was a girl. Anyone sixteen and over could play, as she recalled. Men and women had brought their own bats and balls and the necessary bases. Teams had been formed by drawing names from a hat. The park didn't have bleachers or an official ball field, so spectators brought blankets and lawn chairs. She wondered if the games were still done the same way.

She looked at Derek. "Are you going to play?"

"Can't right now. I've got to head home to take care of the animals. They need to eat before I do."

The disappointment she felt was unexpected. Then again . . . maybe it wasn't.

"Is it okay if I leave Miss Trouble with Alycia? She offered, but I wanted to make certain it's all right with you."

"I don't mind."

"Thanks. It won't take me long." He passed the dog to Alycia. "I'll look for you when I get back."

CHAPTER 19

Derek completed his evening chores in record time. Afterward, he took a moment to wash up in the house before he got into his pickup and drove back to town, eager to find Brooklyn again. Parking spaces within two or three blocks of the park were at even more of a premium now than they had been earlier in the day. Fortunately, nobody had blocked his grandmother's driveway, as had happened a time or two through the years.

Before he looked for Brooklyn — and Alycia and Miss Trouble, of course — he made his way to Gran, checking in with her again, the way he always did on this hectic holiday. Although she ventured forth from her spot under the elm trees now and again throughout the day, much of the town made its way to her, if for nothing more than to say hello and to wish her a happy Fourth.

"Hey, Gran."

"Oh good. You're back."

"Why? Did you need something?"

"Heavens, no. I don't need a thing." She raised an eyebrow. "What about you, dear?"

"Not sure what you mean."

"That's okay." She grinned. "You're smart. You'll figure it out."

Since he truly didn't have a clue what she meant, he shrugged. "If you say so."

"Where's Miss Trouble?"

"Still with Brooklyn and Alycia." He glanced toward the western end of the park. "They were headed over to watch the game the last I saw them."

"Well, don't waste time here with me. Get on with you."

He grinned as he leaned in to kiss her cheek. "I'll do that."

"And if the dog gets underfoot, you bring her back here to me. She and I get along quite well together."

"Okay."

He set off across the park, greeting people along the way. Shouts from the ball game reached him well before his arrival.

Hank McLean spied him from the sidelines. "Hey, Derek. You here to play?"

"No." He shook his head. "Not this year."

"But we need you. We're losing."

Derek shrugged. "Sorry. Other plans."

Not giving his friend a chance to ask ques-

251

tions or make another attempt to get him to play, Derek moved on. He worked his way around the edge of the crowd. He'd made almost a full half circle before he spotted them, their backs toward the sun that had lowered in the western sky. He stopped and simply observed them for a few moments, trying to analyze what it was that he felt when he looked at Brooklyn. No, more than that. What he felt when he looked at both mother and daughter together. For they came as a package deal.

"You're smart. You'll figure it out." Maybe he knew what his grandmother had been asking him after all. But was he ready to discover the answer?

When Hank McLean hit the ball into the trees at the far side of the backfield, Brooklyn jumped to her feet and screamed her excitement right along with the rest of the crowd. "Go! Go! Go!" she shouted as Hank rounded third base and headed for home.

As the crowd continued to celebrate the home run, a fresh sense of belonging washed over Brooklyn. An even stronger one than what she'd felt the day before. For most of her life she'd felt invisible, an outsider. First in Thunder Creek. Then in Reno. But no longer. Right now she felt a part of it all.

252

She turned for a victory slap of hands with her daughter but found Derek approaching them. Her mind went temporarily blank. Her stomach tumbled. He'd said he would seek her out when he got back. Was that only because of Miss Trouble?

His grin and the look in his eyes said otherwise. She felt the latter all the way down to her toes.

"Hank can really hit a ball," he said when he stopped the other side of Alycia.

"He sure can."

"He told me a minute ago that his side was losing. Doesn't look like that now."

"No, it doesn't." Her heart beat erratically in her chest. Silly. Over a home run?

Derek looked down at Alycia. "Who're you rooting for?"

"The blue team."

"Good choice." He glanced up again, his smile warm.

"Aren't you going to play?" Brooklyn asked.

He shook his head. "I think I'll sit this one out. Mind if I join you?"

Like him, she shook her head. She didn't mind. She definitely didn't mind. Part of her was convinced it wasn't smart for her to feel that way. She chose to ignore that part.

They sank to the ground, Brooklyn and

253

Alycia with a blanket beneath them, Derek sitting on the grass.

Another batter stepped to the plate.

"That's Wendy's dad," Alycia said. "He's super nice."

Derek replied, "I agree. Ian's a great guy."

"Wendy's lucky." A wistfulness had entered her daughter's voice and flickered in her eyes. "It must be nice. You know. A mom and a dad and a brother. Being a family like that."

Brooklyn's breath caught in her chest. She'd never heard Alycia say anything like that before. She'd known and yet she hadn't known the way her daughter must feel. But hearing the words aloud . . .

Again it was Derek who answered Alycia. "You know what, kiddo? It is nice. But there's all kinds of ways to have a family." He draped one arm casually around Alycia's shoulders. "This is nice too."

"It sure is, Mr. Johnson."

She stared at the pair of them, comfortable, happy. Envy of her friend hadn't lingered in her daughter's expression. Derek had driven it away.

In that moment, Brooklyn could almost believe in love again.

Strange, how natural it felt to gather up

254

Brooklyn's blanket when the ball game ended and to walk with them to the food court for something to eat before the fireworks began. And it pleased him that Brooklyn and Alycia seemed to feel the same way.

They made a stop to leave both blanket and dog with Gran, who also looked rather pleased. With herself? Or with him?

"We'll be back for Trouble when we're done eating," he told her.

"No hurry. She's well behaved." Gran's gaze shifted to Brooklyn. "Are you having a good time, dear?"

"Yes."

"Me too," Alycia piped in.

Gran's smile broadened. "I'm so glad."

Derek took a step toward Brooklyn and Alycia. "So what is it you want to eat?"

Brooklyn gave a slight shrug, as if to say she didn't care.

Alycia's hunger was more precise. "A party pup. And a really big lemonade."

"That okay?" he asked Brooklyn.

"It's fine."

They moved on, Alycia leading the way. Derek thought she looked like a racehorse at the starting gate. Any moment she would run off, leaving them in the dust.

"She's loving all of this," Brooklyn said.

"No Fourth of July celebrations where you

used to live?"

"Yes." She stopped walking. "But it isn't quite the same in a city as it is in a small town."

Derek stopped, too, watching a play of emotions cross her face. He didn't know her well enough to understand everything he saw there. But he would like to understand. "And you?" he asked after a while. "Are you loving it?" He waited, her answer important to him.

Her smile slipped away. Not unhappy. Serious. At last she answered, "Yes."

Something special seemed to pass between them. Something Derek had never experienced before and couldn't quite define. What he could define was the sudden desire to kiss her, right there in the middle of that crowd. *That* would have given the town gossips something to talk about. But would she welcome it or run away?

Alycia's voice intruded on his wayward thoughts. "Are you guys coming?"

Derek held Brooklyn's gaze a few moments longer.

A flicker of a smile tugged at her mouth, then she turned toward her daughter. "Yes. We're coming."

They went to the booth, where they ordered their party pups — corn dogs slath-

256

ered in mustard — as well as large lemonades. They ate while strolling around the park. They didn't talk. Mostly they smiled for no apparent reason.

At one point, Brooklyn stopped, so Derek did the same. She eyed him a moment, then reached out with her thumb and wiped the corner of his mouth. "Mustard," she said, holding up that same thumb. He licked the spot she'd touched with the tip of his tongue. If he wasn't mistaken, she blushed before she turned away and resumed their walk.

Derek thought of that saying he'd often heard: "Man plans and God laughs." That seemed to fit this situation. Derek had decided to avoid women for the foreseeable future, but God had made Brooklyn his neighbor . . . and perhaps even caused this growing attraction between them.

CHAPTER 20

Eyes still closed, Brooklyn raised her arms above her head and stretched, her fingertips touching the headboard. She smiled. Not over anything in particular. More over everything in general.

The busyness of the hours she'd spent working at the diner's booth had caused her to sleep like the dead. But the charming nature of the entire day — including Derek's company throughout the evening hours — had left her feeling contented and happy. Perhaps more than it should have.

Sighing, she opened her eyes. Sunlight spilled through the slats in the blinds, telling her that morning was well under way. Derek, the farmer, would think her a lazybones for certain if he could see her still in bed.

A disturbing thought. In a pleasant kind of way.

She shoved aside the sheet and blanket

258

and got up. A quick shower was in order. Then there was a long list of things she wanted to accomplish today.

Half an hour later, damp hair caught in her usual ponytail, Brooklyn sat at the kitchen table, laptop before her, once again scrolling through websites of bed-and-breakfast establishments in Idaho, jotting down an ever-expanding list of ideas. She was thankful Internet service was available and affordable in their location. Her continued research and planning would have been more difficult if she had to go into town for access.

Across from her, Alycia looked up from her book. "What are you doing, Mom?"

"Getting more ideas." She met her daughter's gaze across the top of the laptop. "Did you eat enough breakfast?"

As if in answer, Alycia popped the last of the buttered toast into her mouth. "Mm-hmm." She swallowed. "Shall I go take care of Miss Trouble now?"

"I thought Mr. Johnson said you didn't need to go over until after lunch since he planned to be working on his computer this morning."

"Yeah, but his pickup's not there now. I looked a little bit ago. What if Miss Trouble needs out?"

"He probably had to run into town for some feed or something. He would have let us know if he planned to be away for long."

"I suppose."

Brooklyn smiled at her daughter as she closed the laptop, giving up on her research for now. "Why don't you and I do our grocery shopping? If Mr. Johnson isn't home when we get back, we can check on Miss Trouble then."

Interesting how easily she had added herself to that particular errand.

"Okay."

While Alycia put on her shoes, Brooklyn grabbed her shopping list from beneath the magnet on the fridge. A short while later, they were on their way.

The market parking lot was almost empty at this hour on a Wednesday morning, but what customers were in the store all seemed to be standing in a close circle inside the automatic doors.

Georgia Hanover, one of Ruth's friends who had helped Brooklyn with cleaning the house, looked over her shoulder at the sound of the opening doors. "Brooklyn." She motioned the new arrivals forward. "Have you heard? There's some sort of emergency at the Riverside Vineyard."

"Emergency?"

"Deputies from several counties have been called to the site. We heard that a man's been shot. Maybe killed. Could be hostages."

Someone shot and possibly killed. Hostages. Deputies.

Derek.

Brooklyn felt a surge of panic.

The store manager said, "Nobody knows much of anything at this point, but we figure it's got to be serious. Seems it's been going on for hours."

Brooklyn took her daughter's hand. "Come on, honey. We can shop later. Right now we need to go check on Mrs. Johnson. She'll be worried about Derek." Brooklyn was worried about Derek, too, but she didn't want to say that aloud. Not in front of her daughter. Not in front of the others.

Together they hurried out of the grocery store and to the car. It took mere minutes to drive from the market to Ruth Johnson's home, but it felt much longer to Brooklyn. After parking on the street, she led the way to the shop entrance. The sign in the window said *Closed.* She tried the door anyway. It opened before her.

"Ruth?" They stepped into the empty shop. "Camila?"

Silence surrounded them.

261

"Let's go around to the back door to the house," she said to Alycia.

Before they could turn, the door that connected the shop to Ruth's kitchen opened, and the older woman stepped into view. The age lines in her face seemed to have deepened overnight.

"We came as soon as we heard."

Ruth motioned them forward. "We were praying for the safety of everyone at the vineyard."

"Do you have any details? Has there been any word from Derek?"

"No, dear. None is expected. He's on duty. No spare time to contact his grandmother, I'm sure. All we can do is wait." Ruth led the way into her kitchen.

Camila Diaz sat at the table, a mug of coffee held between both hands, her expression as solemn as Ruth's. With a nod, she acknowledged Brooklyn's presence.

"Coffee or tea?" Ruth asked.

"Coffee, please. But I —"

"And you, Alycia? Would you like some juice?"

"Sure. I mean, thanks, Mrs. Johnson."

"Apple or orange?"

"Apple juice, please."

Brooklyn stopped by an empty chair, watching as Ruth poured apple juice into a

262

plastic tumbler. "Can I h— ?"

Camila touched the back of Brooklyn's hand with her fingertips. When Brooklyn looked at her, she shook her head. "It's good for her to stay busy," she said softly. "A grandchild in law enforcement can be a worrisome thing."

Ruth brought the juice glass to Alycia, now seated at the table. Then she turned toward the coffeemaker.

Brooklyn had to fight the urge to follow her there. Her own hands felt much too idle.

The incident at the Riverside Vineyard that had called Derek to work turned out to be a couple of employees losing their tempers. Heated words had been exchanged, and then one of the men involved had waved a gun around. An unloaded gun, as they later learned. But at the time, the action alarmed the other employees, several of whom called 911 on their cell phones.

Several hours later — after doing his part to calm folks down and taking almost a dozen witness statements — Derek climbed into his truck. He let out a breath and rubbed his eyes with his fingers.

"Sorry about calling you in on your day off."

He looked out the open pickup window at

263

Hank. "No problem."

Although it was a problem. After taking yesterday off, Derek had planned to spend the morning catching up on important paperwork, including paying bills. Now he would be up late into the night completing those tasks. But first there were animals to feed and crops to water.

Hank patted the truck door. "At least it turned out all right."

"Yeah."

With a nod, Hank walked back toward the main building.

As Derek reached to turn the key in the ignition, his phone vibrated. Gran's photo appeared on the screen. He answered it. "Hey, Gran."

"Oh, Derek. Thank God. Are you all right? I waited as long as I could bear before trying to call you." His grandmother wasn't making any sense, and that wasn't like her.

"I'm fine, Gran. Why? What's up?"

"Are you still at Riverside? Is the standoff over? Did anybody die?"

"Standoff?" He took a breath. "Gran, what are you talking about?"

There was a lengthy silence. Then in a slightly calmer tone of voice, his grandmother told him what she had heard. Derek wasn't surprised by what rumors had done

264

to the truth, but it did catch him off guard how quickly it had happened.

"I'm sorry you were worried, Gran." He gave her an abbreviated version of that morning's incident. "Do you want me to come over? I need to go home to feed the animals first, but I could —"

"You don't have to worry about them, dear. Brooklyn is taking care of them now."

"Brooklyn?"

"And Alycia. They came to see if I was all right. Wasn't that sweet of them? Anyway, we were told that you were called out in the night, so when we learned that, they went home to see to Miss Trouble and the horses and such."

He hadn't been called out in the night, of course, but apparently the rumor mill had gotten that wrong too. And how would Brooklyn know what to feed or how much? A farm girl she wasn't. "I'd better get home, Gran. But would you let your friends know that everything is fine and nobody was shot? Shut down the rumor mill if you can."

"Of course."

"I'll come over later."

"No need, dear. I'm perfectly all right now that I know you are."

He ended the call, started the pickup, and drove toward home. The first thing he saw when he got there was Alycia and Miss Trouble. By the time he'd parked the truck, he could see Brooklyn, too, scattering feed to the chickens. The sound of his arrival had drawn her gaze in his direction.

"Mom! It's Mr. Johnson."

"I see." Brooklyn tossed the last of the feed to the poultry. Moments later, she was walking toward him. There was hay in her dark hair and clinging to her summer top.

"It's over?" she asked when she drew close.

"It wasn't anything like it sounded. There wasn't any danger."

"There wasn't?"

"By the time I got there, it was mostly paperwork." He relayed the same short version he'd told his grandmother.

Brooklyn studied him with her eyes, as if to see if he told the truth.

"I'd like to catch the person who got the rumors started," he said. "From what Gran told me, the whole town was thinking the worst."

Brooklyn nodded.

He reached out and plucked a piece of hay from her hair, showing it to her as he drew back his hand. "Thanks for taking care of the animals for me."

"We didn't know how long you would be,"

266

she said, just above a whisper.

"They wouldn't have starved, but I'm grateful anyway."

"I called the feed store, and they told me what to do."

He smiled. Seems he hadn't needed to wonder how she would know what to feed and how much. She was smart enough to ask for advice when she needed it. She might not be a farm girl now, but maybe she had the makings of one. That thought made him want to smile all the more.

Alycia arrived with the dog in her arms. "Miss Trouble made a mess in the house, but I cleaned it up."

It was difficult, but he managed to look away from Brooklyn. "I appreciate it, kiddo. I guess it's time for me to put in a pet door so Trouble can fend for herself when I'm busy."

The girl grinned up at him. "You're gonna keep her?"

"Yeah. I guess I am."

"That's great, Mr. Johnson. That's really great."

It seemed great to Derek, too, but the way he felt had little to do with his decision to keep the pint-sized dog.

CHAPTER 21

By the end of her shift at the diner on Thursday, Brooklyn had heard at least a half dozen different versions of what had happened at the vineyard. Like a good fishing tale, the details grew bigger and more harrowing with every telling. It made her thankful she'd heard the real story from Derek, and she said what she could to stop the more outrageous rumors.

Since the grocery shopping had been interrupted yesterday, Brooklyn went from the diner straight to the store. She didn't dawdle in the narrow aisles. All was going well until she rounded the end into the last aisle between frozen foods and produce. That's where she smacked into another shopper's cart.

"Oh, I'm sorry." She looked up from the slip of paper in her hand. "I —" The words died in her throat.

Her dad scowled at her as he jerked his

shopping cart backward, as if she'd run into him on purpose.

Brooklyn took a quick breath. "Hey, Dad." She hadn't seen him since he'd stomped out of the diner her first week on the job. She wasn't certain how she felt about seeing him now.

He grunted.

She decided to be thankful he hadn't sworn at her, the way he had the last time.

Her dad's eyes narrowed. "I heard you plan to turn the Hallston house into a bed-and-breakfast."

"Yes." Perhaps it was silly, but it encouraged her that he'd bothered to learn something about her future plans. Maybe he —

"Something like that takes business sense. You'll be bankrupt in a year."

The encouragement drained away. "I'm smarter than you think, Dad."

"You never even finished high school."

"Not because I couldn't have. And I got my GED a number of years ago."

"Worthless piece of paper." He grunted again.

Brooklyn had had enough, and she didn't need Derek to defend her this time. "You know what, Dad? I'm really sorry you dislike me so much. I'm sorry I'm such a disappointment to you. That I always was a

269

disappointment in your eyes. But I'm not going to let you bully me anymore. Not in private and not in public. Alycia and I are here to stay, so you're going to have to figure out what to do when we accidentally see each other." She leveled her shoulders. "Because this is our home now, and you can like it or lump it." She grabbed the cart and wheeled it around him.

She half expected to cry, if not before she finished checking out, then at least by the time she had the groceries in the trunk and was seated behind the wheel of the car. Only she didn't cry. Her eyes didn't even grow misty. The wound of his rejection was still there. It still hurt. Maybe it always would. But it wasn't going to hold her back ever again.

As she had the first day she went to see her dad, she whispered, "I can do all things through Him who strengthens me."

Only this time she *knew* it was true.

Next year, Derek thought as he leaned on the fence and gazed over his land, the July evening warm on his back, he would try planting a different variety of vegetables. If he made a few changes in the layout of the northeast quadrant of his property, he could add at least another couple of crops to his

270

harvest. And he wouldn't wait to plant those additional fruit trees either. He had the space for them. Also it was time he built a modest-sized greenhouse and added some beehives to his small farm. Bees were always good to help with garden pollination, not to mention the honey he could sell as a by-product.

There was more he could do to improve his three acres and increase his profits. He had the savings he'd intended to use for a down payment on the Hallston property. He would invest it in new equipment and modifications. Should Brooklyn ever decide to sell some of her acreage to him, he could make the down payment from the additional income he would derive from the changes he made now.

Realizing he could still make plans, still move forward with his dream, even if not by the path he'd originally intended, eased a tightness in his chest he hadn't really wanted to address.

"You're lost in thought."

The soft sound of Brooklyn's voice drew him around. It was as if she'd come in answer to his thoughts.

"Yeah." He ran a hand through his hair. "I guess I was."

She held something out in her palm. "I

271

believe this belongs to Miss Trouble." It was the name tag from the dog's collar. "Alycia found it in our backyard."

"So much for my powers of observation. I hadn't noticed it was missing." He took the tag and slipped it into the pocket of his jeans.

She moved to stand beside him at the fence. "Have you heard the stories that are circulating in town?"

"More outlandish than yesterday?"

She answered with a soft laugh.

He groaned. "Spare me the details. Glad I've been too busy to hear any of it. We were harvesting today."

"We?"

"I hire help whenever I harvest. Tough to always be a one-man operation, even on a place as small as this one."

As he'd done moments before, she stared across the fields. "It's a lovely evening."

"My favorite time of day on the farm, when the heat eases a bit and the light gets . . . hazy." He rested his forearms on the top rail. "I like the sounds of evening too. Like the earth is humming."

She was silent for a while. Listening, he supposed. Then she said, "Derek?"

"Hmm."

272

"I saw my dad tonight. After I got off work."

He looked at her. "Where? What happened?"

"We were at the market, shopping, and ended up in the same aisle. He wasn't awful to me. Not like he was in the diner."

Derek wasn't sure he believed her. He knew what Reggie Myers could be like.

"I didn't give him a chance to be unkind."

He felt a strange sense of pride when she said that.

Now she looked at him. "The thing is, I've felt so alone and uncared for most of my life. For a while I thought Chad would take away that loneliness, would help me feel loved, but we were both kids and he was running away too. Of course, I didn't understand that when I was seventeen. Then I had Alycia, and I expected my baby, my sweet little girl, to plug that empty hole in my heart. She did, too, in many ways. Only that's asking a lot of a child. Isn't it?"

A lump had formed in his throat. Unexpected emotions flooded his chest.

"You're right." She took a slightly shaky breath, then smiled at him. "The earth does hum."

By instinct rather than forethought, he reached for her, drawing her close. His eyes

273

asked a question he was unable to speak aloud. Her eyes gave him permission. He leaned down and kissed her on the mouth. Long and deep, slow and sweet.

Derek was no monk. He'd kissed his share of girls and women in his lifetime. But this kiss was different. It was something . . . more. And he didn't want it to end. The last of his reasons to avoid romantic involvement were carried away on the soft evening breeze. Even if they still made sense — and he wasn't sure they did — he didn't care any longer.

At last he broke the kiss, lifting his head so he could look into her eyes. He saw himself reflected for an instant before she stepped out of his embrace, lifting one hand to touch her lips.

After a moment, she said, "I haven't been kissed in a long, long time."

The male population in Nevada had to be blind or crazy. Maybe both.

"I haven't wanted to be kissed."

Well, that made more sense to him.

"This could complicate things, Derek. Between us."

He wanted to draw her close again. He made himself stand still. "Let's not let it."

"Is it that easy?"

"I don't know."

274

She was silent for what seemed a very long time. "Derek, what if I never agree to sell you any of my land?"

It was his turn to be silent. First he was surprised, then he felt irritated. At last he answered. "That isn't why I kissed you."

"No. I didn't think so. But what if I don't?"

"What if . . ." The two words seemed to reverberate in his chest. "What if . . ."

Her smile, when it came, was tinged with sadness. "Think about it. Before we take it any further."

This time she kissed him, but it was so brief he barely felt her lips brush against his. As she walked away in the gloaming, he wondered if it was the kisses they'd shared or her question that he would lie awake thinking about for most of the night.

CHAPTER 22

Ruth straightened on the stool she used when gardening and peered at the wisps of clouds that covered the sky. It was late in the afternoon. Her Sunday dinner guests had long since gone home. The dishes were washed, the house back in order. And since the predicted high temperature for today was only seventy-one degrees — unusually cool for this time of year — it had seemed a good idea to get some weeding out of the way.

As she worked, she prayed for each member of her family — for her sons and daughter and for their spouses, and then for her grandchildren. Eventually, she moved on to prayers for her grandchildren's future spouses. She had no idea who those life partners would be, but God knew.

A smile played across her mouth. Perhaps she did know who one of them would be. If she wasn't mistaken, Derek had a growing

276

interest in Brooklyn Myers. Not that he had said as much to his grandmother, but she was convinced it was true all the same. Whenever she'd seen the two of them together — on the Fourth of July, this very morning at church, out at Derek's farm a couple of times — they simply looked as if they belonged that way, as if they were meant to be a couple.

A butterfly flew up from the flower bed, almost colliding with her, making her smile and reminding her of something. Not long ago, she'd told Sandra Dooley that the butterflies-in-the-stomach kind of love wasn't enough to make a marriage success-ful.

Had Sandra come to some sort of deci-sion about her two suitors? If so, she hadn't let on to Ruth anytime they'd seen each other.

She shook her head, her smile broaden-ing. Her advice to Sandra had been sound, but the truth was Ruth had loved that crazy, fluttery sensation. Oh my. The butterflies Walter used to set off inside of her with his slow smile or that particular twinkle in his eyes . . . From almost the first day they met right up until the end of his life, her husband had been able to curl her toes with such ease.

277

She would wish the same sort of fluttery, whirling feelings for Derek and for Brooklyn. Even if she was wrong and they didn't feel that way around each other. But for some reason, she was convinced she wasn't wrong, and she dearly hoped the butterflies would go crazy inside them.

With a sweet sigh, she bent over and began weeding once again.

Beneath the ancient shade tree in her backyard, Brooklyn straightened away from the old dresser she'd been sanding for the past half hour. The day was pleasant, the sky overcast, although not threatening rain. Perfect for this type of labor. And tomorrow the dresser would be ready to stain or paint. She hadn't decided which she wanted to do with it. But she couldn't do either until she did the last of the sanding. She leaned forward and got back to work.

"Hey, Mom." Alycia pushed with her feet, setting the rope swing on a different tree in motion.

"Hmm?"

"This morning my friends in Sunday school told me there's gonna be a camping trip next month. Before school starts. I'd kinda like to go."

"Camping?" Brooklyn had only slept

outside in a tent once in her life. Alycia had never been camping. "You mean with tents and sleeping bags and all that?"

"Yeah."

"I suppose we could do it. We'd have to borrow all the gear, but I guess we could do it."

"Well, that's just it, Mom. I . . . it's a trip for dads and daughters."

Brooklyn's hand stilled against the wood of the dresser, and she looked at Alycia. "Dads?" Her stomach sank.

"Well, if there isn't a dad, then the girl can bring somebody else. Like a grandpa or an uncle or a friend or something." Alycia brought the swing to an abrupt halt. "I was thinking . . ." She looked up at the sky. "I was thinking, maybe Mr. Johnson could go with me." Her voice was soft, wishful, and full of hope.

"Mr. Johnson?" She felt stupid, repeating her daughter's words, like an echo in a canyon, but that's all she seemed able to do.

"Well, you know, he likes me. I think he likes me." She met Brooklyn's gaze again. "And I'm thinkin' he probably knows about camping. I've never been before, but I'll bet he has."

Brooklyn hadn't told Alycia about Chad's

279

request. Had Derek? No. She was certain he hadn't. This idea was coming straight from her daughter. Suddenly she remembered what Alycia had said at the ball game, about her friend Wendy being lucky to have a dad. It made her heart ache again, remembering. Was this Alycia's way of trying to fill that empty space? Did Brooklyn mind if that's what it was?

"Can I ask him if he'll do it, Mom?"

She blinked, then focused her attention on her daughter again. "I don't know. I'll have to think about it."

Alycia sat back down on the swing and gave herself another push with her feet. Another push and another. Higher and higher. Faster and faster. Apparently satisfied now that her mom had promised to think about her request.

Brooklyn got up from the ground and went inside, where she filled a drinking glass with cold water from the refrigerator door. Then she stepped to the window to watch Alycia on the swing. The nerves in her stomach kept time with her daughter, swinging with wild abandon, up and back, up and back.

Derek and Alycia on a camping trip together. Was that the kind of thing Chad had wanted from his old friend? Was it what she wanted? And what about that kiss? Days later, and her lips still seemed to tremble whenever she thought about it. And she thought about it all the time, even though she'd scarcely seen Derek since that night.

She sighed as she set the glass in the sink. "Is this part of Your plan for me, God? Your plan for Alycia? How am I supposed to know?"

As if in answer, she heard a soft whisper in her heart: *Let go.*

She looked down at her hands, saw that they were clenched into fists that pressed her knuckles against the counter.

Let go. Trust.

Her breathing slowed. "I'll try, God. I *want* You to be in control, but it's hard not to hold on tight to those things that matter. To Alycia."

Let go. Trust. Receive.

She closed her eyes for a few moments, then opened them again. "I don't know what I'm doing, but here goes." Then she unfurled her hands, turning them palms up.

Hands empty and open. And suddenly she understood that open hands were the only way she could receive anything new.

Derek passed a Diet Coke, moisture dripping down the sides of the bottle, to Hank,

281

then sat in a nearby chair on the porch. The two friends sipped their drinks in silence for a time.

Hank finally spoke. "Your dog likes her new little yard."

"Yeah." Derek's gaze followed Hank's to the grassy area he'd fenced near the house. "She took to her pet door with no training. Maybe she had one before."

"You never found out who hurt her?"

"No. Ethan did everything he could. He doesn't think the owner was local. Neither do I. Besides, I don't like to think anybody I know would be that cruel."

Hank nodded, took a breath, and released it slowly. "Speaking of knowing somebody who would hurt something — or someone — more helpless, things are getting worse for Fran."

Derek's stomach tightened as he waited for his friend to continue.

"She went back to Mac. You heard she went away for a week? I was hoping it was for good this time, but she's back. She won't listen to a thing I say. She won't listen to anybody."

"You can't make that decision for her, Hank. She's a grown woman."

"I know." He rubbed his thumb up and down on the side of the bottle. "Just makes me so angry, the way Mac manipulates her. Makes me feel helpless too."

"She's never filed a complaint against him, has she?"

"Never. She thinks everything he does to her is her own fault. It's never his. Always hers." He sighed. "You know how it is."

Sadly, like most cops, Derek did know how it was. He'd seen the cycle of abuse enough times in his years as a sheriff's deputy. "Yeah. I know how it is. And all you can do for now is tell Fran you're there for her, if or when she's willing to let you help. The way you've been there for her in the past."

Hank's voice turned hard. "Sometimes I'd like to forget I'm sworn to keep the peace and just get Mac in a room by myself for about fifteen minutes."

Derek didn't reply. Some men he would worry about. Hank wasn't one of them. His friend needed to blow off steam, that was all. Hank would never take matters of the law into his own hands. No matter how provoked or justified.

"What about you?" Hank took another long drink of soda. "How's the growing season going for you?"

Derek was happy to let his friend steer the conversation in another direction. "Been

283

good. It should be a profitable year, barring anything unexpected."

"Which happens often in farming."

"True enough."

"I've told you this before, but I'm mighty impressed with what you've managed to do here. I mean, this place was nothing much but a little house, pasture, and a few trees when you bought the property. Now look at it. The new outbuildings. The new fences. All those nice rows of fruit and vegetables. Lotta love and labor evident wherever you look."

Hank was right. A lot of love and labor had gone into this place. Even with just three acres, Derek had achieved everything he'd set out to do and more besides. And he'd learned a lot along the way.

His gaze shifted to the yellow house next door. *"Derek, what if I never agree to sell you any of my land?"* He'd heard Brooklyn's question repeat in his head at least a hundred times since that night. And if he'd thought about her question a hundred times, he'd thought of Brooklyn a thousand.

I've missed her.

Sure, he'd seen her now and then, but mostly in passing. Hardly with enough time to say hello or good-bye. A wave of the hand. A smile. There had never seemed to

284

be an opportunity or an excuse for more than that. But did he need an excuse?

"Derek, what if I never agree to sell you any of my land?"

He leaned forward in his chair, realization shivering through him, his friend forgotten.

The question he'd thought about and mulled over and let repeat in his head wasn't the question that mattered to him at all. It wasn't *What if she doesn't sell any of her land to me?* It wasn't *How can I make my farm grow and succeed without those extra acres?* The real question was *When can I see her again?* When could he spend more time in her company? When could he get to know her better than he knew her right now? When could he become an important part of her life, the way she had somehow become an important part of his?

The answer to her question was actually quite simple. It wouldn't make one bit of difference if she wouldn't sell her land to him. Because he wanted her far more than he wanted any piece of property.

Now all he had to do was make her believe it.

285

CHAPTER 23

Farmwork and deputy duties kept Derek busy from dawn to dusk for more than a week, and he spent a lot of those days trying to figure out the best way to tell Brooklyn how he felt about her. How to tell her that he was interested in something more than friendship and certainly something more than her land. The passing of time both relieved and frustrated him. But his gut told him he had to go slow, and giving her some space might be for the best. Even now. Even after that kiss — which seemed to have happened all too long ago.

Brooklyn had two really good reasons not to trust men — her dad and Chad. And like it or not, Derek had given her at least one more reason to wonder if she should trust any of his gender. He wished now he'd never told her that he wanted to buy her land. Since he couldn't take it back, he would have to overcome it. Being a good

286

neighbor wouldn't be enough. He needed to win her heart, not just her head. All he had to do now was figure a way to do that.

And today, he'd decided, was the day to try.

Heat clung to the earth as he strode across the field toward Brooklyn's house. Once there, he knocked on her back door and waited. Strange, how nervous he felt. It wasn't as if they hadn't seen each other or spoken since the night of that kiss. But now that he'd made up his mind to try to move things along, there was more at stake.

When she answered his knock, a fleeting smile curved her mouth. A good sign, he supposed.

"Evening, Brooklyn."

"Hi, Derek."

"Got a minute?"

"Sure." She pulled the door open wide. Another good sign.

Good smells wafted out from the kitchen. "I'm not interrupting your dinner, am I?"

"No. We ate awhile ago. I just finished washing the dishes. Come on in."

"Thanks." He moved past her, stopping near the kitchen table.

She closed the door and faced him. "Would you like to sit?"

"No. Thanks. I . . . I don't want to keep you."

Her head tipped slightly, as if asking a question.

He rushed on. "You remember that they have concerts over at Dubois Vineyards during the summer?"

"Sure. I've never been to one, but I've heard people talk about them."

"In for a penny, in for a pound," his grandmother often said.

Derek continued, "Well, there's one coming up next Friday, and I thought maybe you'd like to go with me. If you're not working that night."

"I'm not," she answered. "I work day shifts on Fridays."

It wasn't a yes, but it wasn't a refusal either. He almost smiled. "So you'll go?"

Brooklyn opened her mouth, about to answer, when Alycia rushed into the kitchen. "Mr. Johnson! You're here. Mom, did you ask him? What'd he say?"

He cocked an eyebrow. "Ask me what?"

"Mommmm." The girl dragged out the word in a pleading tone. "It's been forever."

Brooklyn responded with a soft, "Alycia."

Even he heard the warning in her tone. A flicker of rebellion — something Derek didn't remember seeing before — appeared

288

in Alycia's eyes, and she pressed her lips together in a hard line.

"Honey," Brooklyn continued in that soft but firm voice, "you need to let me talk with Mr. Johnson alone. Go back to whatever you were doing."

"But —"

"Now, Alycia."

The girl released a dramatic sigh. After a short hesitation, she turned and left the kitchen.

"She's not happy with me at the moment," Brooklyn said.

"I could see that."

She motioned a second time to the chairs by the table. "Please."

This time he didn't refuse.

Brooklyn sat opposite him, her gaze flicking toward the doorway. "I'm not sure what to tell you first."

"Let's start with your answer about the date."

Her eyes returned to him. "The date." It was a question, yet not a question.

"*Our* date," he emphasized, just to be sure she understood. "Yours and mine. To the concert."

"Derek, do you really think —"

"I really think. Whatever you were going to ask, I really think."

She laughed softly, shaking her head. "So . . . ?"

She sighed. Not as dramatic as her daughter's had been. More like she was giving in. "All right. I'll go to the concert with you."

"Great." It felt like a huge victory. As if they had both cleared a hurdle. "Dress for the heat, because it's outdoors, and Friday's supposed to be close to a hundred degrees. I'll pack the food. You don't have to think about bringing anything except a sweater for when it cools off after the sun sets." He took a breath and added, "I'll come for you at six."

"Okay."

"Now . . . what did Alycia want you to ask me?"

A tiny frown furrowed Brooklyn's brow. "Just so you know, I didn't accept your invitation because of what she wants."

"Good to know." He couldn't help but smile. "Continue."

"You may have heard. The church is having a father-daughter campout in a few weeks." She hesitated, then rushed to finish. "And Alycia wants you to take her."

He leaned back in his chair, both surprised and pleased.

"You don't have to if you don't want to. I know it's a lot to ask. I mean, I know you

290

are always crazy busy with your farming and with your duties as a deputy. And —"

"I'd love to do it, Brooklyn."

A flicker of a smile appeared again. "You would?"

"I would." The thing was, he didn't want to do it because of Chad's request, and he sure didn't want to do it as *quid pro quo* for the coming date with Brooklyn. No, camping with Alycia sounded like fun. It sounded like something he'd missed out on in the past and could look forward to in the future. Maybe he shouldn't read that much into it, but he did.

"She's never been camping before," Brooklyn added.

He shrugged. "Not a big deal. I've been camping plenty of times."

"But not with Alycia."

He had the insane urge to jump up, round the table, and hold her in his arms. To make her feel safe and secure. Instead, he said, "You're right. Not with Alycia. But I promise I won't screw it up. You can trust me, Brooklyn."

Trust him. Let go and trust him.

Was it possible to do that? To trust someone the way Derek wanted to be trusted? Brooklyn didn't know if she had it in her to

291

trust that way. She could trust God. But a man? And with her daughter? What if something went wrong on the camping trip? What if . . .

He leaned toward her, forearms now on the table, and lowered his voice. "Is it okay to tell Alycia? I'll bet she's out there chewing her fingernails."

Let go.

Trust.

Discover something new.

"Okay," she answered. "She's already waited a long time for me to ask you. Let's tell her."

He stood, then waited for her to do the same. But when she started to walk by him, he stopped her with a light touch on her shoulder. "Brooklyn."

She met his gaze. There seemed to be an ocean of kindness in his eyes.

"I'm not doing this because Chad asked me to. And since you brought it up, I'm not doing it because you said you'd go out with me. I'm doing it because I want to."

Those words, combined with the look in his eyes, caused a lump to form in her throat. The swiftness of her reaction alarmed her, but she was determined he wouldn't know that. So she nodded and hurried onward.

292

When Brooklyn entered the living room, Alycia was lying on her tummy on the floor, the Kindle Fire held between both hands. But something told Brooklyn that her daughter had been straining to hear the conversation taking place in the kitchen, not reading.

"Sweetheart?"

Alycia feigned — and failed — a look of surprise.

"Mr. Johnson has something to tell you."

Her daughter dropped the device and scrambled to her knees. Her gaze shot beyond Brooklyn's left shoulder.

From perhaps a step or two behind her, Derek said, "I hear you'd like to go camping with the church group."

"Yeah." Her face lit up.

"I told your mom I'd be glad to take you."

Alycia was on her feet in a heartbeat. "Really? You'll really do it?"

"Really." He chuckled.

Brooklyn felt his laughter in her chest. In her heart. She wanted to turn and smile at him, to thank him, but she remained afraid of revealing too much. These were uncharted waters and growing more so. Alycia dashed forward, and Brooklyn couldn't help but turn her head to see what happened next.

Her daughter hugged Derek around the waist. "Thanks, Mr. Johnson. I'll do everything you tell me. I won't break any rules. I promise. I won't be any trouble at all."

He chuckled again. "I believe you, kiddo." He ruffled her hair, an action he'd done before. This time Alycia didn't pull back.

"This is the best day ever!" Alycia said, looking up at him.

"We've got a few weeks to get ready," Derek said, eyes serious. "When I've got time, I'll teach you some of the things you'll need to know."

"Great." She whirled to face Brooklyn. "Mom, can I call Wendy and tell her I get to go?" She barely waited for Brooklyn's nod before she rushed off to make the call.

"You couldn't have made her any happier if you'd tried," Brooklyn said.

"It's a start."

She turned to look at him, unsure if she was doing the right thing and yet unable to change the direction they seemed to be headed.

Don't you dare break her heart, Derek Johnson. Or mine.

294

CHAPTER 24

"But you like him," Esther said, her tone both gentle and prodding.

Brooklyn lay on the living-room sofa, staring at the ceiling, as she talked on the phone. "Yes, I like him."

"And you believe he is a nice, decent man?"

"Yes. I'm sure he is."

Esther was silent a few moments. "Then it sounds to me as if you did the right thing. For both you and Alycia."

Did I? She'd been asking herself the same question for a solid week. If only she could be sure. Why didn't God give her an unmistakable answer, like a neon billboard flashing a message?

"You already know what else I want to say, don't you?"

"Yes," Brooklyn answered. "Trust God and stop borrowing trouble."

Her friend laughed, but it ended in a

295

coughing spell.

"Esther?" Brooklyn sat up. "Are you all right?"

When Esther was in control again, she answered, "Yes. I'm fine."

Her friend wasn't fine, of course. Far from it. But she refused to discuss the details of her illness as it progressed. A few weeks ago, she'd told Brooklyn that she only wanted to talk about life and the living, not dying and death. So Brooklyn did her best to honor Esther's wishes. But it wasn't easy. Especially since she believed time was growing short.

Tears welled in her eyes as she wondered how many more telephone conversations they would have. One? Five? Ten? No matter how many, they would be too few.

"How are your plans for the bed-and-breakfast going?" Esther asked, deftly changing the subject.

Brooklyn drew a quick breath and, keeping her voice as light as possible, answered, "I think they're going well. I keep revising my budget and the projected time frame, but I'm getting a good grasp of it. I research something new on the Internet almost every night. Alycia and I have painted two more bedrooms and one of the upstairs baths." She scrambled in her head to think what

296

else she could tell Esther that she hadn't said before. Then she decided it didn't matter if she repeated herself. "Our finances are tight, of course. I knew they would be. But I got a job so quickly, they aren't as bad as I expected them to be. I seem to always have just enough money to pay for the next can of paint or whatever."

"God provides," Esther said.

"Yes. He does."

"You mentioned you were going to talk to other businesses about package deals for your guests. Have you done that yet?"

"No. It's far too early. I need to have a firm opening date in mind first."

"I'm so proud of you, Brooklyn." Esther coughed again. "I'm sorry. I think I'd better hang up now. Call me Saturday. After your date. I'll want to hear all about it."

Brooklyn's grip on the cell phone tightened. "Yes. I'll call you." She paused a second. "I love you."

"I love you too. Give Alycia a hug from me."

"I will."

"Email me some photos. I'm dying to see where you're living. Take some of the vineyard when you're at the concert."

"I will. I'll send some before I call you so we can talk about them."

Brooklyn remained sitting on the sofa a short while after the call ended, still thinking about the friend she hadn't seen in almost four months. Esther had looked so very frail before leaving Reno to live with her cousins. How much more had she changed by now?

"Take care of her, Lord. I know she isn't afraid to die, but please ease the pain of the process."

Drawing a breath, she rose. The house was unusually quiet without Alycia at home. Her daughter was at Wendy Royal's house for the afternoon while Brooklyn tried to plow through the boxes that had been stored in the garage for close to a decade. She'd been halfway through the appointed task when Esther called.

Sorting through the things John and Marie Hallston had chosen to save was proving to be more time consuming than expected. With almost every item, Brooklyn had to wonder if it was something she should save for Alycia because it had belonged to the grandparents she would never know.

She wondered now if her dad had saved anything that once belonged to his own parents. If so, she'd never seen a sign of it. No surprise there. Her dad wasn't sentimental in the slightest. He'd never displayed

298

anything of Brooklyn's on their refrigerator. Her drawings and report cards and other achievements had gone straight into the trash with hardly an acknowledgment.

A sigh escaped her. Not sad. Simply resigned. And perhaps for the first time, she felt a stab of pity for the man who seemed encased in emotional ice. How very sad it had to be to be him. And how grateful she was not to have become like him.

"Are you sure you can spare the time to go with me?" Gran asked, looking over the saddle on Sunny's back.

"I'm sure." Derek tightened Blue Boy's cinch. In truth he couldn't spare the time, but he didn't like the idea of Gran riding alone. She was a decent horsewoman, for someone who hadn't learned to ride until she was in her late fifties. All the same . . .

"Well, I'm glad you can come. You look tired, dear. You could use an hour or so to relax."

He couldn't argue with that. Even he had to admit he'd been burning the candle at both ends for several weeks now.

They finished saddling and bridling the horses, then mounted up and rode away from the barnyard, headed north toward the tree-lined Thunder Creek. The path they followed — ground packed hard by count-less other horses over the years — was wide enough to ride side by side, making it easy to carry on a conversation.

"Did I tell you," Gran asked about fifteen minutes into their ride, "that Brooklyn is coming to the women's potluck tomorrow evening?"

Derek hid a smile. If this was really about the potluck, he would eat his hat.

"She's going to ask for Wednesday nights off come fall so she can attend our Bible study. It's wonderful, the way she's become such a part of the community."

"Yeah," he answered, his eyes watching a flock of birds swoop from tree to tree. "It's great."

"She was worried when she first came back. Afraid she wouldn't ever fit in."

And Derek hadn't done much at first to make her feel more confident. He would do it differently if he could.

There was a lengthy pause before Gran continued, "And I suppose you know I've been asked to stay with Alycia on Friday evening when you take Brooklyn to the vineyard for the concert."

"No." He met her gaze. "That I didn't know. I figured it would be Mrs. Nims."

Her eyes narrowed. "Didn't you think I

would want to know you were dating again? Not that I'm nosy, of course."

"Of course not." He grinned, relieved to know she wasn't really upset with him for his silence. "But I've hardly seen you lately. When would I have had the chance to tell you?"

"Ever heard of a telephone?"

Other than that he'd asked Brooklyn out, there wasn't any news. One date was just one date. Right? Not exactly earth-shattering information that had to be shared instantly.

"However," Gran added before he could voice his thoughts aloud, "I'm not sure I believe your silence is because you haven't seen me or didn't think to call me."

He shrugged.

"All right. I know when someone wants me to mind my own business."

"It isn't that, Gran. It's just . . . I'm not sure what to say. I know how I feel about Brooklyn. At least I'm pretty sure I know. But I don't know her feelings about me. Yeah, she agreed to go out with me, but she keeps a lot of her feelings pretty close to her vest. She's not always the easiest person to read."

"Perhaps not yet. Give her time."

"I'm trying." He looked over at his grandmother. "Seems that's my lesson lately. Be patient. Wait."

"It's a lesson we all have to learn at one time or another, Derek."

He nodded, and then they fell into a comfortable silence, content to listen to the steady beat of hooves against earth, the rustle ofleaves, and the soft sounds of water tumbling over a rocky creek bottom.

CHAPTER 25

Brooklyn worked the early shift on Friday. Off at three, she had more than enough time to shower away the restaurant smells and select the right outfit for the evening. The latter was more difficult than expected. A faded pair of skinny jeans was an easy choice, but picking the right summer top proved frustrating. Too loose, too tight, perhaps too low cut, definitely the wrong color, decidedly outdated. She wasn't a clothes horse. Her income had never allowed for extravagance in that regard, and her choices weren't unlimited. So it surprised her how hard it was to make up her mind.

"Wear this one, Mom." Alycia picked up a short-sleeved, peachy-pink blouse from the bed.

Brooklyn had tried it on twice already.

"It's really pretty on you."

"Is it?" She took the blouse from her

303

daughter and held it against her chest as she looked in the mirror. It was her favorite color and looked good with her skin tone. It was also casual, as if to announce that this date was nothing out of the ordinary. "Okay. That's what I'll wear." She slipped it over her head. "How about helping me decide on my earrings?"

Alycia slid off the bed and went to the small jewelry case on the dresser. Not a lot of choices there either. "Mmm. I think the little pearl ones."

The chosen earrings were the one thing Brooklyn owned that had once belonged to her mother. Whatever else her mother had departed without, her dad had thrown away or given to some charity. But Brooklyn, at the tender age of six, had managed to save the pierced earrings. She'd kept them hidden for the next eleven years, then taken them with her when she and Chad eloped to Reno.

Strange, really. She didn't have special feelings for the earrings. She barely remembered her mother, and the few memories she had weren't good ones. In fact, she wasn't sure they were even true. They may have been planted there by her dad's comments through the years.

Alycia knew none of that. She simply liked

the earrings. So did Brooklyn.

She put them on.

The doorbell rang.

"That will be Mrs. Johnson," she said. "Can you get the door for me?"

"Sure." Alycia raced away.

After a final glance in the mirror, Brooklyn grabbed her sweater from the foot of the bed and left the room. Alycia's and Ruth's voices drifted up the stairs to meet her. She followed the sound into the kitchen.

"Look, Mom. Mrs. Johnson brought ham for dinner. Did you know ham is one of my favorites, Mrs. Johnson?"

The older woman smiled. "Somebody may have mentioned that."

Brooklyn stopped at the counter and watched as Ruth unloaded the food containers from a canvas bag. "This was so nice of you. You didn't have to make dinner for her, you know."

The older woman gave her a patient smile. "Of course I know. I *wanted* to. Just like I wanted to come stay with Alycia. I think it's wonderful that you and Derek are giving yourselves an evening off. You've both been working long days, and this evening will be much more relaxing than the hubbub of the Fourth, as much as we all love that."

305

"Doesn't Mom look pretty?" Alycia asked. "I picked that top for her."

Ruth stopped what she was doing and gave Brooklyn a long look. "You made a wonderful choice. Your mom looks very pretty."

Brooklyn shook her head, as if to cast off the compliment, though it was nice to hear.

"I've forgotten. What time will Derek come for you?" Ruth returned to unloading the food. Obviously far more than ham.

"Six o'clock."

Ruth checked her wristwatch. "Looks like I didn't get here any too soon." Her gaze shifted to Alycia. "Young lady, what say we wait to eat until your mom and Derek are on their way?"

"Sure. I can wait."

"Me too."

The doorbell rang again. Brooklyn's heart beat a little faster in response.

"He's here!" Alycia hurried out of the kitchen.

Ruth smiled. "He's always been a punctual lad." She motioned for Brooklyn to lead the way to the living room.

Brooklyn hadn't dated in the years since Alycia's birth. She had been, after all, still married, even if Chad wasn't with her. Plenty of men wouldn't have cared about

306

that particular complication, but she had. At first her cheap wedding ring had provided her with a level of protection. Later, after she'd finally removed it, she hadn't bothered to explain. She'd simply refused when asked out. It had been easy to do. She hadn't wanted to get involved with anyone.

Until now.

She almost turned back for a drink of water. Her mouth was suddenly dry. But Ruth was right behind her. There was nothing to do but move forward. A metaphor for her life, perhaps.

Derek looked up from Alycia when Brooklyn stepped into the living room. His eyes lit with appreciation. "You ready?"

"I'm ready." She held up her sweater. "I even remembered this for later."

"You'll need it. That much closer to the river makes a difference when night falls."

Derek took a couple of steps toward his grandmother and kissed her forehead. "Thanks for helping out tonight, Gran."

"Gracious." Ruth waved a hand. "Couldn't be happier to do it. Alycia and I are going to have a good time."

Derek swiveled toward Brooklyn again. "Then shall we?" He offered the crook of his arm.

Her heart hammering as if she were six-

307

teen and leaving for the prom, she took his arm and allowed him to escort her out of the house.

There were more than a dozen vineyards and wineries in this corner of southwest Idaho. The majority of them were close to the Snake River. A few were farther north near the Boise River. In addition, fruit orchards flourished throughout the area. Derek thought it made for a pretty drive. He hoped Brooklyn thought so too.

Dubois Vineyards was located on a slope of land overlooking the Snake. For close to thirty years, the owners had hosted concerts on Friday evenings during the summer. People came from far and near with their blankets, lawn chairs, and baskets. Most guests partook of the vineyard's award-winning wine over the course of the evening. After eating their picnic dinners, the guests would visit the gift shop, stroll the grounds, and enjoy the scenery. As the air began to cool, the concert would begin. The music might be country or rock or classical. Occasionally it was blues or jazz. Most of the performing artists were from the area, although sometimes a performer flew in from somewhere else in the country.

All Derek cared about tonight was that

Brooklyn would have a good time.

They arrived at the vineyard as the gates to the amphitheater were being opened to the public. He parked his pickup in the lot between a white Lexus SUV and classic red Mustang convertible, top down, then hopped out of the truck and hurried around to the passenger side. Brooklyn had opened the door by that time, and when Derek offered his hand to help her down, she accepted it.

"I hope I'm not underdressed," she said.

He followed her gaze to a woman in a sleeveless white dress and heels. Her escort wore a business suit, although he'd removed his jacket and had it draped over one shoulder.

"Don't worry about it," he said to Brooklyn. "If you are, then so am I."

Her nervous look disappeared.

Derek released her hand so he could retrieve the picnic items from the backseat of the pickup. "Come on. Let's find a spot in the shade. It's why we came this early."

When she nodded, she did so with a smile.

He liked her smiles. She had about a dozen different varieties, and he was starting to be able to differentiate a few of them. One meant she'd remembered something sad. One meant she was trying to contain her laughter. Another meant contentment.

This one? Maybe that she liked being with him. At least he hoped that's what it meant.

They walked toward the gated entrance and, after presenting the tickets for the evening, followed a narrow pathway around to the backside of the round building that housed the gift shop, vineyard offices, and wine-tasting room. Trees dotted the hillside along the perimeter of the amphitheater. Estimating the course the sun would take over the next few hours, Derek led the way toward some shade on the north side that, with luck, would deepen with the passing of time rather than disappear. Once there, he set the small cooler and basket near the tree trunk, then spread the large blanket on the ground.

"Want to look around before we eat?" he asked when he was done.

"I'd like that."

He reached for her hand again and was glad when she took it without hesitation. Progress. They were making progress.

First, they strolled up one row in the vineyard and back down another. Sunlight painted a buttery glow across the green vines. The clusters of grapes, still six weeks or more from being ready to pick, were mostly hidden by the leaves.

310

"We had a grape arbor when I was a kid," Derek said. "I used to stop there when I got home from school. I'd pick a bunch and eat them right there before I went inside." He remembered the flavor bursting in his mouth. "So good."

"Dad never planted anything in our yard. The roses that are there came with the house, I think."

Derek didn't want her thinking sad thoughts. Not tonight. "Maybe we should plan to come back in September when the grapes are ripe."

Her smile returned. "That would be nice."

By then they'd arrived again at the main building.

"Want to go into the gift shop?" he asked.

"Please."

Inside, they poked around the shelves and tables. Fun, silly items abounded. So did expensive, high-end ones.

"Derek, look at these coasters." She held one up. It had a stick-character man wearing a smile and the words, *Patience is what you have when there are too many witnesses.* "I need this one when I'm working at the diner."

"I'll bet that's not true. I'll bet you're patient by nature."

She crinkled her nose. "Learned behavior

311

at best."

He laughed, enjoying the easy banter, then pointed at the coaster in her hand. "Let me buy it for you."

"No." She shook her head, her smile fading a little. "I don't really need it."

How often, he wondered, did Brooklyn not buy something she would like to have just for the fun of it? Too often, he'd guess.

He decided he'd like to change that for her.

As far as Brooklyn was concerned, the evening was magical. From the food that Derek had packed in the basket to the stroll around the grounds of the winery to the stringed quartet that provided the concert, everything was beyond perfect.

The classical music of the quartet lingered in her mind during the drive home. Overhead, stars twinkled against the black tapestry of night, brighter without competition from city lights. One of the advantages of country living.

When Derek reached her driveway, he didn't pull all the way up to the house. Instead, he cut the engine while only halfway there. His headlights went off too. The night was silent except for the song of crickets.

"You had a good time?" he asked.

"I loved it."

"Good. So did I."

She looked toward him, a shadowy figure turned bluish by the dashboard lights. "You're different from who you used to be."

"You mean in high school? I sure hope so. I'd hate to still be acting like a kid at my age."

"I don't know why I said that." She felt her cheeks grow warm with embarrassment. "I just . . . It's just that there's over ten years of my memories that don't include anybody from Thunder Creek. When we came back, I only remembered you as you were back then. And now you are someone . . . different."

He reached over and touched her shoulder with his fingertips. "I see what you mean."

She hoped that was true, that he understood.

"I'd guess I'm more likable now too."

She laughed softly.

"I wasn't very friendly toward you back then. Chad was the charming one."

"Yes." The laughter died in her throat. "He was charming. Chad was always charming." Charming and thoughtless and selfish and undependable.

An uncomfortable silence filled the cab.

313

"There are more important character attributes than charm." She reached up and covered his hand with her own. "Like love and patience. Like kindness and faithfulness. Charm doesn't hold up against those." She wanted to add that those other words described him, but uncertainty kept her silent.

"Gran's spotted us." Derek withdrew his hand.

Brooklyn looked toward the house. Ruth stood on the front porch, the door open behind her.

"Come on. I'd better walk you up. We don't want to worry her."

As he had done earlier in the evening, he got out of the truck and came around to help her to the ground. But this time he didn't offer his hand. Instead, after she turned sideways on the seat, he put his hands on her waist and lifted her up and out, then slowly lowered her to the ground. Close to him. So very close to him.

"I don't think Gran will mind if I make her wait a minute or two longer." His voice was low and husky.

Until he kissed her, she hadn't realized how much she'd been wanting him to do that again. No confusion this time. No wondering if it was the right thing to do.

Only pleasurable sensations. Only a growing sense of belonging, right there in his arms.

CHAPTER 26

Over the following couple of weeks, a pathway became obvious in the field that separated Derek's home from Brooklyn's. Multiple times a day, someone walked one direction or the other across it. More often than not, the excuse was the upcoming campout. But that's what it mostly was: an excuse.

Derek was no fool. He did his best not to put pressure on Brooklyn in any way, not to ask her for more in their budding relationship than she was ready to give. He watched for a signal that she would welcome another kiss and was frustrated that it hadn't happened yet. On the other hand, she didn't withdraw from those times when he touched her hand or her shoulder. She didn't distance herself when he drew close to her, the way she had at first.

In the days that followed the vineyard concert, Derek and Brooklyn spent what time together they could. They shared a few meals. They watched a couple of movies on DVDs. Mostly they talked. About his family. About Alycia. About people they both knew in Thunder Creek.

But despite their growing closeness, Derek found that Brooklyn remained guarded when it came to talking about her dad or Chad or about what her years in Reno had been like. Sometimes he thought her wariness was more out of habit. At least he hoped so.

Because he was falling in love with her. Falling in love a little more every single day. For the first time in his adult life, he envisioned himself with a wife and child. Not as an abstract concept, but with someone specific in mind. Two specific someones: Brooklyn and Alycia. He wanted a family. He wanted *this* family.

It was a hot Wednesday evening in mid-August when Derek and Alycia made a practice run, setting up the two pup tents in her backyard. Most of the dads and daughters on the trip would share tents, but Derek hadn't thought that appropriate in their case. He wasn't Alycia's dad. He wasn't even her stepdad. But two small tents, pitched side by side, would mean he'd be right there if Alycia got scared or needed something. If they wanted and the weather was good, they could sleep with their heads outside of the tent openings, putting them in view of each other.

"Where's the hammer?" Alycia asked as she stretched a cord on her pup tent to the ground, the stake ready to be driven in.

He handed it to her. "Watch your thumb."

"I know how to use a hammer, Mr. Johnson."

"Sorry." He swallowed a laugh. "Hey, do you suppose your mom would mind if you called me something other than 'Mr. Johnson'? I keep looking around for my dad when you say that."

Alycia stopped hammering and looked at him. "I don't know. Mom's pretty strict about what I call adults. Respect for elders and stuff like that."

He was an "elder"? When had that happened? That made him feel older than being called "Mr. Johnson." He never should have brought it up.

"Derek," Mrs. Nims called from the back porch.

He faced the woman.

"I'm needed in town earlier than expected. Would you mind staying with Alycia until her mother gets here? Brooklyn's due home

318

in about ten minutes or so."

"No, I don't mind. We've got plenty of work to keep us occupied." He turned back toward Alycia. "Don't we, kiddo?"

"Yep." She resumed hammering on the second stake.

"All right, then," Mrs. Nims said. "Alycia, I'll see you on Friday."

"Yes'm." Alycia hit the last stake one final time, then straightened and waved goodbye to the sitter.

After the woman disappeared into the house again, Derek walked a circle around the pup tent. "Good job, Alycia." He stopped and tugged on one of the cords. "Real good job."

"Thanks." She grinned, obviously proud.

"Are you sure it's the first time you've ever set up a tent?"

"Yeah, I'm sure." She walked around the tent too. "It's an old one, isn't it?"

"It's been around." First she referred to him as an elder. Now she said his boyhood tent was old.

"My friend's got one that just sort of pops up by itself." She tugged on the same cord, mimicking Derek's earlier movements.

"Hmm."

"Her dad bought it in Boise especially for this weekend. I'll bet it's cool."

"Must be." Derek resisted the urge to defend the pup tents that had been in his family all of these years.

"Now what?"

He motioned toward the rolled-up sleeping bag beneath the shade tree. "Put your bag in it. Get it ready, as if you were going to sleep in there tonight."

She obeyed in a flash. When she was done, she looked at him with excitement in her eyes. "Hey, can I sleep in it tonight? It'd be good practice for Saturday."

He glanced up at the sky, checking the weather. "I guess you could. If it's all right with your mom."

"But you'd stay, too, wouldn't you? I wouldn't want to be all alone out here."

He hadn't anticipated that question. "I don't know, Alycia."

"Mom'll say yes. You'll see."

"I'll say yes to what?" Brooklyn stood where Mrs. Nims had been not all that long before.

"You're home." Alycia ran to the porch and hugged her mom. "Can Mr. Johnson and I sleep out here tonight? You know. As practice for the trip."

Brooklyn's gaze shot toward Derek. He shrugged, then gave his head a slight shake, not sure if he wanted her to refuse or if he

320

was transmitting his own helplessness to control the situation.

Brooklyn saw Derek shrug. Perhaps she even understood what he was trying to say by the slight gesture. But suddenly, unavoidably, one of those unpleasant memories from her childhood — the kind she'd learned to stuff away and pretend never happened — escaped its little prison cell in her brain and came to the surface.

She was nine and she'd been invited to a backyard campout at her friend Shari's house. Brooklyn's dad told her she didn't have the courage to spend the night outside. Girls weren't meant to sleep on the ground in tents. Camping was for men and boys, not females. Girls got scared. Girls cried.

Girls were worthless.

But he let her go — the first time he'd allowed her to accept an invitation to a sleepover — and she was excited. Right up until the moment her friend fell asleep beside her in the tent and the night turned strangely quiet, except for the occasional hoot of an owl or chirp of some sort of bug. And as predicted, she got scared. Scared enough to make her cry. Scared enough to wake Shari and to alarm her friend's parents. Scared enough to have to go inside. Scared enough never to want to camp out again.

Enough to convince her that she was as worthless as her dad said.

"Hey, Brooklyn."

Derek's soft words drew her back to the present. She blinked . . . and was surprised to find he stood just below her.

"Are you all right?" Concern filled his gaze.

She inhaled quickly. "I'm fine."

Still speaking softly, he added, "It wasn't my idea. About sleeping in the tents tonight. If you think it's a bad idea . . ." He let the words trail into silence.

Another quick breath carried her down the porch steps and toward her daughter. "I have an idea, honey. Would you mind if I was the one who slept out with you tonight? Mr. Johnson shouldn't get to have all the fun."

"Would you, Mom? Would you really?"

Regret twisted her belly. Like the memory, she pushed it away. "Yes, I really would." She glanced over her shoulder. "If Mr. Johnson will allow me to use his tent."

"Sure I will. Sleeping bag, too, if you want it."

She sent him a brief smile. "I'll make do with sheets and blankets."

"Okay." The concern in his eyes had been

322

replaced with unspoken questions.

Avoiding them, she looked at Alycia again. "Are you hungry? How about lasagna?"

"You bet!"

"Then go wash up."

Her daughter dashed into the house without argument.

Behind Brooklyn, Derek asked, "Anything you need to know before I head home?"

"No." She faced him. "I think we can get through the night all right. I'll leave on the porch light."

"Can't see the stars that way."

"No, but we can see the house."

He was silent for a long moment before saying, "Tell Alycia that tomorrow we'll go over those survival techniques again."

"Survival techniques?"

He chuckled softly. "Don't worry. Nobody's going to be in any danger this weekend. But it's best to be prepared when you head into the mountains. Even if we are headed for a public campground and not into the backcountry."

The tension eased a little from her shoulders.

He looked as if he might want to say something more. Instead, he gave her another quick smile. "Have fun tonight." Then he strode away across the field.

CHAPTER 27

Brooklyn awakened to a sky spattered with wispy clouds turned pink by the rising sun. The morning air was sweet and cool. If the earth hummed in the evening, as Derek said, then it sang with the sunrise. Birds hopped from branch to branch in the trees overhead, chirping and tweeting, a melody that made her wish to join in a song of praise. To think that she'd missed seeing this, hearing this, all these years because she'd been afraid.

Fear not.

Oh, that was a hard command for Brooklyn. She tried not to be afraid, but it still popped up from time to time when she least expected it.

Help me not to be afraid, Lord.

Her daughter wasn't afraid of anything. Alycia was full of courage at ten. So unlike Brooklyn at any age. Sometimes even now.

I can be proud of that, at least. I haven't

passed on my fears to her. She took a deep breath as she closed her eyes again. *Maybe I can't take much credit for how well she's turned out. Maybe most of it is despite me, not because of me. You've been looking out for the both of us, Lord. Long before I knew You, You took care of us.*

"Mom?"

Brooklyn opened her eyes as she rolled her head to the side. "Hmm?"

"This was so cool. Best night ever. Thanks."

"You're welcome, kiddo." She had never used Derek's particular term of endearment before, and she wondered what it meant that she had now. She could almost see him smiling at her, as if he approved.

"I'm hungry." Alycia slipped out of the sleeping bag and tent in one fluid movement. "Can we have waffles?"

"Sure." Brooklyn got out of her tent, her movements not as flexible as her daughter's. Her body, she realized, was going to make her pay for sleeping on the ground. Derek had offered her a blow-up mattress, but she'd declined, saying she wanted the whole "roughing it" experience. Perhaps not the wisest decision she'd ever made. But seeing Alycia's face and hearing her delighted chatter helped Brooklyn forget the achy spots

325

on her body.

Inside the house, Alycia pulled the waffle iron from one of the cupboards while Brooklyn prepared the waffle mix. After pouring the batter into the heated iron, Brooklyn laid strips of bacon on a plate covered with paper towels and put it into the microwave. Soon wonderful odors filled the kitchen, increasing their hunger.

A short while later, as they carried plates to the table, Alycia asked, "Do you think I'll be the only girl who's never been camping before? You know. Real camping. Not just in the backyard."

"I don't know, honey. It's possible." Brooklyn sat opposite her daughter. "But even if you are, Mr. Johnson has been camping lots of times, so it won't matter."

Alycia munched on a slice of bacon. "Yeah. He's pretty smart. About a lot of things."

"I think so too." Brooklyn marveled once again over her changed opinions of Derek.

"What do you suppose he's gonna teach me today?" Not waiting for an answer, Alycia speared a large portion of waffle and shoved it into her mouth, leaving traces of maple syrup on her face.

Brooklyn swallowed her amusement. "I haven't the slightest idea what he'll teach

326

you. But I am certain you'll have fun."

"Mom?"

"Hmm?"

"I'm glad we came to Thunder Creek. I like it here. I hope we stay forever."

Brooklyn drew in a slow breath and released it. "I'm glad you feel that way, honey. I like it here too." It amazed her how true those words had become.

She heard a knock from the porch, then Derek's voice asking, "Are the campers up?"

"Yeah!" Alycia answered before Brooklyn could. The girl hopped up from her chair and hurried to meet Derek outside. "Camping is *so* cool, Mr. Johnson. I can't wait for Saturday."

"You'll have to wait, kiddo. Can't hurry time."

The pair of them appeared through the kitchen doorway. Derek, tall and broad, his hand on Alycia's shoulder. Alycia, beaming with enthusiasm. They looked right together. It felt right for him to be here. With Alycia. With her.

The flutter of Brooklyn's heart caused her to look away from them.

Was it possible she was falling in love?

From a chair on Brooklyn's back porch, Derek watched as Alycia filled her backpack

327

with a few articles of clothing and additional camping supplies. Deep in concentration, she had the tip of her tongue poking through one corner of her mouth.

"Why's it so important to keep those matches dry?" he asked, testing her.

" 'Cause if they get wet, they won't work."

"Right. And what do we use to make a fire?"

"Not matches unless it's an emergency." She crinkled her nose. "You've got that starter thingy."

"Starter thingy"? He grinned. Close enough.

"But I don't have one of those, Mr. Johnson."

"No, you don't have one. If we were headed out into the wilderness, just the two of us, you probably would. But we're going with a group to a campground, so it isn't necessary."

Alycia put the last item into her backpack and zipped it closed. "Now what?" She looked up at him.

"Let's go through this book of weeds and other plants you should know about when we're hiking in the mountains." He showed the small paperback to her. "Last thing I want is to bring you home with a bad case of poison ivy. Do you know what that is?"

328

"No. What is it?"

She truly was a city girl. "It's a plant. If the leaves rub against your skin, they'll make you break out in a rash and blisters or make you swell up. It's nasty stuff."

"Is there gonna be poison ivy where we're going?"

"Probably. It likes to grow in the mountains and near rivers, and the campground is both in the mountains *and* near a river." He leaned toward her. "We have to keep our eyes open when we're out walking. That's the main thing about being up in the mountains. You have to be smart. To pay attention to what's all around you. Like you're paying attention to me right now."

Alycia nodded.

"So tell me. What would you do if we got separated?"

"If you got lost, I'd stay with the others."

Derek chuckled. "Good idea. But what if you and I were out walking by ourselves and we got separated? Then what?"

"I'd stay put. I'm supposed to sit still and wait for somebody to come find me." She emphasized the last word by bobbing her chin.

"That's right." He lifted his right hand, and she high-fived him. "Okay, kiddo, back to my book of plants." He motioned with

329

his head toward the chair next to him. "Hop up there and we'll go through it."

Brooklyn came out of the house at that moment, carrying two large plastic tumblers. "Lemonade, anybody?"

"Yeah, me!" Alycia answered.

Brooklyn's gaze met with Derek's, and she smiled. Something told him she'd been listening to their conversation.

"Join us?" he asked, glancing at another chair.

"Are you sure?" She set the glasses of lemonade on the small round table positioned between him and Alycia. "I don't want to intrude on your survival lesson."

"Not possible for you to intrude."

She laughed softly as she settled onto the chair.

When he was a teenager, his mom had told him falling in love was like an intricate dance, taking some steps forward and some steps back, keeping time to the music, watching his partner and matching his moves to hers, trying not to step on her toes while at the same time trying not to stumble over his own feet. At the time, he'd told her it was a dumb analogy, and he hadn't thought about it through the years. But now his mom's words came back to him, and the analogy seemed appropriate.

330

I love you, Brooklyn.

She lowered her eyes, as if to avoid the unspoken words.

Did she understand what he felt for her? Would she ever be ready to hear the words? And how would he know when the right time was to tell her?

"Mr. Johnson." Alycia opened the paperback book. "Show me the poison ivy."

He reined in his thoughts about Brooklyn and focused on her daughter. "Sure thing."

Ruth bid Camila a good evening before shutting the shop door behind her friend. With a weary sigh, she flipped the sign in the window to read *Closed*. Tonight she would be content with a dinner of cheese and crackers or perhaps a bowl of soup. She was too tired for anything more elaborate.

At the entrance to her kitchen, she paused and turned off the main overhead lights for the shop. Then she set the alarm and entered the house.

She wondered how many times she'd passed through that doorway over more than five decades. She wasn't a whiz at math, but it had to be at least thirty or forty thousand times. Before she could reach for a pencil and paper to figure a better estimate, the telephone rang. She went to answer it. "Hello."

"Ruth? It's Fran."

Her heart seemed to skip a beat as she sank onto a nearby chair. "Hello, Fran."

"Can you talk?" The woman's voice was soft and shaky.

"Yes. Of course."

"Mac was fired from his job today."

"I'm sorry to hear that."

"He's so angry right now. He scares me."

Ruth leaned forward on the chair, as if it would draw her closer to the woman on the other end of the call. "If you're afraid for your safety, Fran, you need to leave. Leave right now. Don't take anything with you. Just get the car keys and get out."

"No. I can't leave."

"Would you like me to come for you? It wouldn't take me long to drive out there."

"No. That wouldn't be a good idea." Fran drew an audible breath. "I shouldn't have bothered you. I shouldn't have called. It's all right."

"Oh, Fran," Ruth whispered.

"I shouldn't've bothered you," she repeated. "I'm sorry."

"It isn't a bother. I promise you it isn't. I'm glad you called me." Now it was her turn to draw a breath. "Would you like me to call Hank for you? Or Derek?"

"No. No, don't call them. I'm fine. You know what, I'd better get off the phone. Just . . . just pray Mac will find another job. Will you?"

"Of course."

"And Ruth? Thanks for offering to help. But I'm all right. Really. Bye."

The call ended.

Still holding the phone, Ruth closed her eyes and began to pray. And for much more than a job for Fran Tompkins's husband.

CHAPTER 28

If it had been up to Alycia, Brooklyn would have driven her to the church parking lot before the sun was full up that Saturday morning. She made that clear when she came into Brooklyn's bedroom before six o'clock.

"Is it time to go yet?"

Still lying in bed, Brooklyn covered her eyes with the crook of her arm. "You know it isn't. We don't have to be there until nine."

"I can't wait." Alycia got onto her mom's bed. "Can we go early? I don't wanna miss them."

Brooklyn swallowed her groan. "They won't go without you. Derek wouldn't let them."

"I should ride with him in his truck to the church. You wouldn't even have to go. You could stay in bed. Why couldn't I do that?"

"Because I want to stand with the rest of the moms and wave good-bye to you." She

334

moved her arm from her eyes and gave Alycia a pointed look. "That's why."

Her daughter released one of her dramatic sighs, adding an eye roll for more effect.

Laughing, Brooklyn gave Alycia a little shove with her foot. "You nut. Come up here and give me a hug. Don't you know how much I'm going to miss you?"

"I'm only gonna be gone one night."

"I know. But that doesn't make me miss you any less."

"I'm not a baby, you know." Alycia crawled under the sheet and gave Brooklyn a hug.

Brooklyn pressed her cheek against the top of her daughter's head, breathing in. Alycia's hair smelled faintly of herbal shampoo, but Brooklyn's memories were filled with the sweet baby scents from years ago. "No," she whispered, "you're not a baby anymore." She had to blink back the sentimental tears that welled in her eyes.

Alycia allowed the snuggling for only a short while. Her excitement was too much to contain for long. "Do you suppose Mr. Johnson's up yet?" She drew back from Brooklyn's embrace. "Should I check on him?"

Brooklyn laughed again. "No, you don't need to check on him. He's probably out doing his chores so he'll be ready to leave

335

on time."

"You think so?" Alycia slid off the bed and went to the window. "Can't see much from here, can you?"

It was Brooklyn's turn to sigh. "I give up," she muttered, tossing the sheet aside. Louder, she said, "Let's fix breakfast. What do you want to eat?"

"Anything but pancakes and bacon. Mr. Johnson says that's what we'll eat in the morning. He says nothing tastes better than pancakes and bacon when you're in the mountains. You suppose that's true?"

"I wouldn't know, honey, but Mr. Johnson wouldn't lie to you. So at the very least *he* thinks nothing tastes better than that." Brooklyn followed her daughter out of the bedroom and down the stairs, stifling a yawn.

What she wanted more than anything was a couple more hours of sleep, but she wasn't going to get them. After she saw Alycia and Derek off for their overnight trip, she would head straight to work at the diner. She hoped it would keep her from feeling left behind — a silly notion that had been growing in her ever since she'd agreed Alycia could go with the church group.

In the kitchen, she set a frying pan on the stove to heat before dropping slices of bread

336

into the toaster. Before long, two plates held scrambled eggs and toast spread with raspberry jam. Brooklyn carried the plates to the table, then watched as her daughter gobbled up the food. Brooklyn thought to say that bolting her breakfast wouldn't make time pass any faster, but it would have been a waste of effort. Alycia was simply too excited to help it.

After swallowing the last bite, her daughter said, "Can I go see if Mr. Johnson needs help with the camping stuff? You know. Putting it in his truck. Should I take my backpack over now?"

Brooklyn set down her fork. "Did he ask you to come over, or did he tell you he would meet you at the church?"

"At the church." Alycia sighed. "But maybe he didn't think he'd *need* my help."

"I have a better idea. You go shower and get dressed while I do the dishes."

"We're going camping, Mom. I'm just gonna get dirty."

Brooklyn laughed. "That doesn't mean I'm sending you off that way. Take your shower."

Alycia grumbled something as she left the room, obedient but not happy about it.

Brooklyn rinsed and put the dishes in the dishwasher. Then she went upstairs to take

337

her own shower and get dressed for the workday ahead of her.

She had finished blow-drying her hair when her phone rang. The caller ID told her it was Derek. She smiled as she answered it. "Hey, there. I didn't expect to hear from you."

"I know. Listen. I've got a bit of a problem about this morning."

Her smile vanished.

"I got a call from the dispatcher. I'm headed out to meet Hank right now."

"You have to work? But I thought you had this weekend —"

"They needed to call me in for a bit. I don't expect it to take long, but I might not make the nine o'clock departure from the church. I'll have to catch up with Alycia at the campground. But don't worry. I promise not to disappoint her."

Brooklyn sank onto the side of the bed. Who was he kidding? Alycia would be disappointed, no matter when he caught up with her.

"I've arranged for Alycia to ride up with Wendy Royal and her dad. They'll be looking for her at the church. I'll join her and everybody up at the campground just as soon as possible. Alycia probably won't have time to miss me before I get there."

"She'll miss you, Derek."

He was silent for a short while. "I don't have a choice, Brooklyn. But I promise I'll make it up to her."

He could promise whatever he wanted. Alycia would be upset. And so was Brooklyn. Upset and disappointed and angry. It didn't matter if he couldn't help it. It didn't matter that, rationally, she understood he had a job to do. All that mattered was that he'd promised Alycia an adventure with him and now it wouldn't happen. At least not the way her daughter had planned on it happening.

She closed her eyes, realizing she was even angrier with herself than she was with him. Angry for letting Derek get close enough to hurt her daughter, to hurt them both.

"Brooklyn?"

"It's all right, Derek," she answered stiffly. "I'll tell Alycia what you said."

"Thanks for understanding."

"I'd better go. Alycia . . . I need to tell Alycia."

Derek dropped the phone onto the seat beside him. He'd thanked Brooklyn for understanding, but he wasn't sure she did, judging by the cool tone of her voice at the end of their conversation. He wished he could have told her in person. Maybe then it wouldn't have gone over as bad. Maybe then she would have believed him.

And he'd told her the truth. He didn't have a choice. When a deputy was called, he answered. And if Hank needed him, that was even more reason to go. His friend wouldn't ask for help if he didn't think it necessary.

Derek forced his thoughts away from Brooklyn and Alycia as he pressed his foot on the accelerator. The sooner he got to the Tompkins home, the sooner the situation would be resolved and he could keep his promises to Brooklyn and Alycia.

Surrounded on three sides by large farms and by the highway on the fourth side, Mac and Fran Tompkins lived in a ramshackle one-bedroom house just inside the county line. The half-acre it sat on was cluttered with junk cars, rolls of chicken and barbed wire, rusting fifty-gallon cans, broken farm tools, and an unpainted barn that listed dangerously to one side. Weeds grew everywhere, baked to a pale brown by the hot summer sun.

One of the department's black SUVs was parked on the side of the road. Hank stood beside it, shading his eyes as he watched Derek's approach.

Derek stopped his pickup behind the SUV and got out. "What's going on, Hank?"

Everybody knew that Mac Tompkins had a volatile temper, but somehow he'd managed never to cross a line that would get him arrested. Somehow he'd kept his wife from ever making a formal complaint. That Fran had finally involved her cousin in an official capacity wasn't a good sign for what could be happening inside the house.

Hank repositioned the black cap on his head. "Mac lost his job a couple of days ago. Fran called me early this morning, said he'd been up all night and was busting the place up. She asked me for help." He looked toward the house. "But when I got here, she wouldn't open the door. She said nothing was wrong and I could go on about my business."

Derek waited for his friend to continue.

"She's scared. I could hear it in her voice. Scared in a different way from what I've ever heard before. I don't know what's going on in there. That's why I sent for you."

"Did you talk to Mac?

Hank shook his head. "No. Called to him, but he didn't answer."

"Has he been drinking?" Alcohol never improved a domestic dispute.

"Fran didn't say. But he often does before

341

he flies off the handle."

"Any sounds from the house while you waited for me?" Derek's fingertips touched the badge clipped to his belt, as if he needed to make sure he could be identified as an officer of the law even though he wore jeans, boots, and a black T-shirt instead of his uniform. He didn't do the same for the gun in the paddle holster.

"None that I could hear."

Derek tugged on the bill of his cap. "Okay, let's go see if he's got anything to say to us now."

Brooklyn's heart ached as she watched her daughter join Wendy beside Ian Royal's dark-red Subaru. Uncertainty tightened Alycia's expression as she dropped her backpack at her feet. The excitement and joy the girl had been bursting with earlier this morning had disappeared the moment she learned Derek wouldn't meet her at the church as planned, that she would ride up to the campground with Wendy and her dad instead. Alycia was the only girl present without a dad or a stepdad or grandfather. Derek was none of those to her, but he had been the much-desired stand-in.

Brooklyn's anger over the situation had long since cooled. After all, he was a sheriff's deputy. He did have an obligation to his work and his community. She understood all of that with her head. It was her heart that struggled to accept it. When her daughter hurt, she hurt, and Alycia wanted Derek to be with her.

Internally she sighed, realizing that if Derek was to be that father figure Chad had asked him to be, she would have to work on accepting him and any more bumps that happened along the way. Hadn't she herself had to disappoint her daughter in the past because of work or lack of finances or who knew what? Of course she had.

Something else to let go of, she thought.

Leveling her shoulders, Brooklyn put on a smile and tried to pretend all was well as she moved to stand before Alycia. "You're going to have such a good time, honey. You do whatever Mr. Royal tells you. Okay?"

Alycia nodded, but her expression remained downcast.

"Derek . . . Mr. Johnson will get there just as fast as he can. You know he will."

"I hope so."

"He will. And in the meantime, you've got Wendy and your other friends to enjoy the day with."

The youth pastor gave the all clear for departure, and men and girls began piling into cars, minivans, and pickup trucks.

Brooklyn gave Alycia one last quick hug and the biggest smile she could muster. "Don't let it spoil your weekend just because you can't ride up with Mr. Johnson. Chin up. You've been looking forward to today. Have a good time. It'll still be fun."

Brooklyn watched as her daughter got into the rear seat of the Subaru and fastened her seat belt. Ian Royal started the engine and pulled out of the parking lot, Brooklyn waving good-bye and hoping Alycia could still see her. Then the car rounded the corner and disappeared from view.

Happy conversations from other mothers and a smattering of grandparents surrounded Brooklyn as she walked to her car. But Brooklyn's disappointment on her daughter's behalf made her deaf to them. All she could do was hope the diner would be even busier than usual this Saturday so she wouldn't have time to think about Alycia . . . or about Derek.

When Mac finally opened the door to Hank and Derek, he didn't say a word. He stepped back into the dim interior and let them enter at will.

The living room had been thoroughly trashed. Derek suspected it hadn't been

344

much to look at in the best of circumstances — thrift-store furniture, a few odd knickknacks on a three-by-three bookcase, peeling wallpaper. But there were holes punched into the walls, and he guessed they were new. The glass in nearly every picture frame was cracked. A couple of throw pillows looked to have been slashed with a knife or chewed by a dog. Empty beer cans dotted the floor beside a dirty, overstuffed chair.

Derek remained near the door, his eyes watchful, while Hank tried talking to Mac. Fran, in the meantime, remained on the sofa, unmoving, her shoulders hunched, her eyes locked on the floor. With the curtains closed and no lamps turned on, Derek couldn't see if she bore any fresh evidence of abuse. And unless she talked, unless she asked for help, there wasn't a whole lot they could do.

Frustration burned in Derek's gut. He wanted to make her get off that couch and march out the door and never come back. He wanted her to tell Hank that Mac had hit her. Or at the very least that she'd been in fear of being hit. Just a word or two of that nature would be enough for the law to take action.

"Woman," Mac growled, his gaze shooting to his wife, "tell your cousin it's time for him to go. We got no need of him or anybody else here."

Fran didn't look up, but her shoulders shook. Derek thought he heard a sob escape her. He took a couple of steps toward her.

"Get out," Mac demanded.

"Mrs. Tompkins?" Derek said. "Fran? Do *you* want us to leave?"

Silence.

"Would you like to leave *with* us?"

She shook her head.

"Are you sure?"

Mac's voice rose. "She's not goin' nowhere. You heard her."

Derek turned around. "I didn't hear her because she didn't say anything."

"Well, you can hear *me,* can't you? I said get out."

Hank gave his head a slow shake. "Okay. We're leaving. Derek." He jerked his head toward the front door. "We've done all we can."

They hadn't done all they could, but they'd done all that the law allowed. Derek followed Hank toward the door.

"Wait." Fran whispered the word.

But Derek heard it. He stopped and turned to face her again.

"Keep goin'." Mac growled the order.

Derek locked his eyes on Fran. Waiting.

346

Hoping. After a long, tense moment, she finally looked up. There was just enough light in the room from the open door for him to see the tears in her eyes. "What? What do you want, Fran?"

"I want . . ." She drew in a breath. "I want to go with you."

Derek barely had a moment to register the movement off to his side, barely time to see Fran's eyes widened in fear. He turned and felt a jab of red-hot pain as a blade entered his body.

CHAPTER 29

The busyness of the diner did help Brooklyn keep from thinking about Alycia. At least from thinking about her too much. And when Zach told her she had a telephone call, she hadn't even a moment's trepidation.

"This is Brooklyn," she said into the receiver.

"Brooklyn." The male voice sounded familiar, but it wasn't Derek as she'd half expected. "Ian Royal here."

"Yes?"

"Brooklyn, Alycia is . . . She's missing."

Her heart went cold, and her knees turned to water. She fell against the wall in the small office. "Missing? What do you mean? For how long?" She looked at her wristwatch but couldn't make sense of the numbers swirling before her.

"I didn't want to alarm you, but you sent her up here in my charge and I didn't think it was right not to let you know."

She nodded.

"Everyone is out looking for her."

Everyone? "Was she with Derek?"

"No. He hasn't arrived yet. There isn't cell service up around the campground, so I couldn't try to call him. Had to drive down the road to use a pay phone to call you."

She pushed off the wall with her shoulder. "I'm on my way." She grabbed a pen and leaned over the small desk, ready to write. "How do I find the campground?"

Impatience growing, Derek waited for the return of the emergency-room physician. He'd been examined and prodded and x-rayed and washed and stitched up. Now he wanted to be out of the hospital and on his way.

He heard a rap beyond the curtain, then Hank appeared in the opening.

"It's about time," Derek grumbled.

"I got here as soon as I could."

"Tompkins?"

"In jail for assault on an officer. For starters."

"And Fran?"

"She's with my mom for now. I don't think she'll want to go back to that house again. I think she's finally realized that he'll

349

only treat her worse if she gives him any more chances." Hank pointed at Derek's bandaged torso. "And you? What do they say about you?"

"I'm all right. Doctor says I'm lucky. The knife missed organs and major arteries on its way in and out. The blade got muscle and soft tissue, probably because of the way I turned just as Mac struck. I'll mend. I think they're about ready to discharge me."

"You were bleeding like a stuck pig at the scene."

"Looked worse than it was."

Hank grunted his disbelief.

"Now I need to get out of here. I've got to get up to the campground with the church group. Alycia's waiting for me. I've disappointed the kid enough."

"I forgot all about that. You think you're still going?"

"I've got to go. I made a promise."

"Well, you sure as heck can't drive. They've pumped you full of pain medication."

"I'm clear enough to drive."

"Friend, you try to get behind a steering wheel, and I'll arrest you and throw you in jail with Tompkins."

Frustration welled in Derek's chest. "Then what do you propose I do?"

"Let me call Brooklyn. I'll tell her what's happened. Maybe she can get somebody else to fill in for you. In the meantime, you can go home and go to bed where you belong."

Derek shook his head. "No. Don't call Brooklyn. She doesn't need to know about this. Not yet anyway. And I *am* still going to the campout. Now, can you go out there and find out what's holding things up?"

"I guess you are all right at that. If being stubborn counts for anything." Hank shook his head. "I'll see what's happening with your discharge." He disappeared beyond the curtain again.

Derek glanced at the large clock high on the wall. He couldn't believe how many hours had passed since he got the call from the dispatcher. He should be up in the mountains with Alycia, their tents set up, their sleeping bags laid out. Or taking a hike after lunch. Or identifying types of wildflowers. Or taking photos of mountain birds.

His gaze fell to his clothes on the chair against the wall to his left. The T-shirt was a goner, but his jeans and boots were okay, not counting the bloody stains. They'd be good enough to get him home where he could change.

He tossed off the blanket and lowered his

legs over the side of the bed. The room seemed to sway slightly and his side complained at the movement. But he ignored both as his feet touched the cool tile floor.

"I'm outta here," he muttered, reaching for his jeans.

Hank returned to the room just as Derek was pulling on his second boot. "What do you think you're doing?" There was the sound of a challenge in his voice.

"Getting ready for you to drive me up to the campground, if you won't let me drive there myself."

"You'll need some fresh clothes first. There's blood on your jeans."

"I know. You'll have to take me home first so I can change. But we've got to hurry. Alycia's waiting for me."

"I always knew you were stubborn. Just not this stubborn."

It was another twenty minutes before they were actually in the SUV and headed toward Derek's place. Another twenty minutes of time ticking away. Another twenty minutes of Derek wondering if Alycia would ever forgive him for letting her down.

Brooklyn drove above the speed limit most of the way. Even on the winding river road as the two-lane highway climbed into the mountains, she drove faster than she should. She knew it but couldn't help it. Panic pressed her foot against the accelerator.

Alycia was missing. Alycia was missing in the mountains. She was a stranger to camping, a stranger to the rough terrain. There was a dangerous river and probably dangerous animals nearby.

What if we can't find her? O God, help! What if something terrible has happened to her?

She never should have allowed Alycia to go. Especially after Derek bailed on her.

That's not fair.

No, it wasn't fair. Even afraid, she knew she wasn't being fair to him. But he'd said it wouldn't take long, that he would join Alycia before she even missed him. Brooklyn had tried to call him before she lost cell service, but there'd been no answer. Was he finally at the campground? Did he know by now what had happened to Alycia? Whenever he got there, she planned to give him a piece of her mind.

Still not fair.

But knowing she wasn't being fair, knowing he had to work, didn't seem to control her careening emotions.

Her thoughts were so jumbled that she nearly missed the turn. She noticed the road

353

sign in the nick of time. This, at last, made her ease off the accelerator, and with the road narrowing, she continued at a more prudent speed.

Ten miles later she saw several pickup trucks parked near the entrance to the campground. The first truck had a magnetic sign on the side of the door that read *Search and Rescue.* Her heart rose into her throat at the sight of it. She'd been frightened enough already. Those words intensified the feeling tenfold.

She parked her car and rushed up the hillside into the campground. It was easy to find the church group. Young girls milled about amidst a cluster of tents. A few dads stood near them, arms crossed and wearing grim expressions. She hurried toward the men. Ian Royal was one of them.

Before she could call out to him, he saw her too. "Brooklyn." He broke away from the others. "I'm glad you got here."

"What happened? What can you tell me?" She felt her panic rising with each word.

"They've called in search and rescue."

"I know. I saw a truck." She drew an anxious breath and whispered an even more terrifying thought. "Was she taken?"

He glanced away, then back to Brooklyn. "No. Nobody thinks that happened. After lunch, the entire group went on a hike. The girls were given disposable cameras so they could take photos of any wildlife they saw. You know, chipmunks, deer, butterflies, blue jays." He took a breath. "We're not sure exactly when or how Alycia got separated. The group was pretty stretched out." He took another breath. "This is my fault. I should have kept a better eye on her, made sure that she and Wendy were always together."

It would have been easy to agree with Ian and to blame him for what happened. But Brooklyn knew how quickly children could slip away from adults, intentionally or because they got distracted.

"Brooklyn, what's going on?"

She whirled around at the sound of Derek's voice. He moved toward her, his gait slow, a frown furrowing his brow. Instead of anger and blame, relief flooded through her at the sight of him. She stepped forward to meet him. Almost of its own accord, her right hand stretched out to touch him. He seemed to wince before grabbing hold of her hand with his own.

"Alycia's missing," she said.

"Alycia?" His gaze swept the campground before returning to Brooklyn. "Who's in charge of the search?"

355

Relief vanished, and she started to cry. "I don't know. I just got here." She swiped at her eyes with her fingertips. "Where were you? I thought you were already with her."

Hank McLean — she hadn't noticed him before now — stepped into her line of vision. "I got Derek here as fast as I could. He was in the —"

Derek cut him off. "Not now, Hank. It's not important what kept me from getting here." To Brooklyn he said, "Stay here. I'll find out what I can." Without waiting for her response, he stepped around her and walked toward Ian Royal.

Her gaze met with Hank's, and for a moment she thought he had something to say to her. But in the end, he shook his head and followed after Derek.

CHAPTER 30

Years ago, Ruth had learned from Walter that once a search and rescue team was called in, those volunteers without training were discouraged from participating in a search, lest one of them get lost themselves and make matters even worse. So when word reached Thunder Creek about Alycia Hallston, she knew the best and most important thing she could do while they waited was to organize the town's prayer warriors.

Since there wasn't cellular service in the mountains where Alycia had gone missing, the information she had was patchy at best. But someone up at the campground would drive to the restaurant located ten miles downriver to use the pay phone whenever there was anything important to report. In the meantime, Ruth sat with others in the church sanctuary to pray and wait and pray some more.

357

The shadows had deepened in the sanctuary by the time Sandra Dooley slid into the pew. Ruth must have looked surprised because Sandra whispered, "I know. I know. What am *I* doing here since I don't pray? But I figured you'd like some company. Besides, I know how close you are to Brooklyn and her girl."

Ruth took her friend's hand and squeezed it. "You just missed Camila. She was here for a couple of hours."

"Actually, I saw her in the parking lot. We talked for a few minutes before she went home."

"People have been in and out all afternoon."

Sandra glanced toward the altar area. "I heard they sent the campers back to town. The girls are disappointed, of course, but everybody is worried about Alycia. Everybody wishes they could do more."

Ruth knew the men of the community would be frustrated, not being allowed to join in the search.

Sandra continued, "Alycia is all folks were talking about in the post office. Everybody in town knows she's lost up there. Even Reggie Myers must have heard by now. You suppose it'll matter to him?"

"God knows, I wish it would." *Miserable*

old fool, she added to herself, then regretted the thought. She closed her eyes to pray again.

But Sandra had never been one to be comfortable with silence. "I'm sure she'll be all right. From what I heard, it wasn't all that long before they realized she was missing. How far could she have gone?"

Ruth had wondered the same thing earlier in the day. Now, with night fast approaching, she didn't feel the same confidence.

" 'When I am afraid, I will put my trust in You,' " she whispered.

"Where's that verse from?"

"Psalm 56:3."

Sandra offered a small smile. "I hope trust is enough."

Ruth was sorry her friend didn't understand or share her faith, but it didn't change what she knew to be true. She would trust in the love and mercy of God no matter what happened and pray for Derek and Brooklyn to do the same.

Night fell early in the mountains, and even in August, hot days cooled quickly as shadows lengthened. It wouldn't be much longer before both of those things happened.

Derek tried to comfort himself with the knowledge that Alycia had paid close atten-

359

tion when he'd talked about survival in the mountains. All the same, she didn't have a jacket or warm clothes with her. She didn't have a flashlight. And she'd already broken the first rule of the wilderness by not staying put once she knew she was lost.

Climbing another hill, he felt a stab of discomfort in his side. The painkiller from the hospital had worn off, but there was no way he'd have taken any of the pills he'd been prescribed, even if he had them with him. Alycia had to be found first. Ibuprofen would have to be enough until then.

"Alycia!" he shouted. He heard other members of the search team calling the girl's name too. No answer. Pausing at the top of a ridge, he scanned the forest for any flash of color in the fading light.

Why did this feel like it was his fault? Sure, he couldn't have done anything differently. He hadn't had a choice except to go to the Tompkins place when called. And he hadn't been given a choice about his visit to the ER. But if he'd been with Alycia, she wouldn't have wandered off because he would have been watching her like a hawk.

The incident commander had said most kids were found within a four-mile radius. But the two search dogs hadn't sniffed her out. Had she made it farther than four

360

miles? Had something disguised her scent? Had the wind been from the wrong direction?

If he was in charge of this search . . .

"Which I'm not," he reminded himself aloud.

It chafed, not being able to take control. However, he'd been in law enforcement long enough to have learned to follow orders. He understood the chain of command. The search and rescue team looking for Alycia had trained for times like this. As a deputy, he'd received some training of his own, which was why he'd been allowed to join them. But those men on the search and rescue team actually lived in these mountains. They knew the area the way he knew his own county. They were more qualified, and he wanted the best right now.

Shaking off his thoughts, he shouted Alycia's name, listened a few moments, and called again.

The waiting was the worst part. Her daughter was out there alone in the gathering darkness. There were cougars and black bears, not to mention rattlesnakes, in these mountains. Alycia knew nothing of such dangers.

Brooklyn had been ordered to remain in

361

the campground. It made sense, even to her. They needed to know where she was when they found Alycia. She needed to be at the command center when her daughter was returned. All the same, the inactivity was about to drive her crazy.

The curtain of nighttime had lowered over the mountains. Someone had made a campfire. Brooklyn sat in a chair near it, for both the light and the warmth. Lucca Phillips — her coworker from the diner — had driven up from town sometime in the afternoon and now sat beside her. A short while before, Lucca had draped a blanket around Brooklyn's shoulders.

The searchers began to straggle in. Exhaustion was written on their faces. Disappointment too. Some others from Thunder Creek had come, like Lucca, to offer moral support by their presence. And, to Brooklyn's surprise, it did help a little, having them nearby.

The approach of someone to her left pulled her gaze in that direction. It was Hank McLean, looking as tired and rumpled as every other man who'd returned thus far. She sent him a questioning look, although she knew the answer. He shook his head.

He sat on a nearby log. "I've got to head

362

back to Thunder Creek. I'm on duty in the morning."

"I understand. I appreciate what you've done."

"They're going to find her." He turned his eyes toward the fire. "You don't know me well, Brooklyn, but trust me when I say that it wasn't Derek's fault he was delayed in town."

She looked at the fire, too, not sure what to say.

"When you see him, ask him why he wasn't here earlier." Hank stood, drawing her gaze back to him. "Try not to worry that they didn't find your daughter before dark. From what he told me, Derek got Alycia as ready as possible for this camping trip."

Brooklyn wanted to take comfort from his words but couldn't seem to do it.

Hank gave her a nod and then walked off, disappearing in the shadows of night.

CHAPTER 31

Derek left camp the next morning while daybreak was merely a promise on the horizon. He hadn't slept much, and he was pretty sure the same was true for Brooklyn, lying in the tent not too far away from his.

The tent and sleeping bag that had been meant for Alycia.

He hadn't spoken to Brooklyn last night after he returned, the last person to check in again, the search called off for the night. He'd had a million things he wanted to say to her, but she'd already retired for the night. Maybe sleepless, but in the tent anyway. Probably just as well that he hadn't seen her. He'd been in a lot of pain by the time he got back, and he hadn't wanted her to know. He hadn't wanted anyone to know. Somebody might have insisted he remain in camp, and that he couldn't do.

Once away from the campground, Derek stopped for a moment to pray and listen.

364

Yesterday he'd prayed but hadn't done much listening. He wouldn't make the same mistake this morning.

Help us find her, Lord. Show me where to go.

Four miles, they'd said. Most lost kids were found within four miles. On a flat road, that was about a comfortable hour's walk. But the terrain here wasn't flat. The road and trails rose and dipped. The mountainsides were often steep, the ravines deep. Sound carried in some places and got swallowed up in others.

"Where did she go, Lord?" he whispered, opening his eyes and turning in a slow circle.

He knew the areas that had been searched the previous day. Closer to the campgrounds. Not as difficult terrain as some others.

Today he was drawn toward the northeast, a more rugged stretch. There were no hiking trails in that direction, although narrow deer tracks crisscrossed the area. The forest was thicker here, the pine trees taller. If she'd gone this way, it would be easy to get turned around and confused in short order. And, as much as he hated to think about it, it also would be easy to take a hard fall down a hillside and be hurt, preventing her from answering those who called her name.

365

He started walking. He looked for signs of her passing, listened for sounds of her presence.

In his mind he replayed another statistic the incident commander had shared. Twenty-five percent of kids Alycia's age would try to find or make some sort of cover when it began to get dark. Alycia would be part of that twenty-five percent. She was a bright kid.

A strong breeze was at his back, pushing him forward, as if trying to hurry him along. He climbed toward a high ridge that was free of trees, hoping he might get a better view. His side throbbed, as it had throughout the night. He gritted his teeth and ignored the pain.

Brooklyn stirred along with the rest of the camp. Beyond the fabric of the small tent, she became aware of soft voices, the crackle of the fire, the unzipping of tent flaps and sleeping bags, the whimper of one of the dogs.

It had been a long night, full of tossing and turning and thoughts that raced to dark places. Time and again she'd followed the advice of her pastor in Reno, trying to take her thoughts captive. With every breath, she'd tried to release her daughter into the

366

care of the Almighty, tried to trust and rest in that trust. A few times she'd succeeded.

She unzipped the sleeping bag. The crisp morning air caused goose bumps to rise on her arms.

Was Alycia cold? Where had she spent the night? Was she frightened, hungry, completely lost?

O God, let them find her this morning. Let them find her soon.

She pushed her unruly hair back from her face and reached for a canvas shopping bag that contained a hairbrush, toothpaste and toothbrush, a change of clothes, some good walking shoes. Someone — probably Ruth — had gone to her home and packed those items for her, and Lucca had delivered them yesterday.

Again Brooklyn was overwhelmed by the goodness of friends and strangers. And of Derek. Derek was there too.

Hank's voice whispered in her memory: *"When you see him, ask him why he wasn't here earlier."*

She pushed aside her tent flap and looked toward the other pup tent. The flap was tied open. The tent was empty. Derek was nowhere in sight.

She'd heard him talking to someone after he returned from the search last night.

367

She'd considered getting out of the sleeping bag and going to him. But she hadn't had the energy. Her strength had been spent in tears, and she'd felt too fragile to ask anybody any questions or to listen to any answers.

But she wanted to see him now. As quickly as she could manage in such cramped quarters, she changed into clean clothes, then brushed her hair and fastened it again in a ponytail.

The search team and others in the camp had gathered in a semicircle on the dirt road to get a briefing. Although she knew she would be instructed to remain in camp, like yesterday, she still wanted to hear what the commander had to say.

She made her way toward the group, looking for Derek's familiar form. She couldn't find him — and somehow she knew in her heart that he was already searching the mountains, doing everything he could to bring Alycia home to her.

Because he cared for her.

Because maybe he even loved her.

A split second before the earth gave way beneath his feet, Derek knew he was in trouble. The next instant he tumbled down a steep hillside. He grunted as he rolled over

368

the uneven earth and large rocks, but he didn't feel real pain until he hit the bottom of the ravine, the air knocked out of him. Fireworks exploded before his eyes. Nausea swirled in his belly.

He closed his eyes and waited for the worst of the sensations to pass. Slow breath in. Slow breath out. Repeat. And again.

"Mr. Johnson? Is that you?"

He wondered at first if he was hallucinating. Maybe he'd hit his head harder than he thought.

"You okay, Mr. Johnson?"

He opened his eyes. Alycia stood over him, looking down with worried eyes. Another time he might have laughed. He hadn't found her. Instead, he'd fallen down a hillside to land at her feet.

"You okay?" she repeated.

"I think so."

"I saw you fall. It looked pretty bad."

He tried to sit up, caught his breath, sagged back to the ground, eyes closed.

"Your shirt's all bloody, Mr. Johnson."

So that's why his side hurt worse than any other spot on his body. He must have torn the stitches loose. He put his hand against the wound. "I'm okay. What about you?" He opened his eyes and looked at her. Her hair was a mess and her face was dirty, but otherwise she looked okay.

"I got lost."

"I know. We've been looking for you."

"I fell down a hill, like you, only I wasn't hurt. But I got all turned around." She lowered her eyes. "I didn't do what you said. I didn't stay still and wait. I kept trying to find my way back. And then it got dark. I was scared." Her chin quivered.

"Hey, kiddo." He motioned her close. "Come here."

She was in his arms in a flash, burying her face into his chest but managing to avoid his injured side. Instead of crying, she shivered. At least that's what it felt like to Derek.

"It's okay," he said against her hair as he patted her back. "I've got you, Alycia. You're safe now."

"I'm sorry I didn't do what you said." The words were muffled against his jacket. "Again."

"We'll talk about that later. Right now, we need to get you back to your mom. She's at the campground, waiting for you."

Alycia pulled her head back to look up at him. "Mom's here?"

"She sure is, and she's pretty worried, not knowing where you are."

"We'd better go." Alycia stood again.

370

He started to get up and felt another stab of pain. "Kiddo, I think you're going to have to help me. I'm hurting pretty bad. Think you can help me?"

"Sure."

"Okay." He held an arm toward her. "Help me up and let's go."

Alycia got under his arm and Derek used her like a crutch. For just a moment, her head was eye level with his wound. "You're bleeding bad, Mr. Johnson."

"Looks worse than it is." That's what he'd told Hank at the hospital. He hoped it was still true after his drop off the side of a mountain.

"We've got her!"

At the shout, Brooklyn shot to her feet, spinning toward the campground entrance. Lucca — who had returned to the mountains that morning to continue the vigil with Brooklyn — did the same. In unison they reached for each other's hands.

"She's all right," the herald of good news continued from somewhere near the main road.

Brooklyn felt her knees grow weak again. She had to force herself to breathe as tears filled her eyes. But not so much that she

371

couldn't see the red SUV coming up the road.

"Is it them?" she asked, her voice breaking.

Lucca answered, "I think so." She squeezed Brooklyn's hand.

The SUV stopped. A passenger door opened, and a moment later Alycia dropped to the ground and ran toward her.

"Mom!" Alycia hugged her around the waist, almost toppling them both.

Thank You, God. Thank You. Thank You. Thank You.

"I'm sorry, Mom. I'm sorry." Alycia pulled back and looked up, tears filling her eyes. "I'm sorry I didn't do what I was supposed to. Mr. Johnson said you were worried. I didn't mean to do that."

"It's all right, honey." Brooklyn pulled her close again. "I'm just glad you're okay. That you're safe." Tears of joy and relief streaked her own cheeks.

"I thought I saw a deer and I wanted to get its picture so I followed it. And then I couldn't see anybody and I kept looking and they weren't anywhere." Alycia took a breath and drew back a second time to look at her mom. "I fell down a mountain and it got dark."

"Oh, honey." Brooklyn ran her hands over

372

Alycia's shoulders and arms, needing reassurance that she was unhurt.

"I was really scared, Mom, but then Mr. Johnson found me."

"Actually," Derek said.

Startled by his voice, Brooklyn looked up.

"It was Alycia who found me." His face was smudged with dirt and his shirt was torn and . . . and bloody. Her heart skipped another beat.

"What happened?" she whispered.

Before Derek could answer, Alycia said, "He fell down a mountain too. Only it was a different one. But I saw it, and I helped him up. The blood's not from the fall though. He's bleeding where the knife cut him."

"Knife?" Brooklyn's eyes widened as she straightened.

Derek shook his head. "It's nothing."

"He got stabbed yesterday. With a *knife*. He was in the hospital and everything. That's why he wasn't here with me. 'Cause he was hurt."

Derek shot a look at Alycia, clearly wanting her to be quiet.

Brooklyn also looked at her daughter. "Did Mr. Johnson tell you that?"

"No." She shook her head. "He told the man who found us, after we got in the car. I

373

was in the backseat, but I heard him."

"Derek?" Brooklyn lifted her gaze again, and her heart gave a strange hiccup.

Even with a suntan and dirt on his face, his skin looked pale. "I'm okay."

He clearly was not okay.

"We'll talk later. I'll tell you everything." He grimaced. "Later."

374

CHAPTER 32

Derek leaned against the headboard of the bed in one of Gran's guest bedrooms, obediently sipping more herbal tea. There were some battles no man was meant to win. Trying to convince his grandmother that he was well enough to stay in his own home was one of them. Trying to refuse her herbal tea was another.

A steady stream of visitors had come throughout the afternoon. Hank McLean and his wife had just left. Adrian and Tracy Vinton had been there half an hour earlier. But so far the one person Derek really wanted to see hadn't come.

Gran reappeared in the doorway. "You're not getting much rest with all of your friends dropping by to see how the hero is."

"I'm not a hero, Gran. And I'm getting plenty of rest. I don't remember the last time I spent a whole afternoon in bed, doing nothing but eating and drinking tea. I

375

should be at home. There's a lot I need to —"

"Your dog and livestock are being cared for and your vegetables are being watered and weeded. There is nothing you have to do that someone else isn't gladly doing for you. You can stay right in that bed for a couple of days. Until the doctor says you can go home."

Derek suspected the doctor, in this regard, would say whatever his grandmother told him to say. No more and no less.

The doorbell rang. Gran sighed. "Here are more friends to see you. Shall I send them away?"

"That would be rude, and you're never rude."

Gran shook her head at him before leaving the bedroom doorway.

Derek chuckled. His grandmother was enjoying her role as nurse and protector way too much. Perhaps he needed to get hurt more often so she could fuss over him.

"Although this herbal tea is for the birds." His gaze fell to the cup in his hand. He would much prefer a bold cup of coffee or even a tall glass of iced tea with a slice of lemon. He wasn't going to get either of those, so no point asking. He chuckled again.

Soft footsteps in the hallway announced the approach of his next visitor. He looked to see who it would be. His breath caught when Brooklyn stepped into view. She looked tired, but at least she'd come.

Even though their eyes had met, she still rapped on the doorjamb. "May I come in?"

"Sure." He pushed himself up against the pillows at his back.

She took a couple of steps into the room, then stopped again. "They whisked you away so fast this morning, we didn't have any time to talk."

"I know."

"How are you?" She motioned toward his torso, the bandages hidden beneath his T-shirt.

"I'm good. How's Alycia?"

"She's good too. The doctor checked her over. A few scratches and a bruise or two. Nothing serious." Brooklyn offered a tentative smile. "She was afraid at first that the other girls would be angry with her for spoiling the campout. But they're not. They're just glad she's okay."

"Good."

Her expression tightened. "Why didn't you tell me what Mac Tompkins did?"

"I couldn't. You were worried enough."

"You were already hurt. You shouldn't

377

have been out there."

"Of course I had to be out there. I love the kid." He hadn't planned to say those words, but they were the truth. He loved Alycia — and he loved Alycia's mom. More every day. There wasn't much of anything he wouldn't do for the two of them.

Brooklyn didn't seem to have heard him. "If you hadn't found her . . ."

"If it hadn't been me, it would have been somebody else. And I didn't really find her. I ran into her."

"At first I was angry," she said softly. "I blamed you for not being with her. That wasn't fair of me."

"I disappointed her. I know that."

She looked him square in the face. "Let me finish, Derek. I . . . There's a lot I need to say."

"All right."

She took a few more steps forward, bringing her to the foot of the bed. She didn't look away from him, although he suspected she wanted to. What he wanted most was to get out of the bed and hold her in his arms. He could. He was clothed. But he had the good sense to wait.

"I haven't . . . I haven't trusted hardly anyone since Chad walked out on me. I didn't want to trust. I was convinced that

378

we were better on our own, just me and Alycia." She took a breath, her shoulders rising and falling. "But I was wrong. I needed others. I *need* others."

You need me, he thought.

Something flickered in her eyes, as if she'd heard the words he hadn't spoken. Then she continued, "I didn't come back to Thunder Creek because I wanted to. I came back because it was my one real chance to make a better life for Alycia." Another breath in and out. "So I was determined to make the best of what I thought was a bad situation."

Again he had to resist the urge to go to her, to shelter her, to comfort her.

"But over the summer, there was Ruth and all of her friends and Zach and Lucca and Pastor Adrian and Tracy and so many others who made me feel that I belong." Unshed tears glittered in her eyes. "And there was you."

There was no resisting it now. Derek tossed aside the sheet and got out of bed, ignoring the jab of pain that the sudden movement caused. He didn't stop until he stood before her. He moved to take her in his arms, but she stopped him with the palm of her hand against his chest.

"You and all of the people who welcomed

379

me home, you all made me see that it wasn't a bad situation, the way I'd expected it to be. You, all of you, made me part of a three-strand cord."

He gave his head a slight shake, not following her exact meaning.

"It's a verse in the Bible. I read it just last week. It didn't mean much to me at the time, but after Alycia and I got home from the doctor's, I remembered it and I finally understood what God had been telling me."

He waited. As much as he wanted to hold her, needed to hold her, he sensed it was important that he let her say what she'd come to say.

"It says, 'If one can overpower him who is alone, two can resist him. A cord of three strands is not quickly torn apart.' " Tears slipped from her eyes.

With the pads of his thumbs, he wiped them away.

"God is the first and most important of those strands, and I'm the second. But my daughter, my friends, my neighbors, my community. All of them are that third important strand. They were all there to help me when Alycia and I first got to Thunder Creek, and they were there to help me when I needed my car repaired and my house cleaned and fixed and when I needed

380

a job. They were all there yesterday when Alycia went missing. I wasn't alone. Not for a moment of it."

He loved her. He loved her vulnerability. He loved her courage. He loved the tremble in her chin and the determination in her eyes.

"But mainly that third strand in those verses is you, Derek. You made me stronger. You lifted me up. I didn't want to trust you, and yet somehow I couldn't keep from it, no matter how hard I tried not to."

He'd waited long enough. He drew her close and kissed her. And if he could have his way, he just might never stop.

A hundred different emotions exploded inside of Brooklyn as Derek kissed her. All of them amazing and wonderful and magical. She didn't resist or try to pull away. She knew now that this was where she belonged.

It was Derek who drew back first, but he didn't go far. His hands rose to gently cup her face, and his gaze locked with hers. "Brooklyn, I never realized how fast someone could become essential in my life. You haven't been back three months yet, but you . . . you . . . You've got to know how I feel about you." He stopped, searching her

381

with his gaze.

"How do you feel about me, Derek?" she asked, hoping he would say it, fearing he would say it.

"I love you, of course."

"Of course?"

He kissed her again, more forcefully this time, stealing her breath away. When he broke the kiss at last, she couldn't have stood without his hands holding her arms.

"Brooklyn, I want to be by your side, helping you do whatever you choose to do. I admire you. I admire your courage and your determination. I admire the way you mother Alycia. I couldn't care less about your land or what you choose to do with it. I just want to be a part of your life. Of yours and Alycia's lives. I love you. I love you both."

Strange. She'd known, walking into this room, that she had fallen in love with him. She'd even believed that he might love her or at least that he might learn to. But now that he'd said the words aloud, she couldn't believe she'd heard right. She was afraid she'd imagined it all.

Uncertainty flickered in his eyes. "Do you think you could ever love me?"

"It's too late," she whispered. "I already do."

He gathered her close again, not kissing

382

her, just holding her tight. She closed her eyes and melted against him.

"Brooklyn, I want to love you the way you deserve to be loved." He rubbed his cheek against her head. "And I don't think that means we'll never be mad or argue with each other. We'll disagree again. Maybe often. I know you can be stubborn. So can I. But that cord that binds us won't break. Not ever. I'll never leave you, no matter what you say or do. I'll always think of you first. That's a promise."

Tears returned to her eyes as she pulled back to look up at him. "You'll think of me."

"I'll think of you. Always."

His promise touched a secret place. No one except God — and she hadn't believed that for most of her life — had thought much of Brooklyn Myers, the girl who'd been abandoned by mother, by father, by husband.

But Derek thought of her, and he would go on thinking of her. He saw her and loved her.

Like balm on an open sore, she felt his words heal the remaining wound in her heart for good.

EPILOGUE

One year later
Momentarily alone in an upstairs bedroom, Brooklyn looked out the window overlooking the special-events garden. Flowers bloomed in an explosion of colors around the circumference, while on the lawn in the center of the garden, white folding chairs sat in perfect rows facing an archway covered in more flowers, predominately daisies and sunflowers. Beyond the archway, hidden by trees and shrubs, were acres of land that had been plowed under this summer in preparation for next year's planting.

She smiled to herself. It pleased her to see everything coming to life, to think of the land growing things again, healthy things. To think of roots going down deep in the earth, the way her own roots had gone down in the soil of Thunder Creek.

It also pleased her that their wedding — hers and Derek's — would be the first one

384

held in the garden they had so carefully created and cultivated together over this summer. In another month, after they returned from their honeymoon, the Inn at Thunder Creek would officially open to guests. And during every growing season, the guests of the new inn would eat fresh fruits and vegetables grown right on the property.

Two dreams — again hers and Derek's — perfectly blended.

"Only You, Lord, could have worked that out."

"Knock, knock."

She turned as Ruth entered the bedroom, followed right behind by Alycia. Her daughter looked pretty in a peach-colored dress, a garland of flowers in her hair. Not really a little girl any longer at eleven years old, already showing the promise of the teenager soon to come.

"Are you ready to put on your dress?" Ruth asked. "The first of the guests are beginning to arrive."

Brooklyn nodded. "I'm ready."

More than ready, she could have added. Once Derek had proposed last Thanksgiving and she'd said yes, she had often wished they could forget the more formal ceremony and just elope. Only she'd tried that before, and it hadn't turned out well — except for

385

giving her Alycia. This time, her last time, she wanted to do it right. She wanted to make her vows before all the people who mattered most to her.

Well, almost all. Esther Peterman wouldn't be at the wedding, but perhaps she would be watching from heaven. And that thought, though tinged with sadness, made her smile.

Then she wondered if her dad would come. He'd been invited, although she hadn't asked him to give her away. *That* she'd been unable to do. She'd forgiven him for the pain of the past, but he would never truly be a father. It was too late for that.

Ruth went to the wedding dress hanging on the closet door. She had worn the gown at her own wedding nearly fifty-five years ago. With a little expert help from a local seamstress, it had become a new creation for her new granddaughter to wear.

Brooklyn's eyes grew misty. She'd never known a grandmother or a grandmother's love. Not until Ruth. She quickly wiped away the tears with a tissue as Alycia helped Ruth carry the dress to her. The sight of the two of them together threatened to bring back the tears. She thwarted them a second time, lest they fall on the gown and spot the delicate satin, and instead let the two ladies

— one older and one younger — help her into it.

"Wow, Mom. You're so beautiful."

She smiled at Alycia before turning toward the mirror. She had tried on the dress numerous times as it had been altered, but it seemed like she was seeing it — and herself — for the first time.

And she heard God whisper in her heart: *This is how I see you, My daughter. You are a beautiful bride in My eyes.*

All of this, her everlasting Father had done for her. All of this, God had had in mind, long before she received an overnight delivery from an attorney on the opposite side of the country.

God saw her. He knew her. He loved her. And He had brought her back to Thunder Creek to create a new family.

Until this moment, she hadn't known such complete happiness could exist.

"Nervous?" Hank asked as the two men, along with the pastor, waited at the top of the aisle.

Derek shook his head. "No."

"You know what? I believe you."

Derek smiled at his mom and dad, at his sister, Cara, and at his grandmother Ruth, all of them seated in the front row of white chairs. Aunts and uncles were in the row right behind them, along with all three of his cousins. Across the aisle and one row back, he saw Wendy Royal holding Miss Trouble on her lap. The dog, a sunflower fastened to her collar, sat up proudly, as if she understood the importance of the day.

The stringed quartet off to his right began to play the traditional wedding march. Derek's eyes lifted to the end of the aisle, and he saw Brooklyn.

His heart just about burst at his first glimpse of her in her wedding gown. He'd always thought her beautiful. Even when he'd believed he didn't like her and would never like her, he'd thought that. But somehow she was more beautiful today than ever before. Maybe it was the way she looked at him, with love and trust filling her eyes. He wondered if she knew how much her trust meant to him. It made him feel taller, stronger, more of a man.

Alycia took hold of Brooklyn's hand and escorted her mom down the grassy aisle toward Derek and the flower-covered arch. Not to give her away, but to come with her. The three of them through this ceremony becoming a family.

Brooklyn and Alycia arrived, and Alycia gave Derek a smile as she passed her mom's

388

hand into his.

"Thanks, kiddo," he said softly.

"You're welcome," she answered the same way, then added, "Dad."

He felt his heart do a cartwheel in his chest, amazed how that single word made him feel. He'd hoped, of course, that's what she would call him, but he hadn't known it would feel this good when it happened.

Alycia's smile widened before she turned and accepted the bridal bouquet from her mom, afterward stepping to Brooklyn's left side. Derek's gaze, meanwhile, returned to the bride. He could see his own joy mirrored in her eyes.

Adrian Vinton cleared his throat.

Derek gently squeezed his bride's hand before looking at the pastor.

"Dearly beloved . . ."

As Adrian began to share about the union between a man and a woman, Derek couldn't help remembering how a few years ago all he'd wanted was to own the land he stood upon now. He'd thought he needed it to achieve his goals. How little he'd understood at the time. About what was important in life. About dreams. About love. About God.

And then he recalled that old saying. The one about how a man made plans and God

389

laughed. Only now he realized God had never laughed at his plans. The Lord had simply planned something infinitely more precious for Derek — and for Brooklyn and Alycia — than he had been able to imagine himself. Something sparkled in Brooklyn's eyes, and somehow he knew that her thoughts had traveled a similar path.

Not caring that they hadn't reached that point in the ceremony, he leaned in and tenderly brushed her lips with his. "I love you," he whispered.

The pastor stopped talking. Behind him Derek heard the titter of soft laughter.

When he straightened, Brooklyn laughed too.

It was a sound full of joy and trust, love and hope, and ever so much more. A great harvest, the farmer in him realized. And Derek planned to go on nurturing and harvesting that special crop for years and years to come.

A NOTE FROM THE AUTHOR

Dear Reader:

I hope you enjoyed your visit to Thunder Creek and meeting Derek, Brooklyn, Alycia, Ruth, and the rest.

Although *You'll Think of Me* is first and foremost a romance, it included some serious real-life issues — most specifically the longing for Daddy that is a tragic common thread in today's society. I am a "daddyless daughter" myself, losing my father when I was an infant, and I have come to understand how that absence deeply affected my life, both personal and spiritual.

Included after this note is an excerpt from a paper I wrote a few years ago about this crisis in our society. I used tidbits in the pages of this novel, but there is far more to share. I hope you'll take a moment to read it. Perhaps if we all understand what the absence of fathers is doing to daughters, we can somehow turn the tide.

Of course, by the time you read this, I will already have another story or two in the works. To learn more about my past and future books, please visit my website at www.robinlee-hatcher.com and sign up for my newsletter and/or blog.

In the grip of His grace,
Robin Lee Hatcher

DISCUSSION QUESTIONS

1. Brooklyn was abandoned physically and/or emotionally by her parents and her husband. Have you experienced the pain of abandonment? How did you overcome it?
2. Derek felt that the loss of the ten acres put an end to his dreams. Have you ever had to put your dreams into God's hands and trust Him, no matter the outcome?
3. Which character in *You'll Think of Me* did you most relate to? Why?
4. Brooklyn's father is a bitter man who rejected his only child. He does not change during the story. Do you think Brooklyn handled that rejection in the appropriate way? Is it possible to honor one's father and mother, even under such circumstances?
5. Although never reconciled with her father, Brooklyn found a new family in the people of Thunder Creek. We are all

393

called to be part of the family of God. What does that mean to you? How do you help others feel a part of that family?

6. Derek blamed Brooklyn for coming between him and Chad when they were younger. Did you think that was true? Could you understand Derek's regret that he never asked his best friend "the hard questions"?

7. Brooklyn struggled with how to relate to God as her heavenly Father. Have you experienced anything similar? If so, how did you overcome it? If not, how has that blessed your walk with Him?

8. Both Esther and Ruth were mentors in Brooklyn's life. Have you had a special mentor in your life? How do you think that mentor's advice and wisdom helped steer you along a better path?

9. What was your favorite scene in the book? Why?

MISSING DADDY, MISSING PIECES

My childhood was wonderful in countless ways, filled with love and laughter. I was nourished, cherished, and to be completely honest, spoiled. However, there was a definite absence of testosterone in my family. My grandfathers died years before I was born. My father died when I was four months old, and my mother never remarried. One aunt was divorced. Another aunt was widowed. My four cousins were girls. The only males were an uncle with no children of his own and my brother, older than me by twenty-one months. While I regretted not having a dad, I didn't understand how deeply that absence affected me — and especially the decisions I made as a young woman — until later in life.

My father didn't leave by choice. His life was taken from him when the small plane he was in crashed and burned during a hunting trip. But the way that he left did not diminish the effect a fatherless home had on me. No matter the reason for a dad's absence, it is felt, and it is felt as strongly in a daughter's life as in a son's. Perhaps, in some ways, more so.

Monique Robinson, author of *Longing for Daddy: Healing from the Pain of an Absent or Emotionally Distant Father,* called the absence of fathers an epidemic in our society: "It has hit homes from east to west, north to south, affecting the wealthiest and the poorest, male and female, as well as all races and ethnicities. Society has allowed it, and the church hasn't been able to stop it. Children, teens, adults, even the elderly are all crying on the inside because of it."*

Furthermore, Bravado Garrett-Akinsanya, PhD, LP, a clinical psychologist, stated, "Despite [a father's] importance in the home, researchers have described the decline of fatherhood as one of the most basic, unexpected, and extraordinary trends of our time. In 1960, only 11% of children in the U.S. lived apart from their fathers. By 2010,

* Monique Robinson, *Longing for Daddy: Healing from the Pain of an Absent or Emotionally Distant Father* (Colorado Springs: WaterBrook Press, 2004), Kindle edition.

396

that share had risen to 27%."[**]

From 11 percent to 27 percent is a drastic change, and it happened in my lifetime. As a child in 1960, I had only one friend who, like me, was fatherless. All of my other friends lived in two-parent homes. Today that is more of an oddity.

Garrett-Akinsanya went on to say

More specifically, the researchers found that the quality of fathers' involvement with daughters was the most important feature of the early family environment in relation to the timing of the daughters' puberty so that girls growing up in father-present conditions reach puberty later than girls growing up without a father present.

The information is important because multiple studies show that when girls reach puberty younger, they become sexually active earlier and are more likely to get pregnant in their teens. Daughters of single mothers are 53% more likely to

[**] Bravado Garrett-Akinsanya, "Growing Up Without a Father: The Impact on Girls and Women," InsightNews.com, November 3, 2011, accessed October 22, 2014, http://www.insight news.com/2011/11/03/ growing-up-without-a-father-the-impact-on-girls-and-women/.

marry as teenagers, 111% more likely to have children as teenagers, 164% more likely to have a premarital birth and 92% more likely to dissolve their own marriages.*

When I read those statistics, I was stunned by how closely they mirrored my personal journey. From a young age I felt the absence of a father in my home — and in my heart. I was determined to fill that empty place by marrying and having a family. I married young and had my first child while still a teenager, and sadly, that marriage ended in divorce when I was in my thirties.

Gabriella Kortsch, PhD, a psychotherapist, said "a little girl needs to see herself reflected in the love she sees for herself in her father's eyes. This is how she develops self-confidence and self-esteem. This is how she develops a healthy familiarity with what a positive expression of love feels like."**

My mother often told me that I was the apple of my daddy's eye, but I never got to

---

* Bravado Garrett-Akinsanya, "Growing Up Without a Father."

** Gabriella Kortsch, "Fatherless Women: What Happens to the Adult Woman Who Was Raised Without a Father," Trans4mind.com, accessed October 22, 2014, http://www.trans4mind.com/

experience those positive expressions of love from him. I know I would have benefited from them.

In a paper published in the *College Student Journal,* Franklin B. Krohn and Zoe Bogan quoted statistics from *Getting Men Involved: The Newsletter of the Bay Area Male Involvement Network* (Spring 1997). The last statistic struck a nerve with me. It said that fatherless children were 20 percent less likely to attend college than those with fathers.*

At the age of sixteen, college should have been on my radar, but it wasn't. True, I don't recall my mother ever encouraging me to plan for college; maybe I simply wasn't listening. Instead of college I got married. Years later, to my deep regret, I never encouraged my own daughters to dream of higher education. Had my father

---

counterpoint/index-happiness-wellbeing/kortsch4 .shtml.

* Franklin B. Krohn and Zoe Bogan, "The Effects Absent Fathers Have on Female Development and College Attendance," *College Student Journal* 35.4 (2001), accessed October 22, 2014, http://www .freepatentsonline.com/article/ College-Student-Journal/84017196.html.

399

lived, however, I'm convinced I would have had very different aspirations — for myself and later for my daughters. (Note: Both of my daughters eventually went to college and have their bachelor's degrees, and inspired by them — proving that it is better late than never — I am a part-time college student myself.)

In his book *What a Difference a Daddy Makes,* Dr. Kevin Leman wrote, "A woman's relationship with her father, more than any other relationship, is going to affect her relationships with all other males in her life — her bosses, coworkers, subordinates, sons, husband, brothers, pastors, college professors, and even Hollywood movie stars."**

In addition, Iyanla Vanzant, a lawyer and inspirational speaker, said in an episode of *Oprah's Lifeclass* that "the role of father is to teach his daughter how to be in a nonsexual, intimate relationship with a man. In fact, it's the first relationship a daughter has with a man and therefore teaches her how a woman should be treated." Daddyless

** Kevin Leman, *What a Difference a Daddy Makes: The Lasting Imprint a Dad Leaves on His Daughter's Life* (Nashville: Thomas Nelson, 2000), Kindle edition.

daughters, according to Vanzant, often fill the void in their lives by a willingness to "settle" when it comes to a partner.*

My own experience tells me that Leman and Vanzant are correct. In my early years I was ill prepared for romance or marriage because I had no real knowledge of what those relationships should look like.

When I was in my late thirties, the man who is now my husband took me home to meet his family. He is one of four boys, and during my first weekend with his brothers, I felt as if I'd fallen through a rabbit hole into another dimension. Their masculine behavior toward one another was foreign to me — funny and overwhelming at the same time.

Fortunately, guys do not overwhelm me anymore. Today I count many men among my friends, and as a writer I have learned to empathize with them.

But are there still missing pieces inside of

* Iyanla Vanzant, "Daddyless Daughters: How Growing Up Without a Father Affects a Woman's Standards and Choices," HuffingtonPost.com, July 13, 2013, accessed October 20, 2014, http:// www.huffingtonpost.com/2013/07/13/daddyless-daughters-standards-mistake-define_n_3587142 .html.

me because I'm a "daddyless daughter"? Yes, I'm sure there are. Still, I am more than a girl who grew up without a dad. I am a woman of faith, and I believe that anything that happens in my life can work for my good — even the loss of a father — if I am open to the Lord's healing power and direction.

That is my choice, so that is what I choose.

ABOUT THE AUTHOR

Robin Lee Hatcher is the bestselling author of over seventy-five books, including *A Promise Kept* and *The Forgiving Hour*. Her well-drawn characters and heartwarming stories of faith, courage, and love have earned her both critical acclaim and the devotion of readers. Her numerous awards include the Christy, the RITA, the Carol, the Holt, the Booksellers Best, and Lifetime Achievement Awards from both Romance Writers of America and American Christian Fiction Writers.

When not writing, Robin enjoys being with her family, spending time in the beautiful Idaho outdoors, Bible art journaling, reading books that make her cry, watching romantic movies, knitting prayer shawls, and decorative planning. She and her husband make their home on the outskirts of Boise, sharing it with Poppet the high-maintenance Papillon, and Princess Pinky, the DC (demon cat). Robin loves to connect with her readers online and hopes you'll join her there.

RobinLeeHatcher.com
Facebook: robinleehatcher
Twitter: robinleehatcher
Instagram: robinleehatcher

The employees of Thorndike Press hope you have enjoyed this Large Print book. All our Thorndike, Wheeler, and Kennebec Large Print titles are designed for easy reading, and all our books are made to last. Other Thorndike Press Large Print books are available at your library, through selected bookstores, or directly from us.

For information about titles, please call:
(800) 223-1244

or visit our website at:
gale.com/thorndike

To share your comments, please write:
Publisher
Thorndike Press
10 Water St., Suite 310
Waterville, ME 04901